AN ENGLISH APOCALYPSE

Summer Haven I

Paul J.C. Edge

The Dark Ones

Edge Publications

An English Apocalypse - Paul JC Edge

Contents

I. **PROLOGUE** 5

II. **AN EPICENTRE OF TRUTH IN A WHIRLWIND OF LIES** 7
   1. Light in our Darkest Dreams 8
   2. A Moment of Panic that Lasted a Few Months 15
   3. A Realisation That Mine Was Not A Normal Life (Francisco) 20
   4. Pulling Together People I Could Trust 26
   5. A Choice to Leave the Child Behind Me (Francisco) 41
   6. Immersing Myself in a Dangerous Fantasy 48

III. **GRAND TRUTH; GRAND DECEPTION** 59
   1. Shaping our Lives to Come 60
   2. Big Plans and Bigger Difficulties 71
   3. Months Rolling by With Little Progress 85
   4. El Ángel del Barrio 6C (Francisco) 93
   5. Coming Clean 100
   6. Life or Death Decisions 113
   7. The Weight of Public Opinion 119
   8. The Rise of the Tiger (Francisco) 124
   9. Justification or Vilification 131
   10. Reconnaissance and Aftermath 137
   11. Completing the Vision Under Duress 146

IV. **THE MOMENT OF TRUTH** 153
   1. The Last Day of Normality 154
   2. A-Day: 23rd April 2021 159
   3. A Romantic Night of Shooting Stars (Francisco) 168
   4. The Party for the End of the World 176
   5. The Destroyer (Francisco) 186
   6. The First Few Days of the Rest of Our Lives 192
   7. Redemption in Blood (Francisco) 201

8.	The First Incursions	216
9.	The Battle for Manoel Island (Francisco)	225
10.	Disappointing News from the Seven	235
11.	The Siege of Fort Manoel (Francisco)	242

V. THE TRUTH WILL SET US FREE 250

1.	The Gathering of the Shrooms	251
2.	Escape from Valetta (Francisco)	260
3.	A First Expedition Onshore	264
4.	Venturing into the Big Unknown	274
5.	Inspiration	283
6.	Annihilation	290

I. Prologue

"Crazy people are considered mad by the rest of the society only because their intelligence isn't understood."

Zhou Wei Hui

This is a record of the events leading up to the apocalypse of 2021, plus the immediate aftermath that followed. I don't claim to be a creator of wondrous prose, but neither am I given to embellish the facts. It represents the events as I saw them, to the best of my ability. A simple account for those that follow, to honour those that have given their lives that we may survive.

I have included some sections from my brother Francisco's journal in order to explain the events fully.

If you were given advanced warning of a global world threatening event, what would you do? I am certainly not an influential or charismatic leader. How would you begin to plan for the beginning of a world's demise from the ground up, especially when you have had no germane experience to build upon? It is brutally hard to accept there is only you that can do something meaningful in the face of a disaster on such a scale. When you engaged your friends, they would say you were insane, once they realised it wasn't an elaborate joke.

Can you take significant action based upon what is simply a dream or a premonition? It defies all logic. How do you begin to persuade people that the world as you know it is about to end, and they and their families need to turn their back on their lives, their careers, their homes and to join you in a quest to build a leaky ark to ride out the tidal wave of an impending catastrophe?

What, in a lifetime of wonderful and bittersweet experiences, would ever prepare you for events such as these? You do what you must with the time given to you. I did some terrible things that I am not proud of, under extreme duress. Does it make me a bad person, when ultimately it led to the survival of our species? An impossible conundrum that could have broken me; on my bleaker days it nearly did.

One thing that I have learnt in my life, is that change can only be brought about by embracing uncertainty and finding a path to bring talented people on the journey together with you as equals and friends. Given the deception I was forced to employ, would my family ever trust me again? Would it matter if I saved them? But then what if it all proved to be a fantasy, a hopeless pipedream?

II. An Epicentre of Truth in a Whirlwind of Lies

"There are no great men, only great challenges that ordinary men are forced by circumstances to meet."

Fleet Admiral William Frederick Halsey Jr., KBE

1. Light in our Darkest Dreams

After dinner, at 22:00 precisely, the lights lowered. It was time for the main event. A large screen had been erected at the back; the projector was ready to display the live coverage. The banner 'Party for the End of the World' was illuminated in green. The doors were closed, and the whole complex was locked down. All eyes turned to me as I walked up to the stage, strangely energetic after a hard day. Adrenaline surged through my veins; I would probably collapse into a catatonic state afterwards.

"Good evening and welcome", I began. "Sir Patrick Hastings-Crawley and I would like to formally welcome you to the launch of Summer Haven. As you know this is a working commune designed as a prototype to test the possibilities of survival in the face of global disaster".

"I would like to begin by informing you all that my narrative is a complete and utter sham, everything I have told you about this place over the last few years has been a necessary lie". A few confused looks were exchanged by the audience. I continued, "The first of the lies is Sir Patrick Hastings-Crawley does not exist", the audience gasped. "The seven of us have led the build of the project under our own funding". I gestured for the others to join me on stage. "It's a remarkable achievement, completed under great duress. I hear you ask, why would we create a charitable foundation and fund this amazing facility? In order to answer the question, I will have to wind back the clock a few years"...

I could see I was on a small windswept island, there was visibility all the way to the coast and disgusting creatures, that were once people, drew themselves onto the beaches in terrible numbers.

The monster looked at me. His expression showed a twisted cocktail of rage, hunger, and disgust. To this day I'm not sure if the revulsion was channelled at me or at himself. How much of the original human being, his soul, was still chained into his broken and twisted body? His jaws opened unnaturally wide, and I could see his bloody teeth. I turned and sprinted up the green hillside, but I couldn't outpace him. I ran endlessly and my lungs burned with fire. I kept going beyond all endurance, until he grabbed my legs and pulled me to the floor.

Scrambling in on logs, old broken boats and flotsam, they were drawn by the promise of fulfilling their endless hunger. My last memory was of a raging hideous beast feasting on my eviscerated entrails. I needed to rise and continue running, but my body would not respond. Darkness fell as a grim relief over the bloody hillside.

I sat bolt upright in bed, sweating profusely. I had to get up and swill my face with cold water. It was a really bad dream. I reached for my notepad, which I kept by my bed. The dreams were always depicted in broad daylight and darkness came as I closed my eyes to my death, blood splashing like the waves on the broken coastline below.

The dreams continued, evolving slightly each night, but always ended in the hellish brutality of my death. Was it a premonition of my impending demise? If so, then surely every dream would be identical. We were all going to die, that is the reality of our mortality. But I had the distinct impression we were all about to leave this world prematurely, due to an unquantifiable horror. It was the fearful question that crept up on me in the darkness each night, in the early hours before I woke.

The dreams started sometime in early 2018. I had what initially seemed to be an irrational intention, to jot down the events unfolding each night within the dreams. It was impressed upon me subconsciously, becoming something I just had to do. As time went on, the growing compulsion increased as the dreams continued.

My wife, Kate, didn't like being disturbed at night by my ramblings; she liked it much less when I had to sit up in order to make notes. She enquired about the jottings and asked why on Earth it couldn't wait until morning. She even tried to borrow the notebook to peruse, but I remained keen to avoid that eventuality. I am analytical by nature; Kate was used to me jotting thoughts down during the night, as my subconscious processed difficult problems. However, we were experiencing a whole new level of activity and restlessness.

Seeking better understanding, Kate asked if my work was causing me undue stress, or if there was something else troubling me. I contemplated telling her, but my dreams were too weird, she would undoubtedly become concerned. Attempting to be thoughtful, I offered to sleep in the spare room, but Kate declined. She was worried and wanted to keep a close eye on me. Kate is a kind, caring person; except when she was losing her precious beauty sleep, our relationship was becoming strained. I considered speaking to a therapist or my GP, but the embarrassment built a wall too high for me to climb. It was in the realms of real crazy stuff; how could you sensibly interpret the true meaning of such dreams. A shrink would try to determine the rationale behind my dreams and would find nothing of any substance. There was no rational explanation.

The pattern continued night after night, page after page, until the nightmares stopped abruptly as an insubstantial figure appeared in my dreams. I was feeling strong empathy from the figure. I sensed an urge to act, to save people from the terrors depicted in the dreams. I felt it was in my control to help them. The apocalypse portrayed was nearly upon us, and I needed to prepare. I took the matter seriously in my dream, but it was encroaching on my life as I woke into the sensibilities of the real world.

We all have strange dreams; I've had them for most of my life. Weird jumbled up events from the past few weeks, often surreal and occasionally nice. Kate disliked me describing dreams, but these were different; the visions were so vivid and seemed real. In the stark focus of the morning light, I couldn't see how there could be any meaning in them. Yet in the night, in my sleepy half waking state, it felt all too real.

After the dreams finally ceased, I became more disturbed as the memories failed to fade during the day. Did I need to act? There was little I could actually achieve, without significant investment and domain experts to assist. I had no idea how the said experts would react to my insistence of the dream being a premonition. They would laugh at me, or worse still, humour me whilst calling security. I re-read my notes several times, there was a strong recurring pattern. I eventually dismissed them as nonsense and found simple pleasure in the fact I was sleeping peacefully again.

Life returned to normal: dropping the kids at school, work, dinner, sleep and repeat. Life was pleasant, I had a lovely family, with two great kids. Ciara was at primary school, though she thought she was very mature and liked to carry herself as an adult. She had curly, mousey brown hair and pretty green eyes. Matt was at senior school and hated every minute. He was tall for his age, and a little plump.

Early one morning, Ciara woke me, weeping gently, she'd had a bad dream. Kate was sound asleep, so I padded to Ciara's room and explained that everything was ok and cuddled her back to sleep. I guess paranoia kicked in, I suddenly wanted to know what had happened in her dream, but was loathe to wake her. She fell into a deep sleep, I left her room and silently slipped back into my bed.

On Friday night we watched a late movie, imbibed rather too much wine and consequently Kate began talking in her sleep, which was unusual. "You have to help them!" she whispered suddenly. Her exclamation grabbed my attention, given recent events. An hour or so later she whispered, "You are the first of the seven". It was gobbledygook, but still a little freaky. I whispered gently to her, "Who do I have to help?" She responded in a grumpy tone, it was like she was busy and didn't want to be disturbed, "You know who! The children, the seven families. Those who remain behind when all is gone. The white man said you need to help them".

The sharing of such dreams was an escalation. I could accept my strange dreams but found it incomprehensible that others shared the same experience; it wasn't normal, it was akin to a mass hallucination. The rest of my family, even my teenager Matt, began to experience dreams more frequently. It was significantly more than my id playing tricks on me. The dream must be important somehow, they felt deliberately orchestrated. It was a surreal feeling, I needed to change my grip.

A couple of weeks went by peacefully, and our sleep patterns returned to normal for a while. Then the weather became stormy, and the sky appeared endlessly dark and ominous. At this time, the dreams started in earnest again, however they seemed less threatening and exhibited more of an encouraging tone. The figure asked me to take simple, baby steps and it would help lead to a fundamental truth. The figure urged me to take the actions from my dream into the real world. I needed to start to believe it was real.

Matt began to have terrible nightmares. He screamed in the night, waking us. He said that someone was trying to eat him. Kate woke him gently and explained that everything was fine, and he was safe. He couldn't remember the dream that woke him so violently.

The worst mutual dream occurred on a freezing cold day in February. Ciara murmured in her sleep, so I rose and crept into her bedroom, I observed silently. Suddenly, she sat bolt upright with blank, no-one at home eyes. She murmured that the wobbly man needed my assistance so he could help me save my friends. I gently asked what she meant, and she replied, "The creatures are coming daddy! You must gather the seven".

Initially, she appeared terrified after the eruption, but then she simply lay back down, closed her eyes and went back to sleep. She never mentioned it again, but unfortunately for me it opened up a whole world of worry.

I was anxious for my family, but I was also concerned for the state of my mind, I was becoming a wreck. I needed to get to the bottom of this, I needed closure. I became determined to find to a resolution, one way or another.

2. A Moment of Panic that Lasted a Few Months

I found some difficulty in admitting openly that I was having recurring nightmares. There were spells of doubting myself, my memory, the very fabric of my sanity. But it became more incredulous as I started to wake with new jottings in my notebook, clearly written in my own hand. I had no memory of writing the notes nor of the dreams I experienced. I was confused to find sequences of numbers and names on the pad. Kate caught a glimpse of a number sequence one morning and asked me if I was planning to play the lottery at the weekend, she knew it was a roll over. At this point, for me the penny dropped, I then started to realise that in addition to lottery numbers, there were horse race predicted results with accompanying dates. There were also investment projections, which were more difficult to decipher.

It was an act of mischievousness to attempt a small bet using the data. I was shocked to find I won a significant sum of money. As the tips proved reliable, I became braver with the wagers, up to the point where I was betting tens of thousands of pounds at a time. To me, it was not gambling; I was gambling on certain outcomes. It became even more incredulous as the wagers increased further, I won more and more. I became substantially wealthy as a result. How could it be possible? The worst part was that I could confide in no one. I was losing sleep again; I was trying to juggle making my fortune whilst holding down a job and bringing up a family. I became so tired, at one point I had to grab sleep when I could during the day.

My quality of life improved when I elected to quit my job, I had more than enough funds in my secret bank account to retire for many lifetimes. I worked hard to avoid my family glimpsing the truth; I avoided spending recklessly; it would be a dead giveaway to Kate. The purpose for which I had been given the money was slowly emerging. I rented an office near to my old place of work in Congleton. It was sufficiently distant so my old work colleagues wouldn't spot me, but close enough so my family would see me driving in the right direction. It bought me the time I needed to properly consider the problem. I knew I had to act, but when and how? I finally committed to a course of action, if a vaguely defined one.

Most days I managed to wall off the events of the day successfully and lived a relatively normal home life. But one day whilst driving to work, I was in such deep thought that I failed to see a parked car in the driving rain. The bump was quite an inconvenience, as I was without a car for a few days until the rental arrived. However, it sharpened my sense of purpose and helped me drive any doubts to the back of my mind and focus on the problem in hand.

My success could not be coincidental. Any one or two of the wins could be attributed to luck, but eleven consecutive successes were impossible. It proved there was some truth in my dreams, and therefore I needed to take action, but with great care. My secret funds were in separate accounts, most of them under a charitable foundation I had created.

Clarity followed, usually in the middle of the night after deep sleep. Travelling into Manchester, I suddenly realised I could separate the problem into two component parts and pursue them separately. Embrace the dichotomy and schedule a decision point in the future, then I could plan without knowing the inevitable outcome. I needed to focus on what I could change and stop worrying about the things I could not.

The first scenario was if Armageddon came about and all hell broke loose, the horrors of the dreams were true. In that case, we needed to protect ourselves. I needed to build a safe place, a haven. A grand project, much larger than anything I had ever completed. I could onboard help using a deception, that a rich paranoid mogul wanted to build a survivalist bunker. I could explain to my team that the idea was crazy, but there were philanthropic side benefits, which would ensure folks took paid attention. A believable story could be that we were humouring the guy, whilst demonstrating to the world a range of sensible environmental objectives. When Armageddon happened, the team would be overjoyed they had a ticket to ride out the chaos and might forgive my indiscretions.

The second scenario was if my dreams were nonsense. It could be a huge embarrassment for me, but I could live with that, especially if I blamed a fictional captain of industry. We would be faced with building the bunker but focus more on the philanthropy and achieve some good. We could live well with the remaining money after the years had elapsed.

In the end, both options had the same initial set of actions. The difficult part would be how to transform the building of a bunker into an act of charity. I would need to concentrate on the context of eco friendliness and self-sufficiency. The facility could be an exhibition of how to live sustainably; a blueprint for a zero-carbon future and a germane example of how we could live in harmony with nature.

To be successful, I needed a team to help me move my plans forward, the issue was who I should involve, and the skills required. I drafted a list of people I had worked with over the years who I could contact on social media. I then worked through the list and underlined those I could really trust, the shortlist enumerated six people plus myself, seven in total. I felt a strange comfort in the number which I couldn't quantify. My wife's whispered thoughts during her dream suddenly came into clear focus, 'The first of the seven'.

They say the number seven was mythologized since early days of civilisation. Modern religions apparently grew out of Mesopotamia and its oldest archaeology demonstrates their belief that the number seven had a cosmic significance. The importance surpassed my dreams.

I contacted my six shortlisted friends to get them on board with my idea, one way or another. I began to set up meets and consider how I could approach them with such a delicate matter. The rough aggregate of basic skills we needed didn't match their skills profile exactly, but the guys were smart and could learn quickly.

I returned home and ate dinner; the usual family politics were recounted by Kate. I felt distracted, the issue of how I could sensibly approach my friends was continually running through my mind. How could I make the story convincing? How much of the truth could I actually impart? I did not want to lose my friends, but then I didn't want to fail.

I was met with a range of reactions from the team. I guess it had been an awfully long time since I spoke to them. We may have been close friends in the day, but that was long ago. It was a balancing act where the tipping point was different for each individual. The biggest priority for me was getting the team to seek common ground and appreciate each other's point of view, the difficulty was agreeing a shared objective. People were amazing, they always approached problems from different directions, the ensuing diversity could be enormously creative.

3. A Realisation That Mine Was Not A Normal Life (Francisco)

From the writings of El Tigre

I am a man to whom bad luck clings to, like a cilice. I am a simple man who avoids conflict where I can, preferring to persuade folk to agree, not argue and fight over trivia. However, dangerous events are seemingly drawn to me like a magnet.

You must understand that anyone who I become close to will ultimately die and before the end of their normal term. At the time, it seemed that life was too dangerous to have the confidence to reach out to others in friendship, it felt as if I was passing them a curse.

My Christian name is Francisco, it was given to me by my adoptive mother, Muñequita, who is no longer with us. Her name means 'little doll' in Spanish, she was diminutive but warm and loving. She and my adoptive father Javier brought me up from the age of seven. Javier spent most of his time working in the fields, in order to put food on the table.

I am English born; I believe my birth mother was called Beatrice. I have an identical twin brother. It is not clear to me the circumstances that would drive a mother to separate her two children, though I accept it can be tough bringing even a single child into this world.

I was bullied at school by the older kids, they felt I didn't belong. My first memory of unusual occurrences was at the age of sixteen. My family had little money, and holidays were a luxury we couldn't often afford; however Javier had worked particularly hard one year which meant he had enough money for a short break. He booked a holiday at San Juan beach in Alicante, we had a wonderful time. Even though I was a teenager, the sand and sea were magical and became lost in the days of my childhood. I loved swimming in the sea, it was so refreshing, and I felt like I could swim for ever.

The first time I first saw Lucy, it felt like my heart had stopped beating. She was slim with light blonde hair and deep blue eyes. She was undoubtedly the single most beautiful creature I had ever cast my eyes upon. She looked like an English princess, in her white full bathing suit with a wispy magenta wrap caressing her shoulders. She chatted to me a few times in passing, but it was merely small talk.

The days passed too quickly, but they felt so special to me. The sun and sea were enchanting; but when Lucy walked onto the beach, everything else paled. It was like she was in full technicolour and the surroundings became dreary monochrome.

At end of our holiday, I was looking forward to seeing Lucy on my last day before we had to head back to the mundane reality that was home life. I was happy when Lucy arrived and soon entered the sea.

We didn't own a camera, so I sketched the waves with my pencil. I was looking out to sea when I thought I saw a tintorera following the crest of a wave, I could see the tip of its blue fin. The dorsal fin of a shark is always instantly recognisable to the subconscious mind, it triggered alarm faster than anything I have experienced. The sharks were considered safe enough in these parts, they weren't normally aggressive to humans unlike their close relative, the tiger shark. The creature had a predetermined purpose, and the purpose was Lucy. Fear hit me like a sledgehammer, I shamefully admit I froze. I was not a person who found courage easily.

Time seemed to pass very slowly, as it often does when you are in peril. I remember I feeling a strange apparition beside me, a vague figure in white but too bright to work out any specific features. He quietly spoke to me like a dream, "Put aside your cowardice. You need to learn to fight the darkness in this world before it consumes you. You can make the choice to be brave".

How could I freeze when the shark was heading directly towards Lucy? It happened in the smallest fraction of a second. The thought of my cowardice made me angry. The anger overwhelmed my feeling of fear, it stirred me to action. "Choose to be brave", the words from the figure echoed in my head, I ran headlong into a new and more dangerous life without a second thought.

I charged at full speed into the sea, stumbling over the waves, and I positioned myself directly between Lucy and the shark. At first, I surprised her with my forceful action, and she appeared confused. She then saw the dark outline of the shark and screamed. The shark was upon me immediately. I punched its nose as hard as I could, as I had been instructed by my Father. But the shark was undeterred and opened its huge jaws, taking me by the hips. I felt an overwhelming pain in my torso, as it bit down with its rows of razor teeth. I heard screams all around me as I blacked out. Consciousness seemed to wane in and out over the next few seconds. "Choose to be brave". My sketching pencil was still in my hand, so I rammed it into the shark's eye as hard as I could, over and over. It didn't always hit the target, but it did hit its eye many times. The shark's blood mingled with mine in the foam of the sea. Suddenly, the shark released me, and it vanished as quickly as it appeared. I wasn't sure if the damage I had inflicted had scared it away or it was the commotion on the shoreline. I blacked out again.

As I was carried from the sea, the last thing I remember hearing was screaming, "Ejercer presión sobre la herida! (put pressure on the wound). I woke in 'Hospital Universitari Sant Joan D'Alacant', in great pain. I was aware Mum and Dad were by my side; Mum prayed to God to bring her child back as she fiddled with her rosary beads. Dad remained silent, but he looked worried. I become aware of a third person sat close to me, I could hear her breathing, like a butterfly was sitting on the back of the chair; it was Lucy. I opened my eyes, and Mum shouted at the top of her voice "Está despierto. Alabado sea Dios!" (Praise be to God, he is awake). There was a myriad of activity, I saw the doctor, he explained that I needed to be calm and relax, they were taking good care of me. It had been touch and go for a while, but I had been incredibly lucky. I had lost a lot of blood, but there was little damage to my internal organs. I needed rest, but I attempted to stay awake for a little longer, to linger on Lucy's lovely face. "You saved my life", was all she could say. Lucy was so pent up with emotion, that she lost her ability to enunciate simple words other than repeating the phrase.

Lucy visited me every few hours over the following days. Dad returned home, as his leave was over. Mum stayed, so she could look after me. On the third day I was able to sit up in bed, though it hurt like hell. The nurse said the injuries weren't serious, and I needed to get up and move around. Hell, I had only been bitten by a shark!

When I attempted to stand, I found I was wobbly initially, but soon recovered my balance. "Careful Francisco", Lucy said, "you will hurt yourself". Soon my confidence grew, and I could walk after a fashion. I was hunched over to avoid the stitches pulling, yet I managed to stroll with Lucy around the hospital gardens. The trees were in flower, and it was pretty and therapeutic. Lucy stopped under a blossoming tree and kissed me on my lips. My reaction was like I had been struck by lightning. The pain and worries left me for a little while. We spent the day talking, laughing, and kissing but then sadly it had to come to an end. Lucy had to return to England that night, to a place called Saxmundham. The word meant nothing, other than the simple fact that I was losing her.

It was in the last desperate moments that Lucy said she wanted to marry me. She said she would love me for ever and there would never be anyone else. As much as I wanted it to be true, we were only sixteen; it was crazy and wonderful, but illogical. I tried to explain we were too young, and we couldn't even support ourselves. We needed to finish school, and we lived in different countries. Lucy erupted into floods of tears, which was too much. It was then that we promised, against all odds, we would meet back at the bar next to the hospital, in five years' time. We would both be twenty-one and we would get married, there and then. It was our sacred promise to each other. We chose not to correspond until that time; we would just meet back here and spend the rest of our lives together. It was not practical, but true love rarely is.

After the wild and crazy events of our vacation, we took the train back to Madrid and the next stop was reality. I kept our pact a secret. I lost my father Javier in the fall that year. My Mum never quite recovered from the blow.

4. Pulling Together People I Could Trust

Gary 'Drake' Robinson:

Gary, or 'Drake' to his friends, was from Stoke and he naturally addressed people as 'duck', regardless of their sex. Duck was an old term of reverence rooted from the Latin word 'Ducas'. One day an ignoramus on one of the building sites called him Drake, the fool believed it to be a male duck, the nickname strangely stuck.

Despite my mental preparations, my first mistake was to mention meteorites from outer space. He claimed that I needed to wear a billboard saying, 'Repent your sins or die in the fires of self-righteousness!' and wander around Manchester aimlessly. My second mistake was to mention the enormous funding for the project. Drake felt the build would become a folly when the funds failed to materialise, it couldn't possibly be real. Drake was quite sure I was trying to play a practical joke on him. This convinced me I needed to soften my pitch; it was too much for folks to process and appeared implausible. I was forced to backpaddle rather fast or lose him from the outset. The engagement only improved when I mentioned having a few beers and I was in the chair, then it struck a chord. Beer was always the right thing to suggest to Drake.

Drake was a hands-on builder. He was short stocky man with warm intelligent eyes. He had a great reputation at his peak. The trouble was that he tended to over stretch himself, it became his downfall in the end. He took on a project that was way too big for him. He didn't have the resources or the cash to fund it properly. He borrowed from banks, cards, friends, and it all went 'tits up', as he would eloquently put it. Since then, he had hit rock bottom, he was penniless and living on small jobs where he could get them, plus handouts and benefits.

"Look Drake, it's an opportunity to earn some real cash, it will help get your life back on track. Maybe restart your business. Yes, the sponsor is eccentric, but it's really just a big building project. The only thing we need to do is to keep up the pretence of planning for the end of the world and draft a full disaster plan. The sponsor just wants to see some well thought through schedules, and for that he will put up substantial funding. The trouble is on the big day, when his fears don't materialise, we would be left with a great facility and a big fat bonus".

"I gotta be honest, duck. I really don't have a lot going for me at the moment", he murmured. "I'm broke and I'm going to be thrown out of my flat in less than a month, I can't pay the rent. I need a leg up, count me in", he added with a slight hint of sadness. "We can arrange accommodation on the island for the whole stint if you want it. It would be great for me to have eyes and ears on the ground", I said sincerely. He downed his fourth pint, and added, "I guess I'm in, but is there any chance of a small advance?"

I left Drake on the main street in Talke Pits, near his flat. I had provided him with a mobile phone, which he promised to keep on at all times, and a decent wedge of cash as a retainer to keep him going until the start.

Simon 'Simes' Wheelright:

Simes had a real talent working with people. He was charming and thoughtful, but also he could be thought provoking and stimulating. As I had got to know him, I realised he was genuine, a real gentleman. We had become strong friends since. In his earlier years, he had been an Olympic archer, missing out on a bronze medal by a hair. Nowadays he was an HR professional for a large conglomerate. He looked the part too, he always dressed smartly but not too formally. His build was upright and athletic, but life had relaxed him a little as he had become comfortable with himself. The years had treated him kindly; he was approaching his forties in the autumn. I struggled for weeks to try to think of a way to talk him out of a successful career, into an off the wall project.

We met in the restaurant at his offices in Manchester, situated in the Northern Quarter, near to Affleck's Palace on Church Street. It was a time when the city centres were vibrant, more recently they had become empty ghost towns. Packs of dogs fought over scraps there.

"Nice to see you again, Paul" he offered. "Same", I replied, "it's been a while, how are you settling into the new home?" "Great. We have everything sorted now, but it cost a small fortune", he smiled wryly.

I decided to cut to the chase quickly, Simes was on his lunch after all, and breaks tended to be short in the city. I explained the situation with my benefactor, the apocalyptic dream he had and how I was planning to create a haven for him. He's really keen to build a centre for culture and the environment to help sustain the future. The way he sees it is that when the foreseen apocalypse doesn't happen, he will leave a legacy. A vision of sustainable living, art, culture, books, paintings; possibly even a museum, all of it contained on a beautiful island in the Highlands".

Simes appreciated the culture angle but did see to the heart of the issue and was very direct in bringing my attention to it. "It's all very interesting Paul, but what use is the legacy if it's cited on a remote uninhabited island, will anyone ever visit it?" I responded persuasively, "The way I see it, it doesn't matter where the collection is located. When the day passes and his heart goes out of the project, we have an opportunity to drive the trust and display the collection wherever we want. The other big driver is to prove the concept of zero-carbon footprint living, to influence builders and governments of the future. It doesn't matter where its located, it would just be a test case".

Simon was really not convinced, but he could see it meant a lot to me. He could read me like a book, and he seemed to sense there was a lot more going on than I was telling him. He had a certain empathy and could feel my disappointment, though I thought I tried to keep a poker face. "I'll tell you what", he said, "why not put me down as a consultant on the project. I can negotiate a couple of days a month to help, with limited travel. If I become more interested, I will invest a little more time. How does that sound?" I was pleased with the compromise; it was not a plum high-profile role that would improve his CV.

Steve McFadden:

Steve was a pragmatist, an inventive engineer and mechanic. He could construct functional machines from scraps and pieces of old toys, radios... you name it. The only difficulty was getting his attention when he focussed on another task. I arrived unannounced at his house bearing coffee and doughnuts at around 2pm, I assumed he wouldn't have eaten. Sadly, he wasn't at home, so I attempted a reboot on Saturday afternoon, and I caught him with soldering iron in hand. "Hey Paul, what's up". I showed him I had brought snacks. "It's not like you to just come visiting, you must be after something", he commented slyly. "Beware of Greeks bearing gifts", I replied enigmatically. I opted to stimulate his natural and overwhelming sense of curiosity. He tucked into the Crispy Crème doughnuts and drowned half of his coffee. "I have a potential job for you, Steve", I began. He looked at me with a twinkle in his eye. He was scruffy, sat there in an old hoodie and dirty looking jeans and his hair almost reached his waist. He was around thirty and was a little overweight, but he carried it well. He obviously exercised, but I avoided the subject as I didn't want to offend him.

"I have a millionaire survivalist client", I began. "A bunker nutcase?" queried Steve wryly. "He's looking to equip a base to survive the next war. He is in the market for some serious kit: including weaponry, security, surveillance, drones; even smart agriculture. It's a real chance to get your hands on some decent toys". Steve looked momentarily stunned, "So why on Earth does he think there will be a war right now? The world is calming down a bit if you ignore the terrorist propaganda machine and fake news". I explained he'd had a dream about the end of the world, and it scared him. So much so, that he was prepared to invest some serious capital, he was using it to build a survival setup on a small island. "The isle is a beautiful place, and we could have some real fun there. However, we do have to take the defensive plans seriously. But ultimately, we would be able to start building, buying kit, and researching immediately. We need to get the whole facility done and dusted in a couple of years. It's a significant project, with serious funding", I explained.

"I really like the concept, it sounds like we could have some fun", he pondered, "but I just can't see my way to leaving Kulbir and little Pearly right now, while I galivant around Scotland. I'm assuming I will have to spend a lot of time up there; worse if it's all the way up in the Highlands". "You can fly into Inverness, and it's a short drive from there", I said stuffing another doughnut in my mouth, "OK, you can't commute using the shuttle, but worst case you could stay a couple of nights a week. You would be home in reasonable time, and you could work most days from your office".

Sadly, he was forced to decline. It was a shame, but I was unable to impress the real urgency upon him and the fact that this might be the only way to secure a measure of safety for his family. I politely excused myself, shook his hand, and left. I hoped he would change his mind. I must admit at the time I wasn't sure how he would cope in a ravaged world, where the latest tech was covered in rust and the only machines were crafted from wood or cast from iron.

Kim 'Kimball' Ferrell:

Kimball was a friend who I met in my first job working at London Data Tech in the eighties. Kimball's nickname originated from his love for the old EE 'Doc' Smith Lensman Sci-Fi novels, he'd assumed the forename of the hero 'Kimball Kinnison'.

Reliable and very motivated, Kim was a logistics and supply chain expert. He had olive skin and curly hair with a smart haircut. I knew he would feel sceptical, after a decade with no interaction, I had contacted him through social media. I knew I wouldn't be high on his priority list, so I arranged a late afternoon tea at the Ritz in London. I was out to impress.

Kim arrived ten minutes early, he was dropped by a cab directly outside the hotel. The concierge opened the door for him, and he stepped out in a rather smart Boss suit with a bright blue tie. He smiled faintly when he caught sight of me, though I thought I detected a quizzical look.

"Hey Kimball", I called out rather inappropriately, given the venue, much to his embarrassment. The tack I had chosen to take was to pitch the job as a lucrative investment. I explained that my client was an eccentric who believed the end of the world was coming, he was aiming to build a community on an Island in Scotland to ride out the maelstrom. He was looking to gather good minds in order to brainstorm the needs of a future community, isolated from the rest of the world with no access to external skills, technology, or engineering. My client was looking for me to project manage the creation of a community, its people and all of its needs for the future using a capable team to think out of the box. He was prepared to pay a significant salary for a four-year fixed term contract plus expenses, an initial retainer plus a fat bonus on successful completion. It was a substantial, even life changing, opportunity.

I could see Kim doing the math, his salary would be covered handsomely for the period, plus it would set him up for life if he was shrewd. He could do the job, bank the cash and either resume his current role or have a complete change of career. Maybe he could set up the little vineyard he always dreamed about, somewhere warm in the south of France.

"So, what's the catch Paul? And please don't sugar coat it", Kim requested earnestly. "The client has paid me my retainer and first year's salary up front. He has placed my bonus in escrow pending successful completion of the project. I've had my contract vetted by a lawyer, who literally said he could drive a coach and horses through it in the event of any dispute. It's a great deal. I have met with the client, Sir Patrick Hastings-Crawley, three times to date. He's a trustworthy, good-natured guy who is just looking for some quality thinking and ideas, plus some real drive to get the job done. He's happy with our best endeavours and doesn't have the time to be controlling".

"Think of it this way", I ventured, "the money will pay your salary almost until retirement. You wouldn't have to work again if you decided not to. You have the opportunity to choose what you do next. When in life have you ever had such an offer?" Kim appeared like he had a bad taste in his mouth, "I'll need to sleep on it", he expressed cautiously. I knew he wouldn't decline the opportunity to earn big money for a few years' investment of his time.

Kim left without touching the rather nice selection of cakes and sandwiches, he had clearly lost his appetite. I must admit, out of the seven possible team members I had approached, I worried about Kim the most. Would he really buy in to this project, or would he see it as a gravy train and do what he had to without any real commitment?

Phil Bridgestone:

Phil was a lover of the Earth, a charity volunteer, a bird spotter, a kind and warm person. I could always rely on him to listen and help me out when my mind was spinning, and my path unclear.

He often wore the archetypal country gentleman garb. He had fluffy hair and a bushy beard, but his eyes always looked gentle, wise and understanding. It was a look that he cultivated, as it brought him respect and a considerable amount of work from the right people.

I met Phil at a bird hide at one of the pools at Tatton Park near Knutsford. I had parked my car in the village and walked the half mile to the hide, whilst breathing in the lovely fresh air. It was a sunny day, though a little cool. Deer gathered on the green, their velvet antlers crowning their noble heads.

One eye to the spotting scope, the first thing Phil said was "Quiet! You sound like a herd of elephants smashing through the undergrowth. I've spotted a nuthatch, have a look!"

I waited patiently until Phil had packed his gear. We agreed to grab a coffee from the shop in the courtyard of the old Tudor hall. "The rangers are over-culling the deer here; they have been doing this for years. They are more interested in selling venison than preserving this noble herd. The deer were here long before they were", he complained. "Anyway, you don't want to listen to me ranting, what's on your mind?"

I explained, "I'm pulling together a team to build a self-sufficient community on an Island in Scotland. It's the brainchild of an eccentric who is expecting global warming to bring destruction to the world. He feels the public will start to riot when their materialism is no longer fully satisfied, and food is in short supply. I need someone to ensure we approach the project in a sustainable way, which complements and helps stimulate the environment around us". Phil became animated at this point, as my ideas chimed with views he held dear, as I expected. I continued, "We need to build a place for folks to live, farm and survive. However, it's critical the community has robust defences against anything a post-civilised society could throw at us". Phil laughed at this point, but he could see I was quite serious. "Survival is the driver of our mysterious sponsor; however, if we could achieve self-sufficiency and simply pay homage to his paranoia, then we could make the commune a success for ourselves too".

Phil smirked, "So this guy really believes in all the end of the civilised world nonsense. Why?" "He had a dream", I replied. "So, he thinks he's Martin Luther-King?", he added sarcastically with a wink. "The upshot is, whilst he wants to defend mankind, he is really looking to build a working environment for a group of individuals. Think of it as being akin to the Eden experiment in Cornwall. Isolate a group of people on a small island, provide skills and tools and see if they can revert to the old ways of survival. It's a really interesting concept", I added. "But one that has been done before", said Phil, "and it didn't go so well. Humans tend to go back to their most ancient behaviours in these environments".

He sat back and thought for a while. "Will they pay me for this Paul? I could do with some additional cash to fund a small building project I have in mind. I'm guessing there will be a lot of expense travelling back and forth to the Highlands". He was in, I knew he would be.

Dave 'Spall' Sipall:

I had worked with Spall on multiple projects in the past, he was a solid, dependable guy. His background was in the military before moving into the security business. We were good friends, but somewhat distanced due to the events of our overly complex lives. I hadn't spoken to him for at least four years, but I knew when we met, it would seem like only yesterday. When I called, he was more than happy to catch up in his lunch break near to his office in Salford Quays. He was a couple of years older than me, in his mid-fifties. He carried himself with a natural grace, his back straight as a ramrod and his eyes young and full of mischief. Hard not to love the guy. His stories from his time in the forces had raised the hairs on the back of my neck. He had been in the marines, the SBS, you name it. As I always thought, someone I wanted at my side in a pinch.

We met in a small seedy café near his office. The windows were greasy, and the red paisley curtains had seen better days. I ordered a coffee and sat on a plastic seat at a Formica table in the back corner, it provided me with a good view of the door. The coffee was instant, served with way too much milk, it was terrible. Good coffee might be a small pleasure I would be forced to forgo in the future. You couldn't grow coffee beans in Scotland.

Dave arrived promptly and sat down with a wide grin, "How's it going?" I noticed he liked to keep an eye on the door, no change there. He was dressed in jeans and trainers, with a 'Five

Finger Death Punch' T shirt. His taste in music hadn't improved. We ordered a sandwich and exchanged the usual pleasantries. He was fit and well, but his life had become a disaster story. His job was not going well, and he had broken up with his long-term girlfriend a month ago. He needed a new focus; something to distract him from everyday life.

"How do you fancy a new job?" I asked. "I'm game, so what is it? Who do I have to kill?" he ventured with a cheeky wink. I had to run with the simple truth. If anyone could take it, Dave could. I really needed at least one person I could bare my soul to, a sounding board. I took a deep breath and began my story. "This is going to sound insane, Dave, but please bear with me". "I'm listening", he replied. I explained my dreams and subsequent actions in detail.

I sipped my coffee and continued, "One morning, I woke to find a series of lottery numbers written on the notepad beside me. I invested a couple of pounds out of curiosity, and I won the roll over. The nights that followed brought me more lottery sequences, plus a number of future sports event results and stock market investments".

"It must sound ludicrous, but the initial investment of two pounds was merely a curiosity, it was peanuts. I couldn't help myself. It became a few pebbles that started an avalanche". Dave continued to indulge me, listening intensely to my story, but he started to regard me strangely. I think he was expecting the punchline of a joke at any minute.

"What can I say, the bets and investments came good. My first win was over a million, for Christ's sake. I created a charity as a cover for my activities. I kept the windfall secret from everyone, even Kate. I know it sounds outrageous, Spall, but I can prove it".

I reached across the table holding my mobile phone, it showed my net worth. The net total was nearly £97 million, which made Spall's eyes almost pop out of his skull. This took the wind from his sails a little, it was concrete proof that something odd was happening. My fortune couldn't be explained by sheer luck. Such events didn't happen to ordinary folk, it was implausible.

I continued my unlikely tale, "Nearly three months later, the dream returned, but more impactful. The skies were red, and the presence was a little clearer, it was definitely an old man in white. He was so bright; I had to squint to make out his vague features. I watched a terrible future unfold, underlining the date of 23rd April 2021. In the dream I saw meteorite storms and a great plague. The world was consumed with a terrible airborne virus and it was extremely virulent. The creatures in the dream were driven by rage and hunger. It was like something from a zombie movie, but these people were actually alive although driven insane. I instinctively became aware there were very few places I could escape the ravaging. I knew where we could build a sanctuary and where the other havens would be located. I knew what I needed to do, but I struggled to believe".

I took a deep breath, and looked steadfastly into his eyes, to judge his reception of my story. His face was deadpan. "Don't get me wrong", I said, "I sit up at night worrying if this is a fool's errand, a nonsense. I wonder if I am still sane. I'm unsure how I could ever convince people to listen to my lunacy". Dave cut through all my uncertainty in his characteristic delivery of impassive logic, "The fact you are asking yourself these questions demonstrates to me that you are perfectly sane. It's some weird shit, and I can see you believe it. What I do know is there are no coincidences in this world. You can't repeatedly win money like that, it's beyond improbable. You certainly didn't earn all this money playing pinball. What on Earth do you plan to do with it all? Perhaps we need to follow the thread to see where it leads. It's tough trying to keep your feet on the ground, your head above the clouds, your nose to the grindstone, your shoulder to the wheel, your finger on the pulse, your eye on the ball and your ear to the ground", laughed Spall, quoting the comical proverb.

I explained, "I have been given the funds for a specific purpose, I believe that much, and I plan to act on it. To keep grounded, I have to put my feet solidly in both camps; the dream was real, or it was not. I need to plan for both eventualities. I guess the business-as-usual option is none of it is real, and as long as I don't expose my family to this nonsense, they would be none the wiser". I explained I had decided to give up my job, I had plenty of cash to create a pretence that I was still working. I despised the deception, but it was the least of the lies I was forced to impart.

"I'm starting to take some baby steps", I said, "my first big purchase was one of the Summer Isles in the Highlands of Scotland, "Tanera Mòr", it had come up for sale with a small number of unoccupied residences. I made an extravagant bid of £2.3 million to secure the island, even though contracts of sale were in the process of being drafted for another party at much less. I bought the Island under a new charity I had founded, under the name 'Highlands Environmental Safeguard Foundation'. The island is quite small, roughly a square mile. I gather it's subject to fairly extreme winds and rainstorms during the winter months, but it's surrounded by four other islands that could provide additional shelter from the ocean.

"The irony is the name 'Tanera' in Celtic means 'Island of the Haven'; perhaps it's fate, somehow meant to be. According to the blurb, Tanera Mòr is around 760 acres and reaches a height of 400 feet. The highest hill is Meall Mòr, which means big, rounded hill. The island is accessible by boat from either Achiltibuie in Wester Ross, or Ullapool. It isn't a bad place to hang out, assuming we can protect ourselves from the elements".

I completed my spiel, "I guess what I'm proposing, Dave, is we simply cover all bases. I have the money to build somewhere to ride out any disaster. We could gear up for survival and retain any knowledge and skills we can, so we can continue once all these terrible events are over. If my plans turn out to be a load of hot air, then at least we have the island. I have enough funds to pay for anything we need. I could pay you a decent salary for the years we have to prepare. Plan for the worst and hope for the best". He was in, clearly excited by the challenge facing us.

I explained the rest of the gang had agreed to meet at 9am on 5th September at the Midland Hotel in Manchester; we would make a start then. I was careful to explain that the others were not aware of all the details we had talked through, due to the sensitive nature of the subject matter. I'm sure I saw a new energy in him as he left the café. I dearly hoped I had the gravitas to pull this off.

5. A Choice to Leave the Child Behind Me (Francisco)

From the writings of El Tigre

The first change I made on my transformational journey was to get myself a job and earn some cash. I used some of my income to fund karate lessons at the Dojo in the next village. A day didn't pass by without me thinking of Lucy, but as the years went by, I started to realise it was merely a childhood dream.

The thought of practicing karate worried me, it was a violent sport. I persevered, in the first class we stood in a line repeatedly executing a sequence: a left block, right punch, right block, left punch.

The repetition paid off, as my body tuned in to the movement. It built muscle memory that eventually would become reflex. I found that Karate wasn't focussed purely on violence and pugilism; when practiced correctly, it encouraged you to become at peace with yourself. Karate gave me the confidence to be calm when there was trouble.

I progressed steadily through the grades to brown belt 2nd kyū. It had become more than a hobby; it was a passion. I worked extra hours in the shop, allowing me to attend weapons classes. That was when I fell in love with the sword and the discipline of Kendo. I became proficient with the wooden sword; it became a natural extension of my arm. I even managed to win a few competitions. As time passed, I extended my mastery considerably and started to build a close relationship with my teacher.

After a few years, sensei passed away; it was a complete shock to us all. He was still young, but a small tumour had appeared in his left ventricle, and it remained undetected until it switched off his lights permanently. We had quite a close friendship, over time he had become like a second father to me. After the funeral, his family gave me sensei's precious katana, a token to remember him by. The katana turned out to be a real Japanese sword and was actually of great value financially as well as a memento. There are always lots of fake swords for sale to tourists in Japanese shops, but this was a *nihonto* blade, it could only be purchased from a certified master of sword making. The steel used to make the blade was layered thousands of times, so it could be edged keener than the very sharpest razor.

At nineteen I was expected to get a proper job. I also needed to do more to keep food on the table at home, as Mother was struggling to make ends meet. There were even times when I was tempted to sell the legendary blade, but I couldn't quite bring myself to do it. I started as an assistant caretaker at the zoo in Madrid. My job was to clean out the animal's enclosures after feeding them and perform some basic maintenance tasks.

Mum suffered with depression since the day Dad had died, and I struggled to keep her spirits up. We couldn't afford the prescribed medication, so times were tough. On Mum's darker days, she would sit in a corner and cry. All I could do was to be there for her and love her. It was on one of these darker days when she finally gave up on the world and ended her life. I found her in the bathtub dead, having taken an overdose. I called the ambulance, but they couldn't save her. It was a tragedy; the darkness found its way into my veins on that vile day.

I experienced some really black days after the funeral. I drank to excess, and sank so low I would behave terribly, sometimes I went out looking for fights. At my lowest ebb I drowned a bottle of Jack Daniels before lunch, I was on my way to a hell of my own making. It was then I was visited again by the white spectre. "Choose to be brave", he said. "Why are you talking to me", I asked. "Who the hell are you? Why are you bothering me? Leave me the fuck alone!" He continued unabashed, "You are no use to the world the way you are. Sharpen your senses and learn to fight the darkness inside before it consumes you". He then added, "Or has the darkness already consumed your soul?"

I suddenly came to the realisation the apparition was right; I had to shake myself out of my terrible state. Mother would not be proud of me behaving like this. I was in danger of losing my friends, my job, and my self-respect. I climbed out of the abyss one hand hold at a time, starting by focussing on my job and doing well. I then worked on becoming a better friend to those around me. They proved to be understanding, but I suspect I had pushed the limits a little too far even for them.

My 21st birthday came without event; it went by uncelebrated. I was improving, I had been dry for two months and was well on the road to recovery. My outlook was becoming a little more positive every day. A passing stranger wearing a familiar perfume triggered my memory of a sacred promise. Odours often invoke the deepest and most powerful recollections. I started once again to think about Lucy and the vow we had made. It was approaching the day we had agreed to meet. It was a crazy idea, a fantasy, but I became compulsive in its pursuit. I had illogical thoughts that everything would resolve with Lucy in my life again. It was a lifeline that could so easily be out of my reach. Realistically, why would she want to marry someone she had only met on holiday for a few days. She was older now; she had most likely built herself a life. It was crazy, we were just children when we met, those long five years ago.

The compulsion would not leave me, I was a fool living a dangerous fantasy. What would it do to me if she failed to materialise. It was the most likely outcome after all, if I analysed the situation logically. Against this backdrop, I decided to change my life for good with no regrets, whatever the outcome with Lucy. I sold Mum and Dad's house and paid back the outstanding loans. I quit my job and said goodbye to my friends, who to their credit, tried really hard to talk me out of my craziness. I packed my things, put my precious sword into storage and caught the train to Alicante. I took the bus into the city and boarded the light tramway over to San Juan.

I got off the tram at Costa Blanca stop next to the beach. It was every bit as lovely as I had remembered in my dreams. Perhaps anything was possible here. I felt optimism wash over me for the first time in a few months. Life was going to be good again!

It was the summer of the millennium when I set foot on the beautiful sand once again. I had nowhere to stay and a bag containing everything I had in the world on my shoulder. I wore a pair of old Ray-Bans and scanned the waves for sharks. I gathered my thoughts and headed towards the hospital, which was a kilometre or so inland. I walked down the dusty streets, past bungalows and apartments, the places where locals went about their day to day lives.

It was late afternoon when I strolled into the agreed bar. I had no idea what to expect from the day, and I impressed on myself the need to be cautious. A couple of locals sat next to the bar eating tapas and drinking beer. I ordered a coke and sat down. We hadn't agreed a time, so it could be a long wait. A group of four girls came in and took a booth. They were loud; they appeared to have been drinking for much of the afternoon, I dismissed them as a hen party.

I felt comfortable and relaxed; people watching was entertaining. One girl looked over at me, she was an English redhead with a prominent voice. I attempted to ignore her attention, but she sauntered over undeterred and asked me if I would like to join her group for a few drinks. I politely declined, but the young woman wouldn't take no for an answer. It became problematic, as I was waiting for Lucy.

I guess I had started to believe that she wasn't coming, a fool's errand. I let the redhead twist my arm and I sat down at the table with the girls. Three of them were noisy and were clearly having a good time, the fourth was a little more reserved. She had mousey blond hair and large oversized sunglasses. The redhead claimed they were in Spain for a wedding, at which point one of the others coughed deliberately. The redhead murmured something I didn't quite hear which caused an embarrassing silence. I tried to engage the quieter girl in conversation, but she wasn't in the mood for talking. Before long, the banter started again between the others. "Are you waiting for someone?" asked the redhead, Jen. She had noticed I kept looking towards the doorway. I avoided the question by asking where they were from. "Have you got a girlfriend?" asked another, a curly black-haired girl with a prominent chin called Lisa. The group then became childish, "Have you got a six-pack?" I must have turned red at that point, they saw my embarrassment as weakness, then they all joined in and started to harass me to take off my shirt. "No, I have a disfigurement, please leave it alone". Lisa lifted my shirt. I stood and tried to grab it, it ripped along the hem. The girls thought it was hilarious, and started to guffaw, "Yeah babes, look at...", then all went unnaturally quiet.

On display for all to see was the top of the scar from the shark bite. It was a big brutal scar, the shark had a 35cm bite radius, the teeth marks had stretched as I grew and were substantially larger. The quieter of the girls paled and started to slide down her seat. Jen and Lisa propped her up and tried to rouse her, she appeared to be fainting. I pulled down my ripped shirt and sat down, my face had turned magenta at this point. I became unhappy and considered leaving. As she recovered, the quiet girl's sunglasses fell onto her lap. Suddenly, I realised she was Lucy. She had changed, her hair was not quite as blonde as I remembered, but it was undoubtedly her. Her eyes were still steely blue, although she carried a little more weight, she was still delicate. All eyes were on Lucy, she tried to gather herself, then looked over and asked, "Is that really you, Francisco?"

I nodded, "Hi Lucy, how are you doing?" "You are really here? You have come for me, after all this time?" "I have. My friends all think I'm crazy, but I love you. I have since the first moment I saw you on the beach. There has only ever been you". The other girls ceased to exist at the table, it became just Lucy and me. The shell-shocked girls sobered up very quickly. We talked about our lives since the day we parted and how we both didn't dare to hope. The conversation was mysterious, it felt like we had never been apart, it flowed freely and easily. Jen asked, "So how did it happen, Francisco? I mean the scar". Lucy stepped in, "A shark attacked me. It was a huge blue evil looking one. Francisco threw himself in its path and saved my life. The shark tried to tear him apart, but he stabbed a pencil or a pen or something into the shark's eye until it let go. The locals found the dead shark on the beach near to Benidorm a couple of days later, the other sharks had turned on it. I saw the report in the Spanish newspapers. I knew it was the one because it's eye had been gouged". It was the first I had heard of the demise of the shark, I guess I was in hospital and most of it was a blank. Jen remarked, "I have heard that story twenty times before, and I never really believed it. Now it's all so real, so scary. My god you must have been terrified!"

We talked all night, Lisa asked, "So, are you two still getting married tomorrow?" My logic kicked in at this point and I tried to be pragmatic, but Lucy was adamant. I couldn't argue with her, not like this. It was insanely reckless, but it felt so right. We were married the next day, there wasn't a choice, not really.

We rented a small inland apartment; it was in a cheaper residential area. Lucy acquired a job at the hospital as a paediatric nurse, luckily with children the language barrier was minimal. Within a year or so, Lucy had a good basic knowledge of Spanish and was becoming much more confident. I took a job in the bar where we had re-met. Life was good. We were perfect for each other and couldn't be separated.

6. Immersing Myself in a Dangerous Fantasy

I sought legal help to draft employment contracts and non-disclosure agreements for the team. I wanted to ensure that my friends knew they would be treated fairly and wouldn't be left out of pocket.

A few days later, Steve called to tell me he'd had a row with his boss. He was shouting down the phone, he was so full of emotion, "The guy has the subtlety of Pol Pot, I'm sick of it all. Everything faster, get it done by tomorrow. There's no real teamwork anymore. I have quit, I'm available if you need me".

On the morning of our meeting, I woke gently as the sun rose. I showered and ate breakfast with Kate and the kids. I walked to the station briskly and caught the 8:02 on time. The journey took around forty-five minutes, stopping at every station in the known universe. By the time I arrived at Manchester Piccadilly the train was bursting at the seams with a multiplicity of commuters. It was obvious how easily a virus could spread across a country, when faces were inches apart and everyone shared the same unfiltered air.

I strode down Market Street and turned towards the Central Library at Piccadilly Gardens. The bright sun reflected in the fountains, like crystals. The trickle of the water reminded me of the last time I was there; It was a glorious day, and the children were running in and out of the water streams squealing with delight. My mood darkened as an unwanted picture of destruction unfolded in my imagination, with bodies lying on the ground, some crawling towards me. I shuddered and tried to focus my mind on the objective.

I arrived at the Midland Hotel, as there was plenty of time, I grabbed a coffee and logged on to my laptop. The Midland was a lovely old hotel that had been a significant presence in Manchester since 1903 where Charles Rolls and Henry Royce agreed to start their automobile enterprise.

I decided to ditch my slides and just talk, this would give the guys a chance to get more involved. The team arrived on schedule. I presented the state of play to bring everyone up to speed. "We're all here to work through theoretical disaster plans", I explained, drawing the team from polite chat at the coffee machine. "I thought we could begin by considering the topics we need to deliberate and the initial actions". Spall, in his jeans and a 'Slipknot' t-shirt, looked kind of out of place in the Midland, which was a top end hotel.

In complete contrast to Spall, Kimball stood there in a lovely Saville Row suit, which looked straight from the press. Despite his polish, Kimball treated everyone with respect, regardless of who they were. Phil appeared as if he was on the way to a twitcher's convention. I won't even mention Steve's attire, it looked like he had been wearing it for a month. "Let's introduce everyone", I suggested. We went around the table sharing a little about ourselves. Everyone seemed to get along fine, but there was a little awkwardness. I guess it was the thought of the strange topic of discussion to come.

"This is an unusual project, try to consider it disaster planning; the actions we would take if an apocalypse struck. At the very worst we will generate ideas and deliverables that may add value to the world, and also secure somewhere to take a holiday!" There was a muted chuckle from the team.

I explained I had purchased Tanera Mòr on behalf of the foundation, and I displayed a map of the island. Reality struck; it caused a reaction as they were all cognisant of the kind of resources needed to secure such a place. All my crazy spiel had become real in the space of a few seconds; I could see it registering in their eyes. A sudden focus appeared in the room as I continued, "I propose we call the isle "Summer Haven". Summer, from Summer Islands and Haven from the literal translation of the name Tanera". Spall threw a thought into the pot, "It may be a Summer Haven, but what's it like in winter? The Highlands are cold enough, but the islands can be brutal. We will need good thermal underwear under our kilts". Our childish laughter started to break the ice in the room.

The humour put me in a good position to make a start. "We must focus on the plans and knowledge we need in order to survive on an isolated island alone, for what could be up to five years, maybe more". It was quite an ask. If the worst happened, who knows how long it would be before the mainland would become habitable again? Our mission was to provide a self-reliant community that could live without any interference or trappings from the outside world. We would need to be able to survive when all factories and advanced manufacture had long since demised. "So, let's start with some thoughts. What plans do need to have in order to build a self-reliant community on a remote island?"

Lots of ideas were raised, the team started to build on each other's thoughts. I noted them down on the flip chart, using a pen with a very addictive smell. "Food, farming, crops",

"Fishing", "Hunting", "Scavenging", "Houses", "Transport". The list went on and on.

We examined our collective capabilities and shared the research needed. "As an example, let's look at food first", I said. "We need to have supplies to get us through the first winter: the knowledge, seeds, irrigation plus the equipment to grow produce is a must". Phil added, "Don't forget about the means to pollenate the plants, bees, insects etc". I replied thoughtfully, "We need to think this through completely or the community would die, theoretically. We can discuss the details next time, let's stick to the headings for now". We built up the list and shared out the work. The ideas were germinating and cross pollinating; everyone was getting into the task.

The flip chart was full of useful ideas, it was a good start:

- Farming and produce – potable water, grain, dairy, meat, fish/fishing, vegetables, herbs, wine, pollination PHIL
- Shelter and plumbing – houses, dorms, drainage, sewers, showers, electricity DRAKE
- Defence – munitions, weapons, training, strategy, defence of the island SPALL
- Foraging/scavenging for supplies SPALL
- People – education, health/medicines, leadership, work policies, justice system, entertainment SIMON
- Transportation and machines – electricity generation, vehicles, boats and machines + procedure when they break, communications, a way to hold knowledge for the future STEVE
- Supplies – food stores, Ingredients, materials, sourcing, manufacture KIM

Simon voiced his concerns, "So, we've covered all the practical stuff for a couple of hours now. I thought we were also going to cover our heritage, like building a time capsule to preserve art and culture. How are we going to build that into this godforsaken bunker you are proposing?" "Hold on", I argued, "we haven't actually decided to build a bunker. But yes, you are right, we do need to preserve our culture. I'd like you to give this some thought. We may need to procure cultural artifacts, but we could buy or scavenge them later, assuming the events we have talked about happen. When the apocalypse doesn't happen, then the approach would need to be wholly different. It may be the virus doesn't touch the buildings and their contents". Drake interjected, "Would you really expect a bunch of crazy people to loot fine art from galleries when they are facing the end of the world? I think food and weapons would be more important". "True", I replied, "but we do need to think through all possibilities. Please could you take this one Simon for the time being?" He affirmed and I added it to the flip chart.

"I guess if the apocalypse doesn't happen, then we need to be clear what we will be leaving behind. I'm assuming we all agree this is the most likely outcome", Simon queried with a little added sarcasm. I agreed, "Yes, we need to think through the outcome in both scenarios, and both must contribute to the world in some way. However, we do need to show we have achieved something positive to counter the paranoia of our benefactor. After all, he is writing the cheque for all this. I will be sharing our progress with the boss; I need to assure him that we are on the right track". "And ensuring we get paid", added Drake, tongue firmly in cheek.

We agreed to meet again in three weeks, when we would share our plans in more detail. Phil and I would carry out a recce of the island, we agreed to take Drake along to check the status of the buildings. Kimball's final remark was the most telling, "So, what if we have missed something and the worst happens?" "If we haven't planned for it, then we die"; I voiced aloud everyone's thought. Isn't it funny how everyone had got in the spirit of the theoretical task, sufficient to be taking it deadly seriously. "No, I disagree", said Spall, "we overcome it! My old unit had a saying on the wall, 'Follow, lead or get the fuck out of the way". "Thank God he's on our side if it does", whispered Simes in my ear.

Just like that, we became immersed in the roleplay, it was like playing a game. There were long periods of high activity and lots of questions on the private blog Steve had created. The least active was Simon, but then he was only working for us for two days a month. I dearly hoped he was enjoying the task, odd as it was.

The following Monday, Drake, Phil, and I took an early flight to Inverness out of Manchester. It was a small plane, and its flightpath was quite low, the view was amazing as we flew into the Highlands along the banks of Loch Ness. It was a fair day, but visibility was particularly good indeed. We hired a car and drove for ninety minutes along the A835 stopping for a drink and a packet sandwich at the beautiful waterfalls at Corrieshalloch Gorge. Ullapool was a most beautiful fishing village on the shore of Loch Broom, I felt obliged to sample the langoustines at the Seafood Shack. The shack was a small take out which reputedly served the very best langoustines. Phil laughed, "Well if I had to live on these for the rest of my life, I would have no complaints". I decided to lob a metaphorical grenade at Phil and suggested, "Well you'd better find out how to fish them then!"

The Ullapool ferry terminal had regular trips to Stornoway on the Isle of Lewis, which was extremely popular in the summer months. I was more interested in the boat trips to the Summer Islands for obvious reasons. I chartered a vessel from Captain Rusty, his girlfriend Sheena was quick to point out we couldn't land on Tanera Mòr, as it was privately owned. Rusty was surprised when I informed him I was the new owner.

It turned out that the sea was too choppy to sail, so we arranged an early start the next morning at 8am sharp. We had a few beers that evening and some more of those fabulous langoustines and we were in bed by 10pm. I'm not sure the full Scottish breakfast was a great idea, as it nearly came up on several occasions during the passage. Also, the haggis gave me the most terrible wind. It was fortunate we were all suffering, but despite this Rusty commented, "Ye reek lik' a pigs bahookie". Not sure what that meant, but it can't have been a good thing.

It took well over an hour to sail to the island. Rusty informed us it would have been a much faster crossing from Achiltibuie, which was by far the closest point. We landed at a small harbour just south of Ardnagoine, at the old quayside. It was half a mile walk up to the unoccupied café, there was a rough path but no roads whatsoever. Drake commented that he thought it was impossible to live here, it wasn't habitable, "How are we gonna grow food on a big heap of shitstone?" Phil was quick to counter by describing the natural beauty of the stone and the heathers, he highlighted the possibilities of how we could start to build agriculture in harmony with the beauty of the island. Drake looked unconvinced. He would come around, he had to. We had no choice but to make this work.

An old sketch of the island converted to PowerPoint by Steve

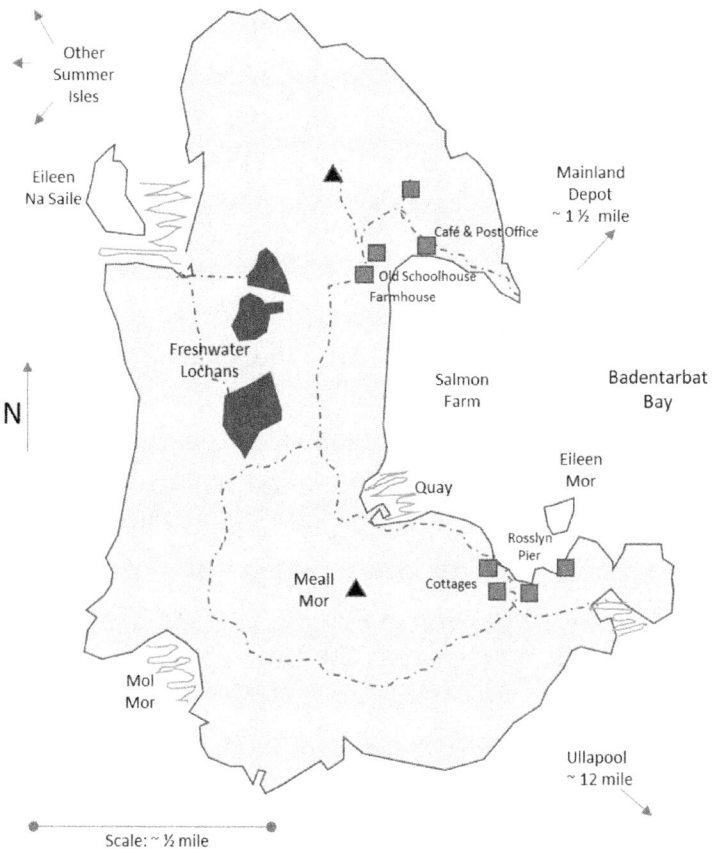

Over the next couple of days, we walked the length and breadth of the Island many times. We found cosy rooms in the Old Schoolhouse, which we managed to make habitable when supplemented by a few items from the large supermarket in Ullapool. Rusty's knowledge of the area proved invaluable. I know availability is not a skill, but we were pleased his business was quiet, due to the departure of most of the summer tourists.

As it turned out, Rusty was only in his early thirties. I guess the life at sea had made him appear more rugged. "Ye dinnae ken whaur yer gaun. Ye dinnae ken wha yer!" he said with a big toothy smile. Sometimes I didn't have a clue what he was talking about, so I investigated. I determined this meant 'You don't know where you are going. You don't know where you are!' Nice.

The islands only natural defence was the sea. However, it has proven to be most effective as a defensive barrier for the UK over the centuries. That is, provided the virus infected people had limited intelligence and couldn't sail an invasion fleet. From the images I had seen in my dream it looked very unlikely; they appeared to be rabid beasts. They weren't like the undead shown in movies, they were no faster or slower than a normal human in a state of extreme fear or anger. My guess was they could be taken down just as easily with the right weaponry. Plan for the worst and hope for the best. I'm not sure the construction of a bunker or a stockade would be well supported by the environmentalists or the county planning department. One worry at a time. Spall was planned to arrive on the following day; I decided to discuss it with him then.

After a couple of days, Drake had settled in and was adamant he didn't want to reside on the mainland. We had to ask him to stop fixing up houses and start to think strategically. He needed to work with Spall to consider the steps needed to resolve the accommodation issue, and specifically how the facility could be defended from attack. We were also unsure of the number of inhabitants we could house on this small island. It was certainly not Noah's ark, where pairs of every kind of animal and a multitude of families could be accommodated. We needed to think smart. Just fifty people would eat a huge amount of meat, fish and produce in a single year. We may be forced to survive for quite some time on the island.

We found the means of producing electricity on the island using generators and a handful of wind turbines, supplemented by a large battery array. However, the existing equipment would be woefully inadequate for our needs and was too old. There was a saline water treatment works, which we may be able to adapt in the absence of fresh water. I hadn't found any large stream or waterways on my walks, but there were a few freshwater pools for emergencies, which were fed by gullies running down the hillside. The main schoolhouse building had nine small self-catering flats; it had been converted for tourists presumably. We weren't going to make many friends locally by flattening them. I had no idea how to apply for planning permission for the extent of building works that was permissible. We needed to investigate further, so we could avoid any issues.

The next day Spall arrived on Rusty's boat. He quickly identified the best observation points using the high ground on both sides of the island, Meall Mòr being the highest at roughly 130 metres. He pencilled them on his map, plotting ingress points and defensive positions. I left him to his work. He looked business-like in his khaki combat trousers and 'Green Day' t-shirt; though he did quickly pull on a camouflage jacket when he walked up the hill, as it was bitterly cold.

Phil and I left for home the following day, as we were travelling under the pretext of a business trip. Spall planned to spend another 24 hours on the island, whilst Drake had moved in semi permanently, although he had agreed to return for the next meeting. It was amazing how quickly things were moving, however, we only had three years or so. The clock was ticking like the timer on a neutron bomb.

The flight back would have proved uneventful, if it weren't for the myriad of thoughts spiralling through my head. I got back just after lunch and by 5pm the whole family was home, and normal life continued unabated. The days were rolling on rather too fast.

III. Grand Truth; Grand Deception

"Do not go gentle into that good night"

Dylan Thomas

1. Shaping our Lives to Come

Our second meeting was on the last Friday in September. An overcast sky was the backdrop for my walk from the G-Mex down to the Midland Hotel. People were moving around the city going about their usual daily business. Was it possible all of them would be gone in less than four years' time?

After hitting the coffee machine and some homemade cookies, we sat down and prepared for business. I gave a quick overview of our trip to the island, and we bedded in and started to go around the table to share progress. Kimball kicked off sarcastically whilst chewing, "So how the hell do we grow pistachio nuts for these cookies on that freezing island?" We laughed, but it was a germane point. There were lots of things we would have to go without, if we were living on the island. If we can't grow it, we can't eat it. "The sell by date on a bag of nuts is only around a year, we are F.U.B.A.R." I remarked. "What's Fubar?" asked Phil. "Everything", chipped in Steve, which made me laugh. I clarified the US military slang for Phil's benefit, 'Fucked Up Beyond All Recognition'.

Kimball started his review. He displayed a slide with a few headings to structure his thinking:

Supplies
- Food - staples, ingredients, herbs, spices, emergency rations, dried and tinned goods
- Means to produce food - fertiliser, pesticides, tools, seeds and tubers, water, warmth, sunshine
- Materials – building, farming etc
- Spares – machines, vehicles, weapons, water, plumbing, energy
- Munitions
- Medicines and surgical equipment
- Manufacturing equipment and raw materials

Kim took a deep breath. "Ok, if we find ourselves in a war situation, we would have to establish a clear supply chain. We would need extensive stores on the island, the location of which Drake will be considering". Drake nodded his agreement as Kim continued, "But also, there would have to be a means of growing new food and manufacturing new equipment, which isn't my baby. I'm going to focus on what we are going to store and how we will store it. We can worry about how we procure these items later. As far as I can see, we will need to move large quantities of provisions and equipment onto the island: everything from foodstuffs, to building materials. The existing small quay simply isn't up to the job and constructing a new goods quay will raise suspicion from the locals. I recommend a model whereby we secure a large storehouse on the mainland with a decent crane and lifting facilities. We could then use an industrial barge to move stuff to the island when we need it. It could also be used for storing vehicles and weaponry needed for scavenging trips onto the towns". I contributed, "We will need to keep well away from the mainland if a virus is airborne, we would have to survive on our stores on the island for at least a couple of years". Kimball balked at this, "Hold on a minute, when did we start talking about a bloody virus". I quickly clarified it was part of the apocalyptic vision our benefactor had seen; he had seen a need for isolation and defence. Kimball was clearly suspicious about the driver for the initiative, but I had to hold back with the details, or I would lose them all.

Drake noticed my discomfort and cut in to change the subject. He reassured Kim that he would ensure his plans would provide plenty of clean dry storage. "So how will you get all the building materials onto the island?" asked Phil with a look of concern,

"We simply can't industrialise the existing quay, we would be strung up". Kim shared his plan for another 'off the radar' quay at the southeast of the island. "There is a beach which leads up to a tidal pool. It has rock walls around it, onto which we could mount a large industrial crane. We could sell the concept of the crane as a temporary measure while we built... whatever", he added with a wink. "The big issue here is the crane would require a barge to enter the ravine, so we would have to dredge and possibly excavate to provide the necessary depth of water. An additional issue is finding a way to stop the barge running aground on the rocks, but let's save this problem for another day". I suspected we would only be able to operate the barge when the sea was calm. We may be forced to go long periods during the heavy seas of winter without the ability to access the onshore stores.

Kim went on to explain the varieties of canned and dried foods that could be stockpiled as their shelf lives were sufficiently long. The list grew when we considered methods to extend the expiry dates of foods, such as cooking and freezing, desiccation, vacuum sealing, and other techniques. However, the maximum longevity of long-life foods could still be counted on one hand, excluding army ration packs, which was measured in decades. The issue remained that in the long term, we would need to be able to produce our own food. He proceeded to cover clever ways of storing ammunition and machinery which would maintain its operability for long periods. How ever we stored the spares, we would ultimately be forced to move back to old-fashioned ways at some point. Steve chipped in, "If we're smart about how we select machinery we could extend its usage. For example, if we buy rugged 4WD pickup trucks, we could use them for transport, mobile gun stations, scavenging trips etcetera. We could give the trucks a longer life, when the engines finally give up. If we reverse the truck and strip out the engine, it could then become a carriage for horses to pull, with a minor adaptation. The only issue would be the axle and tyres. While tyres would last a long time, they would ultimately perish, so we'd need a solution for that. However, spare axles can be stored indefinitely if we cover them in oilcloths and vacuum pack them to protect the more sensitive rubber parts".

Kim's input initiated a rumble of approval from the team. Discussions were heating up as our collaboration improved, and the topics became more interesting. We then considered how to handle manufacturing, which identified a need for machines to cut and shape wood and steel. We would store the raw materials, plus spare parts for the lathes, welders and cutters. We would also need the capability and skills to use the machines if we lost electricity. Spall added, "We will need to store ammunition in a way that keeps it operable for a long period of time. They are explosives and require great care!"

His input was timely, as Spall was next up covering defences for the island. He explained how we would construct an observation point on the smaller hill and a crow's nest at the highest point, they would both would be disguised as photo viewpoints. He suggested that we could build a defensive perimeter around the central accommodation, but the main building must be secure. Steve commented it would be tricky to shoot someone on the coast from the crow's nest, it was half a mile away. Spall grinned, "You haven't seen the weaponry I'm proposing, nor the skill of the team I'm gathering". Spall outlined the weaponry needed, but strangely mentioned nothing about where he would procure it, the items were illegal! We would need to be careful how we shipped such items onto the island, ensuring they couldn't be traced, the trail mustn't come back to us. He explained we could leave the purchase of the more exotic items nearer to A-Day (as it was now being dubbed), which would be less risky if we had knowledge of the potential adversary we faced. We could take a lot more chances if we actually knew the world was really going to end. We wouldn't want the risk of buying weaponry if it all turned out to be a hoax (which the team passionately believed it was).

Simon interjected, "Hold on, no one said anything about buying weaponry and bombs. I don't want anything to do with that!" We spent some time reiterating the fact that we were simply executing a planning exercise, we were not buying anything. This placated Simes and the tension left the room, though I could see Spall was trying hard to retain his poker face. Spall continued, he explained how we could recruit a team of trusted professionals and seasoned ex-soldiers as 'consultants' to work through the plan. If A-Day became certain, then they could become a training team to give the community basic instruction on how to use weapons. It would cover self-defence and engagement strategies. "We would also source Kevlar body armour to protect us from weapons, knives and potentially teeth as we would need to be prepared to face a variety of adversaries. When the virus subsides, we would need to organise scavenging trips as the mainland starts to open up to us. Even though much of the equipment and goods would be spoiled, we could start to move out as the land became safer". Spall displayed a map with key supply points, such as the supermarket in Ullapool, plus larger strategic city locations, for example a large cash and carry in Inverness. He also explained how we would require more conventional weapons such as swords, knives, bows and crossbows for longer term defence and hunting, when the machine guns and pistols ran out of useable ammunition. It would add a requirement to build significant skill in more archaic ways. "I can certainly help there" said Simon, "I can handle a bow".

The key to the defensive strategy was how we built safe accommodation. Drake intervened, "The buildings we have are not fit for purpose, I prefer to knock them all down and build a large fort ideally". Phil chipped in, "You'll never get planning permission for that, *duck*" and chuckled. "True", acknowledged Drake, "Demolishing the buildings will make it way too obvious we are up to no good. We need to leave all the existing houses in place, and then demolish what we need to on A-Day, if it proves necessary. I will need your help with that part Mr Spall. I think we are truly short of options. To avoid suspicion, we would have to fabricate some buildings and defences close to A-Day, otherwise it would be too obvious to the locals. It's really high risk as it would be too late and we would have little or no time, I'm not sure how we would do it. I wouldn't like to build a tent village or a shanty; we may have to live there for years, maybe longer, and the weather can be severe. We could build a Norwegian style wooden village, but the hill is the biggest obstacle", he was looking rather disillusioned with it all. "We'll find a way", I added.

Drake described how we would build a wind farm and use solar panels to charge long-life lithium batteries. He also talked through his plans to upgrade the sea water processing plant, conceding it wouldn't be a long-term solution. We would not have spares or electricity forever. When the mainland opened up to us again, we would have access to the streams and reservoirs for water at that point. The batteries would provide sufficient power until that time, by a considerable margin. Drake felt he needed to investigate the viability of keeping and preserving spare batteries, as they tended to get polarised if they weren't fully discharged regularly. It was pointed out by Steve that this was old fashioned thinking, and polarisation wasn't such an issue these days.

Phil went on to describe how we could dump good soil on the island and improve and terrace the landscape to grow vegetables and remove some of the trees that had been planted in recent years to give wind cover for the paths. He proposed to replace them with fruit and nut trees. He also mentioned about widening the footpaths to make makeshift roads between key points of the island. It would protect other parts of the land by restricting traffic to a small number of established routes. Phil also planned to reintroduce colonies of bees onto the island to help with pollination and provide a source of honey. He identified fishing spots and proposed we could use a fleet of sailing boats, baskets, and nets to harvest cod, mackerel, crabs, and seafood. He added, "There is also an established salmon farm in the bay. I am concerned that there simply isn't enough space to grow significant amounts of root veg or grain, such as wheat for making bread". Steve noted a few points, he needed to consider providing a mill for making flour from grain. This was where Simon had a small revelation, "Just thinking out of the box, but what about the other Summer Islands? We have three other islands we could use for farming". Drake quickly pointed out we didn't actually own those. "But we can use them to plan", said Simon. "We could assume ownership of the islands at A-Day, there would be no one to contest us. We could dump materials and soil on the island a week or two before, nobody would realise until it was too late. We could say our suppliers had dropped it there by mistake", I suggested. Phil caught on quickly, "Greenhouses" he said, "we could build greenhouses on one, and use another for livestock". I added, "We should keep livestock everywhere where it is feasible. Chickens and sheep do extraordinarily little damage, they fertilise the soil and help us to keep inedible vegetation down. It would improve the viability of the disaster plan, hopefully".

Phil admitted further work was needed regarding the types of animals required to supplement the island, whilst respecting the indigenous population and plant life. Most of the fauna was heather from what I had seen, so who cares? A side bar discussion started concerning booze, and the need for our own distillery and possibly a vineyard. "There isn't room for everything", I said. "But we do need to have fun too, or life won't be worth living", pleaded Simon, it was a fair point. We agreed to park the discussion for the time being, there were lots of distilleries on the mainland, and it was too cold for growing grapes.

"We haven't talked about communication", I pointed out. Steve interjected, "Leave that with me, I'm on it". "You didn't communicate that very well earlier, Steve", said Spall with a laugh. When Spall started chuckling it was rather infectious, and we all started to fall about, though we weren't quite sure what the joke actually was.

After lunch, Simon took the time period commonly regarded as the 'graveyard slot'. He talked about stockpiling medication, taking care to ensure we had a number of doctors in the community, including a dentist and a vet. He discussed democracy and having an elected leader when martial law was no longer required. He covered laws, which comprised of basic do's, and don'ts that we all needed to buy into. He talked about everyone having to do their share of work, rotas, jobs for the infirm (like knitting clothing), providing music and general feel-good activities, including parties and fetes. He proposed a library, and galleries of art distributed around the buildings. He led an inspiring session, but in the end things turned a little frosty. Spall asked, "Why do we care about a few paintings, if we are about to wage war?" I quickly cut into the discussion as it was spiralling downwards, "We do need to think about life after the virus or whatever it is. We should expect to return to something close to our current living standards. Also, we need to have a cover for the whole operation, and the culture and environment part is critical to create a camouflage net under which we can operate, assuming *the end is nigh*, of course". The atmosphere settled down a little. "How far are we prepared to go, when we are ultimately planning for a huge hoax? The actual development won't go very far will it?" said Steve, who seemed to be voicing the idea that others were avoiding, like the proverbial elephant in the room. I agreed it was a particularly important point we shouldn't lose sight of; we needed to ensure we left something valuable behind.

"First we need to design what the facility will look like; the vision of whatever the island will become. We must then plan in detail the steps to get us there, and make sure we can do it with time to spare. The real or hoax decision point is critical to the plan". I suggested we went ahead with our planning, and we could get together on the island at the beginning of November to share our individual schedules and harmonise them. We could then start to work out how we delivered it. I also agreed to give the benefactor a full briefing of our progress, I was certain he would be satisfied with the work so far. The group went their separate ways, leaving me deep in thought on that day in the Midland Hotel.

I wandered home in a daze. When I arrived, Kate asked "Bad day?" I knew this wasn't going to go well from instinct. I replied, "No, it was a good day, but I have lots to think about". She countered, "I really don't get your job. It just seems like you float around the country having meetings to me. You're never here to help me look after the kids. You need to help out more!" It was true, I did.

I received an urgent phone call the next morning from Phil. "I have an idea for the dwelling", he said, "can we have a quick get together with Drake and Spall?" We met at the M6 motorway services at Tebay, luckily it was early and there was a quiet corner available.

Drake was in a fairly miserable mood; I suspect he was losing focus, as he was feeling he hadn't contributed much. This may lead him to worry about how secure his job was, and therefore his precious accommodation. We grabbed a coffee and a pastry and settled down to business.

Phil started excitedly, in the manner of a university lecturer. "The problem we have is that great hill, it's slap bang in the middle of the island. It gets in the way of everything. But the problem might be our salvation", he said with an air of mystery. "What do you need from our building in order for it to keep us safe?" he asked. We talked it over for a while and a list emerged: 360-

degree observation, strong walls and gates, defensive installations, warmth and shelter. The list was quite short really. "What about using the hill itself? It is made of Torridonian sandstone, and it's covered in peat and grass. We could burrow into the hill and build whatever we want without harming the habitat too much, if we're careful. It would be virtually invisible from prying eyes. We as a species have been burrowing into sandstone for centuries, it is quite soft but can be easily reinforced with steel to make it almost bomb proof. We can also use the retained heat of the hill to help keep us warm in winter, it will protect us from the elements but keep us cool in summer too. We can use light tubes to make it bright and airy".

It was the breakthrough we had needed. Spall started to share his suggestions regarding how we could lay out the exterior and interior to make it defensible. We enthused about the idea for a couple of hours, but the discussion inevitably dried up. In the end, we agreed to part company, to give Drake time to investigate and draw up plans. Drake's darkness was replaced by a boyish enthusiasm, he almost skipped out of the café. He had a lot to think about, and he now knew he could really contribute. It was going to be a really significant project for him to get his teeth into.

2. Big Plans and Bigger Difficulties

We met again in the post office Café on the island, on a cold day in January. I arrived on the previous day and met Drake at the schoolhouse to check how he was getting on. He had made great progress with the design of our *stronghold* and had begun to test the feasibility by making small excavations into the hill itself. He had tested the ability of the rock to hold the tunnels without collapsing and it was looking good so far. He needed funds for equipment and materials, he had used his retainer up to this point. I ensured he was recompensed and explained we would be allocating funds shortly. Phil had popped in from time to time whilst I was away, I think he had fallen in love with the island. Drake had also met with Spall to discuss the defensive issues around the design. In the back of my mind, I remembered my dream where the door opened in the green hillside and hands were seeking mine, aiming to pull me to safety. I staggered, suddenly hit by a debilitating bout of déjà vu. I realised it was the place I was attacked in the dream; I started to feel uneasy.

Our new friend, Rusty, was in his usual good form, he was always cheerful, and I could see his grin through his red wiry beard as he spoke in his unintelligible brawl, "Ye come 'n' gang a' th' time 'n' achieve hee haw, yer lee is a shite". I started to gather that he was deliberately adopting a rather jovial pose as he threw a hard-hitting insult at us, knowing full well we wouldn't understand a word. I intuitively sensed his comments were banter and intended to be in good fun, but all the fun was on his side so far. I had acquired 'The Wee book of Scots Slang' and was starting to get the drift, which was greatly amusing. He had said 'you come and go all the time, and achieve nothing, and your life is worthless'. He was surprised when I retorted with "Ah hawp sae!" (I hope so). I felt we needed to get on a more formal footing with Rusty, or else we would lose his invaluable local knowledge and our ferry to the island when the tourists started to flock back in spring. The sea crossing was really choppy, and the wind was piercing. I needed to invest in warm clothing, so I asked Rusty to pick up ski jackets and thermals before the others arrived, whilst he secured basic provisions for our meeting.

The café proved a suitable venue. It was a significant wooden construction, in a ski lodge style. The wooden tables and chairs were basic, but functional. I rearranged them into a rough circle with interspersed electric heaters, they needed a little coaxing but worked. The temperature in the room was tolerable, but certainly not warm. We weren't going to venture to the bench seats outside, unless Steve needed a cigarette break.

Simon called in the eleventh hour asking to be excused, as his wife was ill. He updated me, he had compiled a list of medicines we should stock, and how we could prolong their shelf life. He also sent through some ideas expanding on the culture and work ethics. He pragmatically suggested we should deprioritise collecting books and art. He argued that if a genocidal virus came to pass, we could collect and stockpile art after the event. If there was no apocalypse, then we could compile the collection retrospectively. Either way we would be able to purchase or liberate the artworks when things settled down. He felt the big issue was retaining knowledge, it was paramount. We needed to be able to manufacture materials such as steel, electronic devices and machines. Also, we needed to retain service based knowledge such as catering and farming. Using a computer and optical disks such as DVD's was folly, as we may not have the ability to read them in a decade or so. The luxury of electricity could not be relied upon. Books, slides, films, microfiche, and other media would rot, so retaining books was an issue, they needed to be retained in a different form. I passed my thoughts on to the team as part of the meeting.

The guys arrived on the boat looking like they had frostbite. I noticed they had adorned themselves with the ski jackets, woolly hats and thermal gloves. They warmed up a little on the brisk eight-minute walk up to the café. They gathered around the heaters for a few minutes to defrost. "This is a lovely island guys, but we need to harden up a little. It's freezing!" exclaimed Steve with a shiver. Kimball had been the first to complain about the cold, but then he had initially refused to wear the thermals Rusty had given him, because he didn't like the brand. However, he soon changed his mind as the boat began its passage.

We sat down and enjoyed a warm drink. Rusty went back to the boat and gathered the provisions, for which I had paid him in cash up front. There was rather a lot of food, real heart-warming stuff too. We did have the facility to warm some of it in the oven in the kitchens, luckily. Rusty left through the café door, pausing for a second to say "Ye kin stuff yourselves sideways wi' this lot, ye pie-eater bastards". "What the hell was that?" said Kimball. I explained he had told us there was lots of food, hope you enjoy it. "I'm pretty sure I picked up the word 'bastards' somewhere in that", laughed Spall. I explained it was just banter, and the guy was golden, we could rely on him. My feelings went much deeper though, which Spall picked up on, "I'd be happy with him at my side at the walls of Troy, I'm thinking", Spall ventured, "can we bankroll him?" I think the mood in the room was broadly in agreement. "I'm on it", I confirmed.

First order of business was an ultra-quick tour of the island in the 4x4 pickup, Drake had upgraded it with Steve's help. It carried four in the cab plus three in the pickup, sitting on a rough bench seat. The pickup had huge bouncy off-road tyres, which made the ride rather fun, but then I was in the cab.

On the way up, Phil shared a list of produce he thought we would be able to farm in the Highlands climate, he suggested that we could use more than just the fields, we could utilise building windowsills and terraces, plus the large greenhouses included on the plans he'd shared with us. Spall insisted the greenhouses had bulletproof glass, in order to make them secure enough to withstand a small assault; but also, to be resistant to pebbles the sea might lob at them on rougher days. Phil expressed a concern that the glass would be expensive and also hard to construct as it was thicker and heavier. We finally agreed it was a good idea and could be feasible, providing we could get the glass panes onto the island without too many breakages.

Back at the café, Phil shared a list of important items we couldn't easily produce, which he passed to Kim to secure adequate supplies. He also shared plans for bottling and storing the produce in summer, so we would store food for winter. He also showed us on the map where he planned to place beehives, not only on this island but on the others too.

Phil grinned widely when he explained where we could locate a still for whisky, and how he would gain the expertise to run it. His plans showed where he would plant general vegetables, plus the location for irregular fields to grow grain and commodity vegetables. Then we needed to allow space for livestock and their feeds, for which we would need the ability to gather and store the stalks in autumn as winter feed for the livestock. He shared plans for water towers, which would feed the main water supply for each island, fed from both the sea water treatment plant, the freshwater lakes (in an emergency) and scavenging. He proposed having a large tanker which we could take to various streams on the mainland to gather additional water in the summer. I noted that we needed to look at our realistic ability to generate food, versus how many people we could realistically accommodate on the island. Phil looked disturbed at the thought but agreed to investigate further. As Phil went through his plans, I could see Spall was becoming increasingly agitated. Given he had more information than the others, he had started to consider the risk of unwanted visitors coming to the island, and the damage they could incur, it could impact our ability to survive. I made a mental note to discuss it with him later.

Drake took the next turn to present his thoughts. He unrolled a plan across the table, it explained the construction of a significant structure by burrowing into the hill. The facility would be all but invisible from the sea. There would be large expanses of glass which would be green tinted and mirrored in order to blend into the environment, and the glass would be bulletproof to provide the security as recommended by Spall. Even though there was little chance of attack with conventional weapons, you never know. It was possible a band of uninfected could attack us to liberate our stores and supplies, we needed to protect against every eventuality.

The drawings showed a total of four floors and had a burrow-like structure. Lots of small corridors and rooms led to a central atrium, it would be illuminated by the main window and also light tubes, it would provide access and linkage to all levels. The plan showed a multitude of storage spaces and a variety of sociable areas. The uppermost area being a large hall for gatherings and mustering defences. Every space had multiple uses.

Spall had ensured the layout was defensible, access was via two large, reinforced doors, each with defence positions and a killing ground up to a second set of doors. The design raised a few eyebrows, but they all respected the work that had gone into it. Drake promised to show an example structure after lunch. He explained, "The accommodation could house roughly ninety people at a push, the rooms could be organised by family. Each dorm has a double bed and two twin bunk beds for kids. The shower facilities are communal, as I know Phil is concerned about the amount of water they will use. We may need to restrict showering to alternate days or worse".

In the apex of the atrium was an access hatch and dumb waiter for passing supplies and munitions from the stores on the lower floor to the crow's nest above. Drake explained that the observation point would be a wooden construction with metal armour which would need to be added on A-Day to avoid it being noted by nosy neighbours.

The building's drains fed into a pipe ending three hundred metres out to sea to avoid pollution of the shores and to let the plankton do their work. The building would use the latent heat of the rock and geothermal bore holes to maintain habitable temperatures. "The pumps on the bore holes will need electricity to operate, it will come from the solar panels and wind farm we would place at the remotest part of the island". Kimball approved of the idea, but he noted we would need to make sure we had plenty of spares. Kim queried, "What happens when electricity finally fails, as it's bound to?" Phil clarified, "We will need to use log fires and good clothing to keep warm. Drake nodded, "Perhaps we could place some log burners in the plan?"

Kimball took extensive notes through the sessions, as all of the plans would require supplies, fuel, spares, and storage. It had become quite a logistical challenge. Kim outlined the supplies list he had drafted so far and encouraged the others to talk to him as new needs landed. He would have three tiers of supplies. The first tier would be housed on the island in the main storage areas. The second would use a handful of bunkers located on the other islands. The final tier would be a significant fortified warehouse located on the mainland. He requested that we found candidate sites where we could locate the facility. I also needed to consider how we could obtain planning permission for such a large structure. I agreed I would take this one with Drake. Spall agreed to help think though how we could access this from the sea without taking risk of being attacked or being infected. Also, how we could build defences, should we use this as a base for conducting any scavenging missions. Therefore, we confirmed we needed armaments and vehicles as well as a quay and a crane for offloading supplies. Obviously with all mechanical items, we would need a means of using them manually if electricity failed or if the parts wore out and we couldn't replace them.

Kim reiterated the plan for building a landing on the island in the gulley where the sea lake appeared at low tide. It looked promising, but the excavation to lower the water to a sailable depth would be significant. It may well attract unwanted attention.

Kimball's last section was manufacture, he requested help from Drake and Steve to better understand the machines we would need for the future, from kilns to lathes and industrial saws. Drake was interested in the space that would be required for all the materials and equipment; the list seemed endless. We would have to prioritise when we understood the full extent. Manufacturing could focus on the onshore facility, as we hoped it wouldn't be needed immediately, it was an investment for the future.

After lunch, Drake led us around the top of the hill, to the far side of the island. There, he had rigged up an entrance to a fake mine, complete with a sign: 'Danger Abandoned Mine – No Entrance'. Inside he turned on a small three phase generator, which lit the tunnel. On the floor were a several unusual tools which looked like large jack hammers. From deeper inside the tunnel we heard drilling sounds, a lot of banging and no shortage of loud expletives. Drake proudly showed us around, "I have recruited a few locals to help me to build this 'mine'. I have told them we are excavating a seam of lead, but I'm fairly sure they suspect we are looking for something more valuable, I have done nothing to make them think otherwise", he added with a wink. "Men coming through" he shouted, and the drilling paused, I could see another generator humming quietly in a corner.

Drake continued, "So far we have excavated a simple tunnel through to the centre of the hill. It's about 100 metres long. We have also dug out a small central chamber". "So how will you stop the workers from being suspicious when you start to widen out the plan into the rooms and chambers you are proposing, not to mention the separate floors and steelworks?" asked Kim. "We'll cross that bridge when we come to it, I think they are happy to keep quiet if we keep the money coming". Drake also illustrated how the rock was damp but was starting to dry out as the ventilation in the passage improved.

Drake explained his work to date had demonstrated that the plans were feasible, but the biggest challenge was supporting the roof of the atrium, as the space was exceptionally large. Transporting the necessary lengths of steel into the site and erecting it would be a horribly complex task, as he couldn't deploy a crane; but Drake had a plan.

We headed back down the hill exploring the feasibility of the build. Positive, constructive ideas and questions were always welcome. But then Kimball chose to have a whinge, "I couldn't live in a rotten cave! It's damp and musty, and we would all be on top of each other". Spall and I exchanged a look; I knew what he was thinking, 'What a plonker!' I explained we hoped it wouldn't come to that; we were just planning a project. Kimball had immersed himself into the role play too deeply and was really taking it personally. Spall interjected, "You could have a nice comfy place in the schoolhouse instead, if you like. It would be really helpful; if the infected attacked, we would be alerted by your girly screams".

Back at the schoolhouse, using the map, Spall showed us where we could locate lookout points and CCTV, both off and onshore. He proposed a loud tannoy system to sound an alarm in the event of an attack. We would use battlefield radios for communications, and we would build a full defensive perimeter using sectional wire fencing just before A-Day. Also, he mentioned how we would fortify the main depot on the mainland. We would sequester a number of 'gunships' there for the scavenging expeditions. The pickups would be able to tow water tanks and trailers depending on the need. He also outlined an impressive selection of weaponry, from sniper's rifles through to assault rifles and shotguns plus an extensive array of ammo. The munitions would be deployed in stores at various points on the island, where defensive positions would be constructed. The crow's nest would be the main lookout point. He made a request for advanced night vision goggles and binoculars. Then he proposed an array of movement sensors, to easily monitor ingress. He seemed to have covered everything.

Steve asked "What will we wear? Will we have armour or protective clothing?" He suggested a company in Sacramento who made a comfortable weave of Kevlar which was stretchy and extremely durable. "It wouldn't tear in a motorcycle spill and couldn't easily be pierced with a conventional blade. A standard Kevlar overshirt would provide great protection from bullets. I could easily adapt some of the gear with light aluminium panels to provide additional armour, if we needed to go further". It sounded like a great idea, we could source all our stock clothing from there and it would provide significant protection from the wind too, it could be branded with the foundation logo.

Spall reiterated that weapon and unarmed combat training would have to be mandatory for everyone, we all needed to get involved in our defence. In addition, training in more sustainable weaponry such as longbows, spears, and blades would be needed in the longer term.

Spall continued, "For the scavenging trips we deploy small 4-man teams in a 4x4 gunship, they would be small, focussed missions to gather supplies under the cover of the big machine gun. The teams would move fast and focus on clearing the roads to supply zones. For this purpose, we would need to specify winches on the 4x4 trucks, so we could drag heavier objects out of the way". Steve made a note of the requirement in his notebook. "The main priority would be to gain intelligence on the enemy and their combat ability. The teams would need to make excursions to the mainland during the early stages of the infection and may need to be equipped with breathing apparatus and skin protection". They would be dangerous expeditions indeed.

Steve took last watch, and described the generation station, the manufacturing facility and the variety of barges and boats required. He gave particular focus on a fast shuttle, a hydrofoil RIB as used by the navy seals, which lit up Spall's eyes. He enumerated the spares we required, how we would store them to maximise their life and the expected approach when technology finally failed. Horses seemed to be central to the plan for transport and agriculture. Phil started to worry at this point, it was additional livestock and feed he would need to account for.

Finally, Steve came around to storing knowledge for the future. "Obviously, we could employ a number of student researchers to locate information and build manuals for all the skills we needed, such as farming, foodstuffs, manufacture, building etc. During vacations, students will queue up to work on a good cause like this, if there's money to be had. Obviously, the internet will go down piece by piece a few months after A-Day. Therefore, we will need to take offline copies of the information onto our computer here at base. However, after a decade or maybe a little longer, the technology would eventually fail, and we would need to fall back on more traditional means. I propose we print all of the materials and build a physical library".

Kimball quickly cut in, "But we discussed this last time, the paper will perish, no matter how dry we keep it and how carefully we handle it. We can't start copying out everything like the Benedictine monks used to, it would be a brain killer". "No, you are quite right", said Steve, "We will print onto either long life plastic or ultra-thin aluminium using etching paint, it will last for centuries. Etch primer is a paint designed to physically bond itself to the substrate made by combining an acid with the paint, so the acid microscopically etches the surface, it forms a strong bond". "Ok enough detail", added Spall. Steve queried, "Have we got funding for all this stuff?" he enquired with a wry smile.

The funding query brought me neatly onto the topic of budgets, "I have set up each of you with foundation bank account containing a balance of £10 million. You need to carefully audit your spend, so I can provide audit data to our benefactor's financial consultants; you are free to use the funds for legitimate purposes however you see fit. It is a charity, so please remember to be sensible". They could all see it showed enormous faith; but I knew I could trust them. I would have to keep an eye on budgets and ensure no one went rogue. It was a simple way to get stuff done without bureaucracy.

This room became silent; their jaws had metaphorically hit the floor, except for my friend Spall, who had seen it coming. He calmly announced, "It demonstrates a lot of trust gentlemen. Let's take it seriously!" "Oh my god, is this for real?" queried Steve. Drake raised his bushy eyebrows, "Is the guy totally nuts, we are talking about millions and millions here, it's no hobby project". "He is preparing for the end of the world, guys. We need to build something to satisfy his paranoia, but also leave a legacy that people will be talking about for decades to come". "But what is the legacy really?" said Kimball. "It looks like a load of stores and equipment, and a big rabbit hole to me". He was right, there was no real value to a lot of our current plan. It wasn't going to help the environment, nor build something of any architectural merit that tourists would visit. "We said we could badge it as a variation of the Eden project", I followed. "The marketing will need to clearly explain that we plan to demonstrate how people could survive in face of an apocalypse. Lots of younger folk will be interested in how we could survive a cataclysmic event, for example a zombie attack. Perhaps we can push that line of thought, but the marketing will need to be exemplary. The theoretical planning exercise would need to be presented in a state-of-the-art audio-visual presentation, with lots of information signs around the patch similar to museums. We could create a nature trail, perhaps set up a prototype community. It could be really cool. It would be a bit off the wall for a tourist attraction, but quite a good deflection for the general public. They would think we were nuts, investing such funds. But then everyone loves an eccentric, don't they?" "Ah think th' fowk o' Scootlund ur a bawherr mair practical than that", added Rusty. We all turned around and stared at him, he had spooked us.

Everyone froze, they hadn't really soaked in the reality of the situation. They were struck dumb by the revelation that someone was prepared to front so much cash to implement these crazy plans. Hell, none of us were really experts in their fields and were delivering on best endeavours. We all agreed to get the wheels moving, and we opted to schedule regular video calls to review progress. We agreed to meet back on the island in early June when the weather improved.

I hired Rusty on a more formal footing as 'Transportation Manager', which seemed to please him, a generous regular income was of great value to a seasonal businessman. He was still able to schedule tourist boat trips when he wasn't needed, which in turn would help us control what the tourists saw of the island. I hired a public relations agency for marketing our approach. We would announce our plans to the public before we made any material change to the island.

3. Months Rolling by With Little Progress

The marketing of the project had gone well, and the media had received the announcement sceptically, with a raised eyebrow. There was a lot of discussion, ranging from a 'waste of money' through to it being pivotal in order to properly explore sustainable life on Earth. For the moment, we had the younger social media crowd on our side, and they virtually marketed our plans to all corners of the globe. The wider positive vibe really helped counter the concerns of the local community. We managed to sell our proposal to the folk on the mainland, focussing on the significant boost in tourism for the area, helping their businesses to thrive. We emphasised we would only use local tradesmen for the build. The inherent risk was that our true purpose may slip out.

My wife, Kate, was watching my project feature on the news over dinner and started to discuss it. She became overly excited; she was aware I was second in command on something that was high profile. She wondered, "But what a strange thing to do. Why would someone spend so much money on something that isn't going to happen?" "It's just a study", I replied, "he wants to prove it's possible, that we can start again without technology. To demonstrate we still have the skills to survive, and our species hasn't become weak. It's a study into the psychology of our species, it's esoteric stuff. Also, we aim to prove we can live in a sustainable way that is ultimately better for the environment". The problem with bullshitting was I needed to be consistent over time, as Kate always spotted the inconsistencies and loved to throw them back at me. "I think it's cool", said Matt, "Scientists are creating diseases to turn people into zombies, so they can build cheap armies to conquer the world. One of these viruses could get out real easy". He said, as if it was really possible, and he'd seen significant evidence. It exemplified the power of fake news and conspiracy theorists on social media, especially now they had a real platform for their paranoia. "I'm not sure it's really possible, people just like thinking up things that sound exciting". "Yes, it is real! You just don't understand how bad people out there are". I left it there; you can't ever win an argument with a teenager. "I saw a zombie yesterday, he was feeding his dog some sausages", added Ciara helpfully.

The local Planning Department were provided with a conservative set of schematics as part of the planning application, they didn't include the full extent of the excavations into the hill, and the administrator requested to inspect the exploratory construction site. They intended to make regular inspections over the course of the project.

We employed a structural engineer to gather stress data on the rock superstructures and recommend specific steel support assemblies needed to make the build compliant. We agreed to start the construction in anger in mid-2020, and the Planning Department could make a full inspection at that point. I dearly hoped we would be complete by then. It would take months to process any necessary objections, by then the build would be a fait accompli. If the world was going to end, then it simply wasn't an issue. If it didn't, then we would be able to sensibly negotiate and potentially close part of the build in the very worst case. We pushed back on early official requests to visit the island on the basis of safety and potential damage to the environment. The real driver was to keep away prying eyes. The team were well briefed regarding the timings of boat trips, based on Rusty's intel, and we used camouflage netting to obscure all the unusual items we were storing or building. Deliveries were always scheduled at dusk, which greatly pulled on the knowledge and skills of Rusty and his instinctive experience of the shoreline and reefs. However, he was really happy with his new toys; the barge was equipped with night vision, sonar and radar. He behaved like the proverbial kid in a sweet shop. There was a significant presence of engineers and equipment on the island but we had mitigated by explaining the rationale in advance with media announcements. We made it very clear the work was a temporary installation to assist with the building works when they were finally approved.

It was a cold December at the end of 2019 (T-16 months to A-Day) and a skittering of snow littered the ground. I had pulled the team back together at the Midland Hotel to try to accelerate the plan. I suspected they had become unsure about spending the allocated funds, apart from Drake who had royally blown much of his budget.

We had a long discussion, and I realised a lot of the remaining work was subject to dependencies on the building projects. We couldn't buy provisions or build defences until the core construction was complete. Phil continued his work on the island. He had installed a range of well-concealed growing boxes and greenhouses; he had already created some great spaces for livestock and crops; however, it was not enough. Phil explained the facility as planned could only feed roughly thirty people over a full year, allowing for possible wastage. Things would improve when we cultivated the other three Summer Islands.

Kimball had secured ten acres on the mainland, near to Polbain, with good access to the main road. As luck had it, it was already classified as industrial land, and he had managed secure planning permission for a large warehouse. The approval was on the basis that much of the footprint was below ground, but it brought immediate concerns from Spall, as height was always a tactical advantage. Kimball assured us the section above ground was around seven metres high and would be easily defensible. The sides would have no access, the rear would be adjacent to the water and the front would be encircled by a heavy gauge chain link fence. Razor wire could be added to the top near A-Day.

On the top of the building, the roof would be constructed with reinforced steel, which would be sufficiently solid to add additional buildings and defensive emplacements. Spall added, "We could dig trenches around the fence, which we could flood with kerosene, piped from a tank on the top of the facility. No one could cross it and remain in one piece. Kim added that construction was due to start in two weeks' time, well ahead of plan.

The excavation of the new quay remained on hold. I urged the team to prioritise it, as we couldn't land anything on the island of significant size without it. Drake was at the point of needing to bring in large quantities of steel to support the major constructions in the Haven, he had begun to excavate the larger chambers and the atrium. I had no idea how he would transport the steel from the quay into the tunnels and hoist them into position. It sounded impossible. It would take a lot of hands, some serious pulleys, and much ingenuity. Drake planned to use the winch on one of the pickups to pull the RSJs up the hillside. It emerged that Drake had rigged up, with Steve's help, some large wheels with soft tyres to attach to each of the ends of a steel, so they could be rolled into the tunnels.

Drake's progress had accelerated with the new larger equipment, but it was noisy. Because of this they had to keep a look out for nosy sailing vessels nearing the island. However, we were no closer to making the space habitable. Kimball agreed to start work on the quay urgently. The crane was already in place, but the excavation to make the sea navigable wasn't yet thought through properly. It would probably require an expensive sea platform with large scale digging and dredging equipment.

Later, Spall updated me privately that he had obtained the name of an intermediary. A friend of a trusted friend who could secure us the weaponry we needed from an arms dealer in Armenia. He could arrange the first delivery in six months' time, but we would need to store it somewhere secure and away from prying eyes. The ammo and larger weaponry would be arriving in a second consignment later in the year. There would be so much gear it would fill the farmhouse and possibly several of the other buildings near the quay. It worried me, as we would be taking our first illegal step. I encouraged Spall to defer the delivery until we were much closer to A-Day, and we were absolutely sure we needed to go down that path. Spall said he would see what he could do, but we might lose some of the critical items in the consignment if another agency put their money down first. We were forced to take that risk. I needed more confidence in our path to be able to sanction such a risky procurement. We had to keep it quiet from the rest of the team, but the delivery was hard to hide. We needed an excuse to get Drake and Phil off the island when it arrived, but that would only cost me a few rounds of beer.

By late December, I started to dream again. It began with the usual progression of events, but then there was a radical shift in the content. I continued to note down the details of the dreams, it remained compelling for me. The dream went further back in time and showed a myriad of small meteorites travelling across space and entering our solar system. Even to a luddite like me, I could recognise Saturn, Mars, and Earth in their ellipses around Sol.

The meteorites were spread into groupings. There were a handful of small meteoroids way leading the group, a significant gap, then a larger cluster of meteoroids which seemed to go on for some time. The first group hit Earth in the landmass a little north of Europe. A few months passed and then the larger body pummelled the breadth of Earth systematically, every single land mass was hit. The flow of the dream moved into my original nightmare, but the crazy people were infected by the meteorites, it was the source of the virus. I woke with a start. The dream had a very different message, it had become a timeline of events. One thing that really stood out was that the events started earlier than I originally thought, with a small number of isolated impacts. It provided me with confidence, as I could demonstrate the vision was real in advance of A-Day. I could use it to commit to our course of action.

I called Spall the next day and shared my new intel. We agreed to urgently meet at a quiet coffee bar in Salford. Firstly, he unfolded out a world map and asked me to show the location of the collision. We roughly identified the impact site as being close to Kostroma in Russia roughly at the end of the year before A-Day. My memory would normally be a little hazy, but these events seemed to have more substance.

The target location was somewhere between the Volga and Kostroma Rivers. Temperatures would be icy at that time of year, reaching on average -6 degrees Celsius. We needed eyes on the ground to confirm the aftermath. Spall felt the arrival of the meteorites would trigger an infection as per my dream.

Due to the small, isolated population involved, the infection might be quarantined and completely censored by the Russian government. It was likely there wouldn't be any news coverage, leaked news in social media would be denied and targeted by Russian spammers. Positioning someone on the ground would provide the ability to confirm the vision was real. We could also gather critical information about the virus, and the aftermath we would face. One of my dreams had indicated that the virus was fungal and used spores to propagate. We discussed giving the operative a heads up about wearing a suit or gas mask to protect him from the potential virus. Spall laughed, "And you think he would fit in and be inconspicuous in a bloody hazmat suit? In Russia? Anyway, if the meteorite hits, then the dream is true, right? And if the dream is true, then the guy is going to die. I don't see how we can change that". Spall decided to reach out to another of his military friends and we left it there.

Spall strongly recommended that I started to bring the team into our circle. I must explain there wasn't a benefactor, and it was me who had the dream. It was inevitable, it was just about timing really. I guess the next meeting would be roughly a year from A-Day. Spall mentioned that a few of the team fostered suspicions already.

I had scheduled the next face to face meeting to be hosted on the island in April, and I was looking forward to seeing the new facilities being close to completion. It was probably good timing. I just hoped they wouldn't react too badly and decide my plans were now a wild goose chase and split. Simes was able to attend the meeting, it had been some time since we had seen him. It would be good to catch up on his progress in person.

4. El Ángel del Barrio 6C (Francisco)

From the writings of El Tigre

In 2011, Lucy announced that she was pregnant, completely out of the blue. All was looking good; she had sailed past the rocks of the first twelve weeks unscathed. We were excited, Lucy started to buy baby clothes, and I decorated the small spare room as a nursery. "What colour do we paint it?" I asked, knowing there was no sensible answer at this stage. "Pink", she said with no hesitation. She hadn't told anyone other than her Mum so far, but the news wouldn't stay secret for long.

A couple of weeks later we were looking forward to visiting the hospital for the first scan. We arrived early, registered and joined the inevitable queue. We waited for quite some time, and I became restless. I decided to grab a cup of coffee, we were 13th in the queue, so I had plenty of time. It was fortunate I wasn't superstitious.

The coffee machine was broken, so I headed for the adjacent ward. I walked to the coffee machine and faintly heard aggressive shouting beyond the doors; the language was inappropriate for a hospital. A motorcycle gang was causing havoc in the next ward. I looked at my feet and took a deep breath, I felt a faint presence at my side, but no white figure and no message on this occasion. I felt a quiet reassurance, a reminder to 'be brave'; it didn't need to be said. "Why me?" I asked the white presence, but as usual there was no reply.

I walked into the ward, being careful not to look confident, I was not aiming to draw attention to myself, so I could assess the situation. My face was angled down towards the floor, but my eyes were attentive.

Five guys in motorcycle jackets, with 'Hijos de la Muerte' (The Sons of Death) on their backs, watched as one of them was admitted to the ward. There had clearly been some disagreement with the staff; often nurses see motorcycle accidents as self-inflicted and are not always too sympathetic. It would be sufficient to set off an argument with this crew. The guy in the hospital bed was shouting expletives at the top of his voice. A smaller grey-haired guy grabbed a nurse by the throat, choking her violently as he screamed at her. Two of the others drew blades, they slashed them menacingly.

I noticed blood on the floor, I realised the duty doctor had been stabbed and another nurse had been cut. It was already a nasty situation; and the trouble was escalating dangerously. The guy with the long beard shouted, "If any of you even think of calling security, you'll get my knife in your gut! Then security will get the same treatment". Hospital wards were fitted with CCTV these days, so security would have already called the police. Hospital guards duties didn't include breaking up knife fights, it was way above their pay grade.

The guy with the beard clocked me entering the ward and raised his knife as I walked directly towards him. "Quieres un poco de este bastardo?" (you want a little of this, bastard?) he yelled. I walked up to him calmly; he stabbed out and I blocked his knife hand. I delivered a uraken strike to the bridge of his nose, a whiplash back handed technique which was fast and harder to block than a conventional punch. It proved enough of a distraction for me to break his arm and force him to drop the knife. He sat on the floor with his nose streaming blood; he screamed and kept on yelling as confusion reigned.

Two of the other gang members charged me, one with his knife out in front, the other lining up his fist for a vicious blow. Telegraphing a punch like that was ridiculous, it would not end well for him. I took out the man with the knife first, with a low kick to his knee, which put him down quickly. I then disarmed him. The second man tripped over his fallen friend and took an off-balance swipe at me. I deployed a basic Aikido technique to add to his momentum, and throw him to my right, whilst holding onto the arm and twisting it. His arm made a terrible cracking sound as it snapped in several places. Seeing three of his friends taken down with a vengeance knocked the confidence of the fourth, who started to back off as I approached. "I don't want any trouble", he shouted. "Well, I do, you motherfucker", I replied calmly, and hit him with the palm of my hand under his chin. His head jolted back violently, and his legs folded beneath him. The guy in the bed stayed put, good move.

I dragged the bikers into the corner by their hair, conscious or not, and assessed the situation. It was worse than I feared. The Doctor was down and bleeding badly, two nurses had been cut and another was looking bad, but there was no evidence of blood. I shouted, "Is there a doctor in here?" The nurses indicated there wasn't, so I instructed the ward admin to request an ER team, urgently. I then asked her to call security, I didn't want any of the bikers getting away, though I guess in hindsight they were going nowhere. The guy in the bed was trying to get up and dress himself, but he caught my eye, and he sat back down and sighed. A couple of the injured staff might not last until the team arrived. I had no medical training other than basic first aid, I felt powerless to help.

The familiar presence materialised by my side once more. An unnatural knowledge and confidence filled me, it was like someone else had taken over my hands by remote control. I triaged quickly, then asked two mobile patients to grab towels and apply pressure to the wounds of the bleeding nurses.

The doctor exhibited a serious knife wound to his abdomen. I gently lifted him onto a bed, I cut away his clothing and examined the wound. It wasn't deep, but it was bleeding profusely. An injured nurse had recovered sufficiently to bravely offer help. I suggested she use a swab to clean the wound, and to find a sterile needle and with dissolvable suture or thread. I quickly stitched the artery, cleaned the wound, and sutured the laceration. I left the nurse to dress it. The doctor was waning in and out of consciousness, but he had regained a little colour, it would suffice.

I asked the uninjured nurse for an update on her colleague. She explained that she had been strangled violently, her trachea was crushed, and she was struggling to breathe. Her face was a deep shade of purple and she was starting to panic. I pinned her to the floor and asked the other nurse for a scalpel. I retrieved a ball point pen from her top pocket, took off the top and dumped the ink cartridge onto the floor. I located her trachea with my fingertips and made an incision in her neck. I inserted the tube from the ball point pen into the windpipe. She instantly started to breath and calmed. I felt like I was in a dream, and my body was reacting as if by remote control, it was the weirdest sensation.

The ER team arrived with security, the guards had seen the CCTV footage and knew exactly what to do. They formed a cordon around the biker gang until the police arrived and took them away. The medical team triaged, and instantly assisted the nurse with the damaged windpipe. "Good tracheotomy", the doctor remarked, "take this patient to the ER and ask for Doctor Carlos. He'll fix her up". He moved to the wounded doctor, removed the bandage, and examined the wound. "Take Dr Parsek to ultrasound and check out that wound". Finally, he assessed the remaining nurses. He carefully checked their wounds and sutured them, and the team dressed their cuts.

The doctor turned to me, "Thank the Lord you had medical experience my friend, good job". "I haven't any experience", I replied as I sat beside the wall. My fingers had been guided by someone else, I have no idea what I did or how I did it. My confusion gave way to darkness. I didn't realise I had suffered a wound to my stomach, I had not been aware of the injury during the heat of the fray. The adrenaline had disguised the pain, allowing me to function as normal.

I awoke to see the worried face of Lucy, "Thank God", she said softly. "What on Earth have you been getting into this time? You nearly died you stupid, stupid man. I couldn't face this world without you!" She cried softly with a strong sense of relief, "I almost had the damn baby when I heard". A crowd of nurses and doctors were standing silently behind her with expressions of relief on their faces. One nurse said, "El ángel está despierto!" (the angel is awake). Then the TV camera pushed through the throng to focus on my battered face. "Get them out of here", shouted a loud voice, and security appeared and escorted the cinematographer off the ward. "It's a hospital, not a party", he added more softly, "this man needs his rest". Hearing that I had no medical experience, those present had seen my work first hand and assumed it could only be divine intervention.

It was three days before I was discharged. Each day, well-wishers brought flowers, fruit, and religious paraphernalia; it made me feel privileged. Lucy and the baby were fine, that was my main priority. "How did the scan go?" I asked, suddenly remembering the reason we had visited the hospital in the first place. "She is fine", replied Lucy. "She?" I enquired, "how wonderful". My abdomen was still causing me pain, I managed to walk from the ward to the lift without any issues.

Unfortunately, this time there was a lot of newspaper coverage. My bandaged body was splashed over the front pages with the headline 'El Ángel del Barrio 6C'. There was talk of erecting a statue in front of the hospital building, depicting my fight to save the doctor and nurses. I really hoped it didn't happen, but my optimism was failing, it started to seem inevitable.

Suddenly, everyone knew me and wanted to shake my hand. It brought lots of business into the bar, but Lucy could sense I was becoming more and more uneasy with the attention. A few weeks later, Lucy explained the well-wishers weren't actually calling me the angel of ward 6C. They were claiming an angel had helped me. I felt a little arrogant; but in the end it made me laugh, but my ribs still hurt.

In the fall, the statue was finally erected. It was nearly three metres tall, and it had a fair likeness of me. It was unusual in the way it depicted me fighting at the same time as healing, both scenarios merged into one magnificent modernistic statue. The backdrop for the scene was an angel, with his hand on my shoulder and his face turned towards heaven. It was a beautiful work, but I'd rather they got rid of it. I walked to work past the statue every day, and I'd started to hate the bloody thing with a vengeance. It symbolised all that was wrong with my life, when I wanted to focus on all that was good with it.

By far the best thing that happened in the fall was the birth of my daughter. The labour only lasted an hour or so, and out she popped. A big, beautiful baby girl. The staff at the hospital made a huge fuss, and we were given all the clothes and toys we would ever need for the child. She was healthy, and boy did she have a good pair of lungs. It felt like five minutes later she could say 'Dada', and it seemed as though five minutes after that she was up and walking. There was never a dull moment with Colletta. Lucy was a wonderful mum, and she doted on our little one.

5. Coming Clean

One year to A-Day, on a misty wet April morning, we gathered at the island café. We were getting close to the deadline, and we needed to get down to the more esoteric parts of the plan. I was hoping the major works would be complete.

I didn't quite know how to explain my misdirection, so I stumbled straight into it. "Guys, I have a confession to make to all of you. I'm sorry, but I haven't been totally honest and transparent with you about this project. I hope you will understand when I explain my reasons". All faces turned to me, waiting for a revelation.

I elucidated further, "It was me who had the dreams. It is also me funding the operation, there is no mysterious benefactor". I walked the team through the dreams I had, and how serious they had become. I also conceded I had my doubts, but after the long string of lucky gambles and investments I was forced to believe it was no coincidence. I chose to have faith, plan for the worst, and hope it wasn't true. I took the team through the reasons why I felt I had to hide the truth. The fear of rejection, fear of making myself a laughingstock, the fear of failure in case all of it was true.

Drake kicked off boisterously, "Bugger off! You started telling me this load of old pig shit once before. I wasn't having it then and I'm certainly not having it now. Why on Earth would you waste a fabulous amount of money, when you could have done so much good with it?" He sat back and looked thoughtful for a few seconds and let it all soak in. The others were in deep thought. "If you weren't utterly convinced it was real, why would you do all this?" said Kimball, he then voiced the more important concern to him, "So we will still get paid?" "Of course, yes you will, you have a contract with the charity, and I have put your money is in Escrow, you have the documentation. However, if my dreams prove true, then you won't have any shops to spend it in!" Kim laughed and said if it came true, he would be rather happy to share this damp cold shithole with us all. It did lighten the mood a little.

Spall timed his interjection well, "Listen guys, if Paul thinks this is real then we have to take it seriously. I have known him an exceedingly long time and he's not someone who has flights of fancy. We finish the job, for which we are getting well paid, and we go our separate ways in a years' time". Drake grinned, "Well, duck, at least we'll have a nice holiday home for the forseeable". Kimball laughed, "You think I'd come here for my holiday?" Phil said, "Well I would. It's absolutely great in summer; I wouldn't be anywhere else. It has been a dream come true for me".

"Of course, I knew all the time", muttered Steve, "It was obvious, the benefactor was suspicious by his absence, all his money was being spent like waves breaking on the rocks in Badentarbat Bay". He received cat calls from the group after his response. I saw how his jaw dropped when I broke the news in the first place, he was devastated he hadn't seen it coming, as he prided himself on being in the know. But he did enjoy his moment of false bravado.

My revelation received a cool reception from the guys, but they grudgingly acknowledged that it didn't really make much difference to them in real terms. They had a contract of work for someone with too much money. They conceded it was such a strange story that they totally understood why I didn't disclose it from the start.

It was a good time to share the news of my latest tranche of dreams, the team agreed they provided an early warning to validate the authenticity of the message. The group were concerned that a mere few months warning was not sufficient, as the plans would force us to break the law. Steve interjected with a well thought through argument, "Do you really think you only have a few months warning? Our telescopes, and more so the radio telescopes, will see meteorites coming long before they enter our solar system. These meteorites will hit the news at least two to three months before they actually impact the ground. It would be big news and the BBC and CNN love stuff like this. They'll have the scientists and astronomers on the show. It'll be a really big deal". Everyone went quiet, while they were worked through the math. "So, if the first group is scheduled to impact Earth on 20th December 2020, there would be newspaper reports in September. We would have a definite go/no-go decision at that point. We would then have six months to break the law, if we are forced to", said Simes trying to look nonchalant. It was only five months from now!

Spall commented, "That's a plan, I can order the munition deliveries in October. I guess I can cancel, at a price, if we don't need them. "Hey, hold on", I said, "these are very rough timelines. We need to allow a month either side of that as a contingency". "Ok, end of October it is", replied Spall. He added, "We can begin to build the perimeter fences at the start of the new year. On that subject, here is the latest defensive plans for the island". "Lets hope we don't need them!" Phil interjected, and everyone agreed.

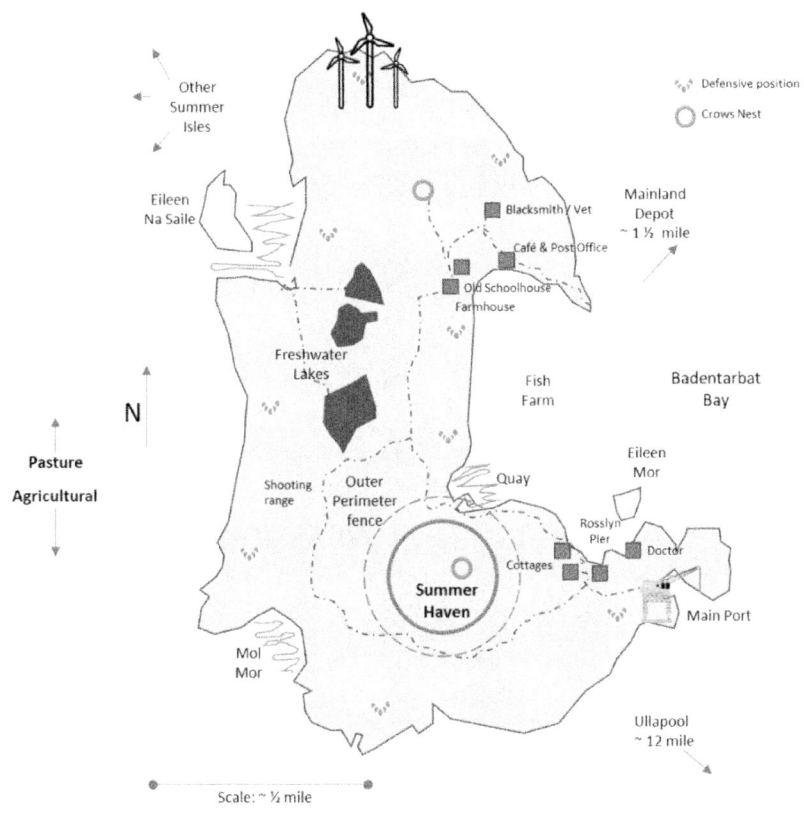

"We plan to have 2 crow's nests, one atop Miall Mor at the highest point, and one smaller lookout post on the hill at the other side. I aim to provide full arms caches at defensive positions all over the island, which we will build from sandbags just before A-Day, and we will surround some of them with razor wire. We will also perimeter the key positions with movement sensors and CCTV. Large gatling guns will be installed at the main ingress points, plus the crow's nest. These would bring down a hundred infected in a couple of seconds. The M134 GAU-17 'Vulcan' cannon is a six-barrelled, air cooled, machine gun which fires up to six thousand rounds per minute".

Spall's briefing elicited a wow from the team. I think at the time I would have dared a whole company of soldiers to attack our island. But it was nonsense really, we didn't have an army to deploy to the positions. Spall had previously explained that from A-Day, everyone would need compulsory weapons and basic soldiering training.

After a long discussion, I allocated the remainder of the budget to the team and retained a meagre £10 million for emergencies. The money was starting to run down, but then look at what we had achieved.

We spent the evening in the 'Ferry Boat Inn' in Ullapool. We decided to take some time off, to give our minds a chance to mull things over, discussing the project was banned. I invited a few locals to join us, and our pal Rusty. We had some great seafood and more than a few beers. But as the guys warmed up, I stopped drinking. I really had to be careful to ensure we didn't let anything sensitive slip.

As Drake's tongue became a little loose, I had to call a halt to the party. I promised we would have a few more drinks back on the Island. Rusty's girlfriend, Sheena, had emerged as promised at 10:00pm after her shift at the hotel. She was ready to see him home, but she kindly agreed to take us back to the island first, Rusty was not sober enough to pilot the boat. It emerged that Sheena had marine skills, they met in the Royal Regiment of Scotland, they were soldiers before Rusty joined special forces, he had also served in a special attachment of the Swiss Guard.

The next morning, we all felt a little groggy after several drams, we met in the Café. Phil shared plans to set up a still and a beer brewing vat in the old post office part of the building, Phil had chosen the wrong day to discuss booze, and we couldn't muster any enthusiasm. He had visited to the still on the Island of Jura to understand the distillation process. He'd agreed to purchase their old still. I ensured we all grabbed a hot drink, and we commenced the walking tour of our new facility.

We entered Summer Haven through the abandoned mine tunnel at the rear. The windows and main entrance were taking shape on the east side, the elevation was inconspicuous from the shore. The green tinted mirrored glass worked very well, angled slightly forward to reflect the grass. Drake announced proudly, "This is the way we will bring the planners in, having covered the front window areas with fake astroturf boards. The entrance covers about a third of the construction, for the benefit of the planning inspectors. However, when you go through the 'Danger of Collapse' area you will see the larger space: the atrium and the lower floors".

He continued into the main area and uttered, "Voila", as he threw back the large double door with the warning symbols. The expanse opened into the atrium. It was amazing, its high ceilings drew in plenty of light from the windows and the light tubes. It was an industrial construct, with the steel supports, pipes and cables fully visible, but it was a really effective space. marble tiles and some of the basic fixtures were being installed by his crew.

Drake continued his tour past the bore holes and the heat exchangers, which when commissioned would warm the Haven. The solar panels would drive the pumps extracting the heated fluid from the bore holes, some two hundred metres into the Earth's crust. "The engineer estimates that these babies will generate enough heat to keep the Haven at around 18 degrees, even in winter. It should be comfortable", Drake explained. "Where are the radiators?" asked Kimball. Drake explained, "I have installed underfloor heating, it runs throughout the whole building excluding the larger storeroom in the basement. The storeroom is insulated from the rest of the complex and will be our cold store. The ambient temperature of the stone should keep the lower floor at around four to six degrees centigrade depending on the time of the year. Almost as good as a fridge".

Each bedroom and dorm featured whitewashed stone walls, operational sinks and a toilet closet. "Showers will be communal as we need to manage our use of water, as Phil suggested. Drake added that the newly installed wind farm on the north point of the island would generate all the electricity we required. Occasional log burners were installed, and flues had been cut into the rock. The complex was impressive, and remarkably close to completion. It was great to see the things we had discussed becoming a reality.

The defence positions, perimeter and killing ground surrounding the front doors would be erected a week before A-Day, but we could see their intended location.

Phil continued the tour past the limited pasture, including the emerging flocks of sheep, cows, pigs, and other livestock. In the near future, the main pasture and farmland would be placed on the other islands. He had constructed a horse ranch close to the old sailing school and away from the new training ground, utilising the existing huts and cottages. However, the most impressive development was an array of small agricultural terraces appearing on the hills. They were laden with vegetables and herbs, in various stages of growth. It looked wonderful, like a Hobbit's garden. They gave way to uneven plantations of crops, wheat, corn, barley, larger vegetables, and fallow.

The island would make a reasonably interesting tour, if our plan B was put into action. It was as if we had terraformed the island, from a crag into a garden. Phil built on this point, "The island is essentially just a big rock. The soil was mostly of poor quality and there wasn't much of it. We've had to import all the soil onto the island, there are millions of tons of it. But imagine how hard ploughing will be if the equipment starts to fail, these are not flat fields that a combine harvester can process. I hope we would relocate to the mainland before that happens". The sleeper constructed retaining walls would be critical to keep the soil in place as the winds ramped up in winter.

We completed the quick tour as the rains started to move in. Sheets of rain pounded the hills, it ran off through age old rock gullies down to the sea or the 'Lochans', the three small but surprisingly deep freshwater lakes in the middle of the island.

In the afternoon, we took to the boat to see the new building on the mainland. We got soaked on the 30-minute ride over to the facility, luckily our coats were very warm and waterproof, but my trousers were sodden. Spall talked about the defences to be positioned on the top of the new facility with enthusiasm. He explained how we needed to run some attack scenarios and war games to ensure their effectiveness. I'm not sure anyone was really listening, except for Rusty. I gestured quickly to Spall to cut it, waving my open hand across my throat, but it was way too late.

Not surprisingly, Rusty had lots of questions. "Ah knew ye bastards wur up tae something", he guffawed, "Urr ye starting a pumpin' war?" Our carelessness had become a problem. Rusty's army training kicked in; it became clear he missed nothing. He had clocked all the building materials and tools, and some of the more unusual constructions, however he had said nothing at the time, not to anyone.

I was forced to explain the unusual gimmick we had adopted to help market our sustainable eco-friendly tourist attraction. "We are positioning Summer Haven as a place where you could survive a world ending event or a chemical warfare attack". Rusty replied, "Aye ah read that in th' paper. Ye mist think that a'm soft in th' heid". I was forced to explain our situation fully and have faith in our friend. I gave him the full story, bringing him to the same level of understanding as the others. It was Spall's turn to use the flat hand across the throat gesture, with a wide grin. Rusty took it all in his stride, he thought it was funny. "Yer a' pumpin' mad, bit dinnae worry yer secret is safe wi' me", he laughed.

As we neared the mainland, I started to consider Spall's words. I realised we could use my notes to test our defences. The dreams mapped out typical attack scenarios, which could be useful to us. It might explain why the dreams had evolved and changed, and why I was urged to take notes. Spall and I needed to sit down and work through the details when we returned home.

The new facility was bland in appearance. The main building shell was complete, it was like a big airy warehouse. Drake mentioned the planners were confused why we were wasting money by grossly over engineering the steel support structure, and why the walls were thick steel rather than lightweight alloy. He had told them the owner was American, and it was how they did things over there, he laughed. Already the space was separated into areas for vehicles, stores, and weapons. The walls had sealable defensive slots every few metres 'to allow good air flow', the water side had a sizeable quay with protection from the waves.

Several locals had complained about the quay. Drake had explained to the planning team that it was not documented on the plan, as it was only a temporary facility to allow freight access and would soon be removed. The extraordinarily strong wire fences and gate at the roadside of the building gave way to a wide driveway. Spall commented, "The preparations are in place for razor wire at the top of the stanchions. The wire fence will keep the enemy at bay whilst we hit them with the Gatling gun from the rooftop gun emplacement. If they breach the fence, we will use the slats in the main building for 2nd tier defence. We will run our scavenging trips from here, so this will be our base: Ground Zero. The risk is if we hit the fence with the gatling gun it could rip through the mesh, so we will position the weapon where we can fire over it".

A makeshift meeting room had been built in the corner of the facility; we took our seats for the last part of our meeting. The team looked drained; it had been a long couple of days with too many revelations. I empathised; the foundations of their faith had been shaken a little. Simon finally took his turn; he passed around a small booklet he had prepared. He explained he had been working with English Law students on a mini project to consider communal regulations. It was extremely basic but was built from the assumption we were a primal culture with no modern-day trappings. "Please have a look at this, it has been distilled into some really simple principles. I've tweaked it to our remit. Text or email me if you have any thoughts or suggestions. Please don't ring me, as I do have a day job", he added.

Summer Haven Community Regulations

All matters will be resolved by a democratic court

Capital offences which could lead to the perpetrator being ejected from the community.

- Allowing outsiders into the community without authorisation
- Introducing disease or infection
- Killing or seriously injuring another
- Stealing
- Rape
- Destruction or damage to community assets
- Gross cowardice or negligence – causing harm by your failure to act
- Not following the chain of command when under attack
- Not contributing or persistently not completing assigned tasks

Behaviours to be encouraged.

- Democracy
- Not coveting possessions - Everything is shared by all
- Being vigilant
- Learning to defend ourselves
- Learning new skills – partnering with those with experience
- Working hard
- Sharing knowledge and helping each other
- Being positive and building on each other's ideas
- Listening to what others say and being prepared to change your point of view
- Keeping your areas clean and tidy
- Recycling rubbish and composting food waste
- Being brave for each other
- Being kind and thoughtful

The last question before we broke was lobbed into the group by Simes, it was incendiary. "So, if the inevitable happens, whose lives are we going to choose to save, and how do we get them here?" It's strange how enthusiasm transitions into stress when the rubber hits the road. At some point a conceptual exercise moves from the hypothetical, into something real; in just four months we would know if my dreams were true.

6. Life or Death Decisions

In June we met in Manchester. The faces around the table were tense, and body language was awkward. I had been giving a lot of thought to the last question posed by Simon, who do we save? The first item of the session was even more telling, how many do we save?

I had called Drake and Phil the week before, requesting we finally come clean on numbers. They needed to quantify how many people we could feasibly accommodate and feed. They would present their thoughts at the meeting.

Drake's view was the facility could accommodate seventy people, excluding the cottages and the old schoolhouse, which we would use for stores. Possibly ninety if single folk used the dorms, but then these rooms were spartan, like an army barracks, simply an array of beds in a room.

Phil had been conservative and roughly calculated the food could sustain around fifty people long term, if we worked hard to preserve our produce. However, in the first year or so it would only be thirty to forty as the crops would not be fully established. In the following years it would increase to around eighty-five people as we cultivated the other Summer Islands.

We each listed our immediate families and came to a figure of 49, plus a handful of locals such as Rusty and Sheena. "It's too many", argued Steve, "we must bring in needed skills. Let's add them to the list, excluding those already possessed by our families". "We can't bring all our families and close friends, it's just not possible. If they have the critical skills, then we can make a concession". As horrifying as my line of thought was, I couldn't invite my parents. They were old and wouldn't contribute much, they would panic and within five years they would be infirm". The thought of this made me nauseous. Seeing my distress, Spall cut in, "Steady on mate, it might not happen. Remember?" "It gives us a total of 105, still twenty too high, but hopefully, we can find multiskilled couples to reduce the number", I pointed out.

Kimball had a dark breakthrough when he mentioned the concept of attrition. "What I mean is", he explained, "some simply won't come. You may have 105 people on day one, but sadly some will die. There will be illnesses we can't treat; people will die in combat. In the first couple of years, we could lose a significant proportion of the team. If we can accommodate them, then we should let them in. In the first two years our numbers could halve". "Jesus", said Phil, "that's not a welcome message, but sadly I guess it is realistic".

Kimball built on his idea, "What you have to remember is, we only need to grow enough produce to feed our families for a few years. Given the shelf life of dried products and tinned food, we could ensure we had sufficient stores to feed everyone for the first 12 months, until attrition kicks in". Drake added, "Well then we could initially fill the schoolhouse and a couple of the cottages. We could simply invite the full 105 and just manage for a while". His idea was pragmatic, but we would feel hopelessly sad leaving many of our loved ones behind.

We reviewed the list of additional skills. Simes suggested that we should start to reach out to people in the local Scottish community plus our network of friends and acquaintances to identify candidates for the additional places. "But we must bear in mind this is the seed from which the new human race may be formed", said Phil, "we must have a significant bias to younger people, those who can adapt and can bear lots of children to begin the next phase of life on our planet". "Right, so all of us old lags can sling our hook?" said Spall challengingly. "No, we need experience and genetic diversity too. But we must ensure we can introduce children into our community, if we want to survive", countered Phil. "So, it's all a done deal then" laughed Drake. Phil hesitated, "No, I'm thinking hypothetically. I guess I may be overthinking, it's starting to feel deeply personal".

"How do we gather everyone on the list in Summer Haven for the evening of A-Day, without explaining the apocalypse to them?" asked Simon. He added, "We obviously can't tell them we are transporting them to a damp stone bunker on a remote island in case the world ends". Steve strutted, "We invite them to a big party; a huge event; one that's impossible to resist". "Hey dudes, drive 300 miles then take a rough boat crossing to a remote island for a huge rave. It'll be so cool", laughed Kimball mocking Steve.

Simon appeared thoughtful, then slowly added, "No, but what if we throw a launch party on behalf of the Charity Foundation to introduce Summer Haven? We could make it really ostentatious, inviting the guests formally from the office of Sir Patrick Hastings-Crawley". Steve added sarcastically, "Yeah, and maybe we should create a bogus Wikipedia entry in for the guy. The first thing they will do is google the big guys name. I did, and it came back with nada, that's why I was suspicious from the start. You really need to cover all bases if you want it to work".

Steve agreed to fabricate the fake persona on the web and link it to the project as background. We decided to throw the party of all parties, one that people would be crazy to turn down. "It will be the long-expected party", grinned Steve, "Paul can start with the Bilbo speech, in our very own hobbit hole". "I don't know half of you half as well as I should like; and I like less than half of you half as well as you deserve", I chipped in with my hands crossed on my belly, laughing.

The formal invite from the sponsor's address looked expensive on gold leaf letterheaded paper. It offered guests a limousine service to their local airport and an executive helicopter shuttle from Inverness to the island. We built a makeshift helipad on the western side. The stated purpose of the party was to wet the head of the new project on the day of the formal press launch.

We offered fine champagne, fancy hors d'oeuvres and a remarkable banquet created by a celebrity chef. It promised attendance of the rich and famous. On offer was the very best luxury accommodation. "They will have a shock when they get here", Drake mused. "Too bloody late then", laughed Spall. "We could make the main atrium look ostentatious and post pictures on social media in advance. It would be event of the year. No one could refuse the opportunity, surely?" added Simes.

I agreed to send out the invitations quickly as it was such a huge event. I secured the services of our PR agency to pull it together and add the necessary glitz, money was no object. Steve made sure the event was splashed all over the web, and

I had the invites sent out the following week. My family was really excited, I hoped the others reacted in the same way.

"My goodness Paul, you must have really impressed the guy", exclaimed Kate, "I really can't wait, it looks fabulous". Even Ciara and Matt went bananas, all the kids at school were jealous as they had seen the event posted on social media.

We had titled the invite 'Party for the End of the World', which not only chimed with the theme of the project, but the irony played to the darker side of our sense of humour. The thought of the indulgent party lifted our spirits at a time when the UK and most of the world was locked down with the COVID-19 virus. COVID was just a little taste of what was about to come. The lockdown slowed progress a little, but we still had sufficient time.

Spall and I worked through the attack scenarios using my notes. The planning went well, but we found a critical weakness. The proposed defences struggled to cope with a sustained mass attack, as we would be unable to clear the dead before spores were ejected by the fungal mycelia. Spall later discussed the issue with Rusty and Steve, and they came up with the idea of a sulphur bomb. An aerial grenade which dispersed a cloud of sulphur. The ordnance would be for emergency use only.

Steve would arrange to have a consignment specially manufactured under an R&D banner. If we could get the spreading mechanism right, it might be highly effective. There was a risk to dispersal in high wind, the sulphur cloud would drift, we would have to allow for wind displacement when we deployed. Spall clarified their efficacy in simpler terms, "I guess it's not too different from the terrorist weapons used in Afghanistan, where the plastic explosive is covered in nails and dog shit, in order to kill those nearby but also poison and maim those further from the blast. When deployed the payload wrapping the explosive is distributed over a wide area". Nasty stuff. Steve would work out in what form we would need to deploy the sulphur, it could be pressurised containers such as an aerosol, in a solution or dry powder form. Also, we should have a backup if the sulphur didn't eliminate the fungus as we hoped.

7. The Weight of Public Opinion

The main efforts of the PR team had hit the street. They facilitated prepared interviews with newspapers and magazines, there was also limited publicity on natural history TV shows plus a big push on social media. The papers progressed from showcasing to mild mockery, to trying to probe into the business sense of making such a huge investment. Overall, the hype came and went, a quick news blip and onto more pressing world matters. They were waiting to see how our innovations would save the world; their knives were being sharpened in readiness.

The mainland had seen the publicity and had heard about the fancy party, seeing the press launch but tending to deride or turn their noses up. They thought it was a fancy party for the big wigs and the filthy rich, so what? But opinions started to change as they realised the guests would need accommodation, food, and other trappings; it could lead to an early April tourism boom. Generally, people across the breadth of Scotland remained neutral about the whole idea. It was ideal for our apocalypse plan A, but a terrible disaster for the backup plan. It was unlikely we would ever recoup any of the ridiculous sum of money invested. However, it would all be preferable to the alternative. What the hell, I started with nothing. I could sell the island and go back to work.

The summer rolled on; we were all waiting with trepidation regarding our September meet. The midges came in their clouds at the end of August, I felt like every square inch of my entire body had been bitten, I itched like hell. Worse than the midges were the cleggys, they were large black horse flies. The females offered a more significant bite and were a real pain. Phil advised me to eat more garlic, as it was a natural repellent. The trouble was this would repel people as well, most likely. Phil had planted wild garlic near all the gathering areas on the island, which would help suppress the flies. He also planted eucalyptus, it too was a natural repellent, but a little less effective unless you went to the trouble of extracting the oil.

The Planning Department were keeping unusually quiet. I knew Drake had been bribing some of their more senior officials, in order to prevent them from asking too many questions. However, as the marketing and the newspaper debates matured, it started to make the officials and more senior members of the general public think about the extent of the changes made to the Island. They realised the building work seemed to be much more extensive than the plans they had approved.

The sheer volume of deliveries observed was deemed ridiculous. Then there was the ugly carbuncle further round the coast, the crane. The officials were becoming convinced something subversive was going on. The whole topography of the island was changing, and although it improved it considerably, it was a significant change which had not been signed off.

In early August they decided to challenge, and those we had under our influence were not in a position to impede the investigation. The planners ordered a full and detailed inspection of the island, and the recent works carried out. A more prominent councillor actually went on record as saying we had ruined the natural beauty of the island, the work had to stop, and the Summer Isles had to be reinstated to the original buildings and natural habitats. The only advantage we had was that the wheels of bureaucracy ran slow. We received official notice there would be a full audit at the end of August, and our full cooperation was mandatory.

We mounted a legal push back on the basis of incorrect information, but it never had a chance, they were quite within their rights. It was merely a delay tactic on our part. The legal threats only slowed their pace a little, but they did relent in pushing back the inspection to late October. I hoped we would know more by then. We observed more vessels than usual making their way around the island, with official looking people using long lensed cameras and binoculars. In fact, we could see them much better than they could see us, due to our expensive optics. However, they could only really observe the agricultural changes to the island. The old mine cover, and the fake grass camouflage over the windows made the building virtually invisible.

Most of the large scale building work was now complete; the focus had moved to the second fit. However, there was still a significant amount of cargo being shipped in, such as beds, kitchen equipment, bathrooms and soft furnishings. Our twenty-man team continued to work, and their comings and goings needed to be disguised. The transportation of larger items: such as parts, fittings and building materials, had to be done by night as the port was painfully visible. It was increasingly hard to cover up all the activity.

The extent of the works was preventing some of the indigenous birds and wildfowl from inhabiting the island. Phil had mixed feelings about this, the birds would damage the growing plants and eat the seeds. He hoped things would return to normal when we had finished building.

Several pups appeared on the island; Sheena acquired them from a friend, they were very friendly dogs, a mix of Alaskan Malamute and Husky. Dogs were useful as they had superior olfactory capability, they could smell an intruder from miles away. A couple of cats were also introduced into the residences, Drake explained that they would control the rodent population. One dog, Rosie, took a particular liking to me and we quickly became friends. Rosie had a soft light brown coat, with a ruddy red mottled back and a big smile.

The press noticed the island was becoming a little overcrowded with livestock. We anticipated we could ship them to the other islands over time. Spall was keen to build two-way zip lines between the islands, enabling us to move between them easily, and drop supplies. With Drake's help, he erected a series of towers, the zip lines would be installed on A-Day.

I was making too many trips to the Highlands, and it grated on my family's nerves as I was away for two to three days every week. I tried to use video conferencing for my meetings, but it was not helpful. The internet bandwidth on the island was virtually non-existent, despite Steve's attempts to patch beamed microwave connections to the mainland. He was also working on plans to deploy satellite internet, which was fine for downloading information but terrible for upload, it still didn't resolve my technical issues. However, it improved Steve's research and the printing of manuals and reading materials. Kate finally lost her temper, and I was forced to moderate my travel to a couple of days every two-weeks. The upside was I did find I had a little more time for myself and my family. I had been working so hard, I hadn't indulged in any of my hobbies, and I was becoming unfit.

In order to spend more quality time with my family, Kate and I took a trip to Chester Zoo with the kids. I experienced a strange sensation when we passed the tiger enclosure. I had a feeling the gate had been left open and one of the beasts had escaped. It really spooked me; I continued looking around nervously. Matt picked up on my body language, "What's wrong Dad, you look like you're expecting something to attack us". As we passed the next corner, an overwhelming sensation gripped me, a sensed a large cat leaping from the undergrowth. I lashed out with my arms, but there was nothing there. It really scared me; it was a nightmare occurring whilst I was wide awake.

At the time, I remember feeling a presence beside me, helping fend off the animal, I felt we had faced the threat together, our life forces combined in some way. I knew it wasn't the white being I had encountered in my dream, but more like a close friend or a relative. Kate was concerned, she enquired, "What the hell is wrong with you? You look like you're afraid of your own shadow!" It was a strange sensation, something I couldn't explain. The feelings passed quickly, and we carried on with our day out, we had a picnic, ice creams, and everyone was happy. My little incident was soon forgotten.

8. The Rise of the Tiger (Francisco)

From the writings of El Tigre

Much of the next decade went by in a flash. My beautiful daughter Colletta was growing up. She was the image of her mother, and there was nothing I wouldn't do for her. We spent many lovely summers in the park and by the sea. We had picnics and went to the cinema, doing all the things that families do. Lucy and I taught Colletta to read, she was a bright kid, and she was progressing well at school, so we figured she deserved a special treat for her upcoming ninth birthday. More than anything in the world, she longed to visit Zoo Aquarium Madrid at Casa de Campo, as I had worked there. It was late in the summer of 2020, and a little after my forty fifth birthday. We decided to make a weekend of it. We took the Renfe AVE train which took roughly two and a half hours.

The next day, we aimed to arrive at the zoo early before the crowds; it was always so busy in the tourist season. Colletta was beside herself with excitement. We walked from our hotel, and we were in the zoo by 11am when it opened to the public, it was becoming busy already. I could find my way around easily and still knew a few of the staff.

We headed for the aquarium initially. Colletta absolutely adored the turtles, she could have sat there for hours watching them. We took seats and watched the dolphin show, she was thrilled. Lucy and I had seen many dolphin shows over the years, but Colletta's excitement was infectious; it was like seeing it for the first time. She was less excited when we went into the shark tunnel. Her expression was one of genuine concern, "And one of those actually bit you Dad?" she asked doubtfully. "Yes, but it was the best thing that ever happened to me". "Why? They have rows and rows of very sharp teeth. Didn't it hurt?" "Yes, of course, it hurt a hell of a lot", I responded. "But if that shark hadn't have bitten me, then I wouldn't have married your Mum. See how lucky I was?" Lucy and I exchanged warm glances.

Following lunch, we made our way to the animal enclosures. The pandas were popular, but Colletta's favourite were the koala bears. We walked past an array of caged areas, the last one being a special exhibition of Siberian tigers. We neared the bars, and the hairs instantly stood up on the back of my neck. "What's wrong?" asked Lucy. I had a feeling the gate had been left open, it really spooked me. My eyes flicked around nervously. As we edged forward, I felt a large shape walking on a parallel path to me in the undergrowth. I couldn't see it, but somehow I could sense it. Lucy asked, "Are you ok? You look nervous, it's making me feel uncomfortable".

A class of twenty school children turned the corner, I could hear them long before they came into sight. They were on a weekend trip and approached haphazardly, several of them stared into the tiger enclosure, as one of their teachers lit a cigarette. The gate to the enclosure was open, it wasn't something I had simply imagined. I told Lucy to grab Colletta and get the school kids over to the café quickly. It was about 50 metres away, past the field and picnic garden. She became utterly confused for a moment, but then from her face I knew Lucy had seen the beast stalking us. It had emerged from the undergrowth just behind me. The zoo was designed to look like a jungle, and it provided plenty of cover for the tiger.

I put myself directly inbetween the tiger and the children. "Don't worry, I used to work in this zoo, and the tigers like me", I declared out loud confidently. It was bull, but it helped calm the kids down just a little, allowing them to think and function. It was enough to get them moving to the relative safety of the café. Lucy kept them calm and placed me between the tiger and the kids, so it didn't have a clear line of sight of any of them. The group started to back away slowly, if one of them broke into a run, Lucy knew the tiger would attack immediately.

The tiger's eyes focussed on the children and tracked them. Its tail flicked to and fro, almost nervously. I knew this was a sign of indecision in the cat. I held still for a few seconds, until its indecision cleared. I knew it would consider twenty meals to be better than one.

I attempted to appear more threatening; I puffed up my chest and bared my teeth. I was aware that this didn't scare the tiger in the slightest, but it regained its attention. I estimated Lucy and the kids would have covered around half the distance to the restaurant. I needed to buy a little more time. I lurched forward and growled suddenly. It caught the tiger by surprise, I suspected it was preparing to pounce. It hesitated just for a moment and then it attacked before I had a chance to fully prepare.

The children hadn't quite made it to safety, but I knew they were sufficiently close to minimise the risk of attack. As prepared to leap, the tiger gathered its strength and hunched its back legs. It was one of those occasions when time slowed. I had already experienced this far too many times in my life, however I truly believed this was my last, no one survives a tiger attack. The events of my life swept past me in a blur: waking up to Lucy after the shark attack, getting married, the birth of Colletta. I'd had an amazing journey; life had been more wonderful than I had I'd dared hope. It was the last second of my life, I was going to die. I whispered the words, "Goodbye my love".

I felt a flash of anger; why should I have to leave the world in this way? I experienced a moment of clarity, an epiphany if you like. The words of Dylan Thomas came to mind, "Do not go gentle into that good night". The tiger launched itself, triggered by my fear. I felt a calming presence at my side, and a stillness fell upon me. "What would you do, if your assailant was merely a man?" he asked me. "Choose to be brave!" In a moment of absolute terror, I felt a supernatural connection with my brother, and I knew he could feel me. We were one, he would be there for me and I for him. Together we were strong! I wasn't going out of this life without meeting him.

The tiger leapt through the air; I crouched low. As it came upon me, I surged upwards into an *empi-uchi* elbow strike using the adrenaline-charged strength of my thighs and forearm. I screamed as I struck. It was a powerful technique, the best option in close quarters. I could feel the breath of the beast as it pounced. I put all my strength into the blow and the resulting force was joined by the momentum of the monster. I locked my back leg as I struck, so all my bones were aligned, like a spear. The combined momentum focussed on the tiger's jawbone; it then became an issue of accuracy. A question of which bone would be the weak link in the chain: its jaw, or my forearm. The blow hit just to the side of its mandible; the force focussed on the point just below the tiger's temple where it connects with the skull. The tiger struck and bowled me to the ground. I felt a pain in my right side and my face, then the impact of the ground on my back, plus the full two hundred and fifty kilos of the tiger ramming into my chest and abdomen. But the tiger didn't move, it just left the huge pressure from its weight on my chest. I twisted from under it and rained blows into its face, which had no effect whatsoever, but I started to realise the tiger had ceased all movement as my red mist cleared.

I limped towards the café; a large glass window full of faces stared in horror. I was bleeding from a dozen places, so I must have looked a terrible sight. I eventually approached the pane and spoke to Lucy, "Is everyone safe?" She nodded affirmative, I slid down the window into unconsciousness. The last thing I heard was shouting. It was Lucy screaming for help, over and over in blind panic, "Stay with me!"

I awoke in hospital with Lucy by my side once again. I was really in a mess this time. The doctor said I had physically died, but they had managed to revive me. I was strong, and lucky to be alive. What was this life but a rollercoaster cocktail of love, laughter, fear, and pain? But once tasted, you wanted more. I had been unconscious for five days; I flitted in and out of awareness for three more. I couldn't move, my face and my abdomen hurt. I had three cracked ribs, and my face and stomach had been savaged. I had multiple cuts and bruises all over my body. It felt like I had been hit by a car. It took a couple of weeks to get out of bed this time.

Colletta and Lucy were seated by my bedside, "Hello love, how are you doing?" "Fine, feeling a little better thanks. Time to get myself up!" The nurse overheard and started to object. I swung my legs over the side of the bed and stood shakily. I felt shooting pains, but I didn't topple. "Ouch!"

"My dear god, there's no stopping this man", said a passing porter. The nurse admonished me grumpily. A day or two later I managed to get myself home, the day after that I removed the bandages from my face whilst showering. I attempted to shave, but the skin around the scar tissue was too tender. In the mirror I could see the terrible scars on my cheek from the tiger's claw. Three diagonal raw lines intersected my face from below my ear to just beneath my eye. I was lucky not to have lost an eye or an ear, it looked hideous. Lucy said she thought it made me look heroic. I smiled, but still didn't feel too good about it. She wrapped her arms around me, and we kissed briefly, it hurt.

The newspapers reported I had hit the sweet spot on the tiger's jaw, a thousand to one chance. A combined 350kg of mass from myself and the tiger had applied a huge force to the weakest part of the beast's mandible. The impacted bone had less integral strength than my forearm and it had snapped away from the skull and the momentum drove the shard through the softer tissue, directly into the brain. It was as if I had pressed the tiger's off switch. It was more than simple luck; I knew something extraordinary had occurred.

There was no avoiding the paparazzi this time. I was now well known in both Madrid and Alicante; the papers were plastered with 'El Tigre'. A student had taken a video clip of the whole damn thing on his phone. The clip went viral on social media, not just in Spain but across much of Europe. The lad made a lot of money on YouTube but had been persuaded to donate much of it to the zoo. After all, the zoo had lost a majestic creature, and part of a main exhibit. Everywhere I went they called out 'El Tigre'. Can I have a selfie? Could you sign my autograph book? It was driving me crazy. I hated the attention; I just craved a quiet life. When would I get peace and quiet? I started to suspect I would only find peace in the grave.

The media attention worsened when others came forward to tell their stories of my misadventures, including the shark attack. The very last straw was when someone scratched three claw marks onto the face of the statue outside the hospital in San Juan, as they had connected me with the events on Ward 6C. There was now no escape, I feared to leave the house. I was more afraid that very soon the kids in school would realise Colletta was my daughter, and her life would be impacted too. Why I had been singled out to face these terrible events? It was more than a coincidence. Why me?

The self-isolation I imposed to avoid my unwanted notoriety was compounded by the rampant pandemic of the COVID-19 virus, it resulted in me becoming almost a recluse. I didn't care to leave home even after the lockdown had been lifted. The symptoms were all too familiar for Lucy, as she had suffered from agoraphobia before we married. She was desperate to save me from going down the same track. The factors compounded and drove us to make, what turned out to be, a catastrophic move to Malta in late 2020. To this day I could not be sure why we selected Malta as our new home, I simply felt a pull towards the place.

9. Justification or Vilification

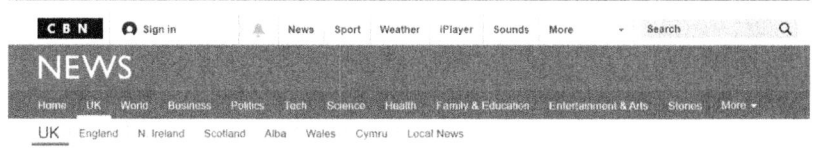

Astronomers track a large group of meteorites, a number of which will be visible from Earth in late September.

Tuesday 5th August 2020

Scientists at Jodrell Bank Observatory are collaborating with academics around the world to track a group of meteorites which are heading towards our solar system and will pass in close proximity to Earth. Their trajectory will take them close to our sun. The path is likely to take the meteorites into Sol's gravity well, which will slingshot them on their onward journey across space. The first, smaller, group of meteorites will be arriving in the last week of September and are likely to be visible to our telescopes as they near Earth. The larger group will pass by in spring next year and will result in a rare display, as some of them will inevitably fall under the influence of our gravitational forces and burn up in our atmosphere as shooting stars.

"This will be an unprecedented opportunity to see a significant body of meteorites, it's an exceedingly rare occurrence indeed. A once in a lifetime opportunity" said Professor T. Roe, Principal Scientist at Jodrell Bank Observatory.

The Lovell radio telescope at Jodrell Bank remains the largest of its kind globally, although the latest technology favours an array of smaller dishes. Jodrell Bank partners with the SKA (Square Kilometre

Array). international project, which will revolutionise our ability to observe space ...

A call came in from Steve at 6am on Tuesday 5th August, he was almost screaming down the phone. "Paul, have you seen the news? Switch on your TV". I was half asleep and felt groggy to say the very least. Kate woke and asked me which of my crazy friends would be calling at this time in the morning and advised that I should tell them to clear off. I apologised and explained it was a work emergency.

I headed downstairs and resumed the call. Steve continued, "It's on CBN, Sky and the BBC. I'll send you the link. It's the meteorites, Paul, they've seen them! Jodrell fucking Bank have tracked them. They're coming in the last week of September". "Calm down Steve and talk to me. Are they really sure?" "Yes, but they say most of them are going past Earth". "I really hope they do", I replied wistfully. "Jesus, its real! It's really happening! What are we going to do?" exclaimed Steve. "We have a plan", I explained. "We are the only people who know exactly what we are going to do. We will finish Summer Haven and sit this one out. I need to tell the others and expedite the plan". I didn't know if I felt elated that my predictions had been justified, or trepidation of events to come.

I called the each of the team and forwarded the links to the news articles. Everyone was in deep shock, but I sensed that through it all, a deeper determination was building, except Spall, who said, "Well this is what we've been planning for. Time to kick some ass!" Typical. I encouraged them to ensure their friends and family were safe and were attending the party. At least I could offer my team a path which meant those closest to them would survive, even if the future looked unclear and dangerous. At least they would be safe for now.

The following day, I chatted to Spall in my office in Congleton. "We know roughly where these babies will land. Did you manage to secure intel from that area?" Spall explained that a guy from his platoon, Dimitri, was involved with a Russian woman who ran a small factory in Yaroslavl, in central Russia. Their employees mostly comprised of his old squad from the Russian naval engineers. Spall had made a substantial offer to one of these guys to provide three weeks of reconnaissance in central Russia, wherever the meteoroids hit.

Dmitri's comrade was under explicit instructions to report every day by private blog using an anonymous account, so it couldn't be traced. His remit was to merely observe from a distance and keep away from the meteoroids and those who may come into close proximity, to avoid possible radiation poisoning. Dmitri said his comrade laughed at the thought of the danger from radiation, he believed these were merely lumps of stone from space. He'd said, "Rocks of no interest, but if your fool friend willing to pay me well, what the hell. I happy to take money from stupid English pockets".

I replied, "Sounds good. But do you think he will be able to get any meaningful information at such a distance? I guess we can ask him to take a small amount of risk but I'm not keen on putting his life into any real danger, as you said before he can't walk around a Russian village in a hazmat suit". Spall explained, "My contact will monitor army and police radio frequencies, so he should obtain additional information that way. He will also gather data from the locals. He is taking three weeks of holiday from the day before the meteoroids are predicted to arrive. If they don't arrive, we will pay him regardless". Therefore, we had him locked in and we could look forward to a full report. There was no way he would turn his back on the money, as it was significant. I must admit my concerns were that we might fail to classify the nature of the virus. It was pivotal that we knew how it affected people and how to protect ourselves. Any information was a blessing.

OMG it was all real! The thought kept running around my head, even though I really knew from the beginning. My friends were going to need more support and reassurance as the days went by, it would be become a nightmare for them, and they would be losing sleep too. We needed to keep our focus as the days rolled on, or we would compromise the entire project.

My thoughts eventually turned to the people we couldn't take with us. What would I say to them? The fact was that there was nothing I could do or say to help. If I advised them, in real terms it might make their lives worse, they would surely think I had lost the plot. Taking measures to protect themselves might just mean they suffer longer.

The team met again at the Midland. Everyone was in an agitated state; except, of course, for Spall, who was his usual calm unflappable self. "Everything has changed! It isn't a hypothetical project, it's as real as this brick wall", said Kimball with a heretofore unseen level of urgency. I stepped in, "We are the lucky ones; we have a plan. We just have to execute it and make it work. There are six similar locations scattered around Europe; perhaps their leaders had dreams too. Some might be as prepared as we are". No-one understood why all the locations were in and around Europe. What about

Australasia and the Americas? From what I could remember of my dreams, they were all wiped out without exception. I explained I had a rough idea of the locations of the other six havens. It was odd that they were all islands, they were in close proximity to the mainland of France, Spain, Greece, Denmark, Italy, plus Malta. Malta was remarkably close to the other Italian haven near Sicily. The others were well distributed.

We reviewed the remaining work, and how we could accelerate it. Most of the build's second fix, the fixtures, and fittings, were complete. So were the agricultural projects on the main island. The COVID-19 pandemic had slowed us by several months, but we were slowly catching up. It was all about gathering our supplies and moving them into storage now, plus acquiring armaments.

Phil pointed out we also needed to drop huge amounts of soil and materials on the other Summer Islands so we could start their cultivation after A-Day. We would have to do this after the planning inspection, in order to avoid additional suspicion. There was some concern that the inspection would not go well, and we may be forced to undo a lot of the work we had done. "Over my dead body", I said in perfect synchronisation with Spall.

Spall replayed the moral dilemma we had discussed previously. "Ok, so we know A-Day is really happening, we will be the only ones to survive. In the last few weeks, how far are we prepared to go, in order to make it happen?" "I'm sorry, I don't get you", I queried. "Well first off, we need to start buying illegal weaponry: machine guns, RPGs, you name it. In the worst case, let's assume the police find out about the weapons and perform a search and seize, or the planners tell us to take down the work we have done. How far do we go to defend ourselves? Do we let them do this to us? They will all be dead in a few days, so why do we care? Do we just eliminate them and carry on?" It was a difficult thought for us all.

I knew couldn't back track; we had a lot yet to achieve. We couldn't restart the build after A-Day, as we were unable to access the mainland for at least a couple of years. I considered my response carefully, "We can't start murdering people", I explained, "we need to try to delay things like planning inspections and follow up actions as much as we can. We can go on promising and not doing anything for quite some time before they bring in the big boys. In addition, we can sabotage our cranes so they can't bring equipment onto the island. If they try to make arrests or take our supplies, then we need to defend ourselves. There is no other way". "If it comes to lethal force, will you give the order, will you all stand behind me?" asked Spall with grave concern in his voice. "I will. But we need to do everything in our power to avoid that circumstance, or we will lose who we are. It's a last resort, and it may prove to be a necessary last resort", I stated firmly. "Well said", added Phil. We were all in agreement, but it bore a heavy weight on all our shoulders. We knew at some point we were going to have to kill to survive, it wasn't just shooting zombies in a game, these were real people. We would be forced to contemplate murder.

"We need to make some dust, people", announced Spall, "let's talk again when we have the intel".

10. Reconnaissance and Aftermath

On September 22nd, the media announced the first tranche of meteoroids had a trajectory that would drive them directly into Earth's atmosphere in a weeks' time, which was an unexpected outcome for the academics. They assured the public that they didn't need to worry as the meteoroids would burn up in the atmosphere which would create a dramatic light show as they disintegrated.

On September 29th two meteorites impacted central Russia. A further meteorite was lost in the Baltic Sea and the other smaller meteoroids burned up on entry into the atmosphere. We awaited news from our contact on the ground in Russia with bated breath. The blog entries arrived from Sergei at the end of each day and started to paint a rather disturbing picture for us all. However, there was useful intelligence in the stunted script posted.

An English Apocalypse - Paul JC Edge

Unedited Blog Entries from Russia

---- Sergei Votraski 29/9/20 22:45 MSK -5deg Celsius ----
2 meteorites hit 112 clicks SWS of Kostromo at 19:17 small crater no collateral damages.
Dust cloud rises above crater 300m radius / clear after 2 hours no residue seen on snow.
Target in open fields, no building damages, no death people or animal.
No interest from local, nothing on radio, quick mention on news.

---- Sergei Votraski 30/9/20 21:17 MSK-5deg Celsius ----
Watch all day until night fall. Nothing happen, nothing on radio or news. I go back to hostel, TV say nothing too.

---- Sergei Votraski 1/10/20 23:21 MSK -8deg Celsius ----
Boy visit site on ski, dark hair short big blue ski coat – look at crater - leave
Later, boy back with friend, taller thin mouse hair no ski.
First boy collapse choke, fall down not get up, look ill – maybe should help, best keep position.
Illness sudden, not sure cause. Symptom not crater, 2 hours very fast. Thin boy run away, maybe get help.
Adult return with thin boy on snowmobile - stocky blue wool hat
Adult attacked by ill boy, thin boy run away – boy strong attack teeth nail fist.
Ill boy kill man! man dead how? Boy not right. What fuck is this?
3 more adult arrive on ski with thin boy all attacked 2 die, boy eat from freezing body.
Thin boy like animal/bite/kill, boy move fast, strong like adult but crazy.
Man 3 run away, leave 2 men dead behind.
Dog come sniffing, sniff ass sniff crater sniff everything - no affect him? tomorrow perhaps, we see.

---- Sergei Votraski 2/10/20 20:55 MSK -2deg Celsius ----
Dog back, sniff, go away.
Report on radio, police come big vehicle. Short boy look dead. 2 men dead.
Very big mushroom? grow from boy head at neck. What?

An English Apocalypse - Paul JC Edge

Man get up - attack police. Man slower than boy but strong, kill 1 police. Police shoot man – dead. Police bring in scientist many truck – put up tape, tent
5 hour later dead policeman go crazy like boy - kill 3 policeman start to eat from dead body – What fuck?
Policeman no move. Reports on radio go crazy – talk of mad people virus emergency.
Army arrive in truck and armoured car - fence off area.
Too slow, mushroom make pop, dust cloud.
All people behave odd - some run some fall down. More radio talk say virus epidemic – quarantine.

---- Sergei Votraski 3/10/20 12:17 MSK -2deg Celsius ----
Radio say quarantine no work - cordon 50km.
I leave now – army come with gun. Police radio report 150 die – more mushroom grow.
Tupolev Tu-22 bomber plane circle area 3 time – army leave fast.

No further entries.

The media stories confirmed the incident that Sergei's blog described, but without the more alarming details. The meteorites had impacted between Yaroslavl and Kostromo, 50km south of the river Volga. However, Russian media reported zero casualties. The meteorites were said to be rocky metallic bodies compromised of mostly nickel and iron; they were of little scientific value or significance.

No one managed to make contact with Sergei since the incident, he had seemingly disappeared off the face of the Earth. Spall's friend in Russia speculated that the army had taken Sergei, Dimitri was unhappy with the situation. Dimitri accused Spall of not providing all the facts, and became threatening, assuming he was in prison or dead. Spall denied any knowledge of the outcome, his mission was a basic scientific fact finder. Dimitri became suspicious, Spall had spent considerable funds for observation duties on a basic meteorite landing. Spall didn't appear to be particularly concerned. "Sadly, they will all be dead soon anyway", he said dismissively.

Social media started to spread conspiracy theories about events being hushed up in central Russia, and there had been considerable military activity in the area. Locals seemed to have lost touch with relatives in the Kostromo region. Some 1,270 people were claimed to be missing, but nothing was ever confirmed. The Russian government denied all knowledge, and claimed it was fake news and western sensationalism. The worst speculation was that a tactical nuke had been deployed to control the spread of the virus. There was heated activity from Russian hackers, allegedly, who proactively targeted the sources of the conspiracies; we heard truly little from them after that. We were easily able to read between the lines and we were never more than a few steps from outright panic, but we held it together. We had to.

What became immediately clear was we may not be dealing with a virus at all. It was very confusing, there was talk of 'mushrooms' and dust clouds in Sergei's blog. Technically these clouds could be spores of some kind, which made the infection airborne and considerably more dangerous and difficult to contain. Our strategy for decontamination and extermination might be fundamentally flawed.

Steve identified a natural fungus that better illustrated the infection cycle. We watched a BBC David Attenborough documentary on YouTube, it described the malignant lifecycle of a fungus called Cordyceps.

Cordyceps is a killer fungus that invades the body of an insect to grow, its ultimate purpose is apparently to control the insect population. The fungus infected the insect via spores, the infection grows inside the insect and the growth exerts pressure on the brain, like a tumour, sending the poor creature insane. It then finally kills the insect and sends up a fruit (possibly like the mushroom described by Sergei) which transmits more spores. It looked really freaky and sent chills up our spines; it was hard to feel safe that night. The thought of mushrooms growing out of the backs of our heads was not a nice thought to settle us down for a good night's sleep.

The other odd factor in the messages were a seemingly different speed, both of infection and mortality, in the host itself. Also, the different levels of aggressiveness between the two *types* that were observed. The child must have been extraordinarily strong to overpower the adults, it seemed impossible.

Humans only use roughly half of their muscle strength and drugs, or mental states augment their ability. Therefore, manics or meth addicts can be unnaturally fast or strong. Perhaps the infection worked in the same way. There were too many unknowns.

We needed to determine what kind of antifungal agent would work on the pathogen and fast. But we had no way of acquiring the information, we had no samples to test. We were forced to acquire a range of agrochemical fungicides and hope one worked in the field. We could use the agent to kill the fungus before we safely disposed of the bodies, dousing for a few days before incinerating the cadaver.

We postulated if we could also use antifungals to treat abrasions or bites where the spores had entered the wound. The fungal nature of the infection remained inconclusive; we would have to cover all bases as best we could. It could be something alien that humanity hadn't encountered before.

We weren't going to obtain pathogen samples, nor were the Russians about to disclose what had actually happened. I have no idea why they needed to maintain confidentiality, maybe they had employed terrible measures to control the spread, as the conspiracies suggested. One thing, they had clearly acted decisively and rapidly. Even in the face of the quick response, the casualty rumours showed the infection took one hell of a toll, if two small meteorites could have this impact...

Steve circulated a web article detailing the method to eliminate fungal spores.

'Unwanted fungi in a yard or garden can be very difficult to kill because the visible cap of the fungus is only the fruit, and each fruit has thousands of tiny spore seeds. Even when fungi are removed, their underground mycelia sources can remain, according to a study by the University of California State-wide Integrated Pest Management Program. You must get to the root of the source to be able to kill the fungus spores, and there are natural and chemical methods available'.

Steve saw an opportunity, the underground part of the fungus, the mycelia *sources*, appeared to be contained within the human host. If we discovered a means to treat the fungus, it could be applied to the 'fruit' and to the body and hopefully exterminate it. Spall and Steve suggested we treat the fungus with a cocktail of fungicides and or bleach. After a while, we could incinerate the bodies prior to safe disposal. We needed to determine an optimum time window to ensure the spores were dead, as the heat from the fire would send spores into the atmosphere. We set up a conference call to review Steve's proposals in more detail.

Much heated debate concerning the biting comments followed. We had all seen zombie movies, and the creatures mainly attacked with their jaws. In the films blood sprayed when they attacked. In reality, human teeth don't lend themselves to biting, we are omnivores, and the purpose of many of our teeth is to grind and pulverise vegetables. We don't possess a great array of canines and incisors. Even a dog bite doesn't spray, like in the movies. What is the efficacy of a bite? Why did the host have a tendency to bite? I guess it all came back to an animal's genetic coding, which sits beneath conscious thought. A bite is hard to defend against in comparison to a strike; it's similar to a head butt and extremely effective at close range.

We considered obtaining several large tanks, each containing market leading fungicides from each of the major classes: contact, translaminar or systemic. The volumes needed made storage an issue and we faced many products. Using his knowledge base, Steve briefed us, "It says here fungicides in powdered form are usually around 90% sulphur and are very toxic. Sulphur is the active ingredient in most fungicides. Why don't we cut to the chase and store sulphur powder, it will keep for years? We can dilute it when we need it, or just use the powder directly, it might be easier. What do you think?" It seemed like a better proposal. "But what if it doesn't work?" asked Kimball, "we will then be in trouble then". Spall suggested we also stored tanks of common bleach. The chlorine in the bleach provided an antiviral, antibacterial and antifungal activity, "We don't really know for sure we are dealing with a fungus here!" We agreed it was a good idea. Kimball grinned, "If it doesn't work, there will be lots left to clean the floors and toilets for years to come".

Phil commented, "We need to be really careful with these chemicals, we don't want to kill our livestock or the fauna and flora. Our drains eject directly into the sea , a high concentration of chemicals will harm the indigenous species". Spall lost his cool, "If we don't kill this fucking fungus, we'll all be dead. We won't need any crops then, will we?" I quickly interjected to try to calm things down, "We'll all die if we don't eat". I suggested we applied the bleach and/or sulphur to the bodies sparingly and made sure we removed the topsoil with the cadaver after burning. "But this is all theory based on some knowledge from web searches. We need to be very sure", challenged Simon. Steve agreed to consult a professor who he knew at the University of Dundee, where they had created a geomicrobiology specialism.

Phil recommended we planted more herbs with strong antifungal properties around the coastline, such as garlic and turmeric. It may not help, but it was worth a try, we could use them for cooking if all else failed. The garlic also helped with the midges, as he had suggested before.

11. Completing the Vision Under Duress

The Council Planning Department opted to pay us a visit late in November. Spall had seen them coming from over a mile away, having picked their vessel up on the radar much earlier. He called me on the radio, "Should I just send them a gift-wrapped RPG right now? They won't pay us any more visits after that!" I could tell from his tone he was kidding, but I think we had both given it serious thought. They arrived at the main quay, as expected.

At the head of the quay, they were welcomed by Simes and I. We asked the others to take a low profile. It was a really cold, blustery day, so we contrived to keep them outside as much as possible. There was nothing like subliminal messaging. We didn't offer warm drinks or hospitality of any kind. There were five in their party, and they were demonstrably self-important.

After a quick look around the island, they were vaguely approving of Phil's landscaping activities. The improved pathways, the fruit trees, the planting, and crops were breath-taking. They also noted the improvements we had made to the salmon farm, the water processing plant, and the electricity generator. They realised the construction remained in harmony with the island.

However, their mood plummeted when they became cold, and the time came to inspect the main build. They had clearly been patronising up to that point, to put us at our ease. They hoped we would incriminate ourselves; it was a bid to get to the heart of what was really going on. Their officious leader,

Peasebody, was domineering; he wore a crisp suit, expensive tie, and greased back hair. Even though he was only thirty something, on his nose he sported a pair of old-world half-moon spectacles, they looked quite ridiculous. In his hands he clutched a leather briefcase and a long black golf umbrella. Behind his back, Simes regarded him as 'the Child Catcher',

We decided to come clean with them. There was only four months to A-Day, the build was complete, and we had absolute certainty of forthcoming events. We had halted the supply movements, and we had hidden the first shipment of armaments on the mainland. There were no perimeter fences or defensive positions in place yet, they were due to be commissioned in February, just a few weeks from the big day. We gave the planners a full tour of the facility. Their first reaction implied we had impressed them with the breadth of our vision, with its underground complex, impressive atrium, accommodation and array of cosy social spaces. But wonder quickly turned to consternation.

"We have never seen such wholesale blasphemy to our planning rules and laws in this country. How dare you take it on yourselves to completely undermine the law! It beggar's belief what you have done here", Peasebody was not happy. "I demand you take down this unapproved and unwanted disgrace immediately". Simon quickly countered, "So how would you like us to do that? Should we put concrete in all these voids? Should we collapse the hillside? We would do far more damage to the environment that way". Peasebody turned crimson at this point. "You will put this hill back as it was, so no one would ever notice; it's an embarrassment for the planning office, and I will not tolerate it!" His colleagues were clearly divided on the point. Peasebody's number two, a man called Lister, interjected, "Let's not be too hasty, sir. This is a beautiful building; it's a wonderful environmental example, with lots of showcase ecological features. The charitable foundation will do lots of good work on this island and should bring lots of tourism to our area". It was obvious Lister was one of the people Drake had 'influenced', however his points were valid. Lister's comments were not received constructively, we were dealing with an arrogant autocrat. I pointed out, "The building is undermining the hill and does no harm to the island. It's supported by more steel than was recommended by the structural engineers and will never crumble or collapse. It's barely visible from the sea, as was evidenced by your absolute surprise when you entered. It hasn't harmed the island, or Scotland, in any way. Tanera Mòr is a private island; it affects no other soul".

Peasebody was incensed, he left the facility shouting and threatening to arrange for police supervised staff to bulldoze the entire building if we didn't comply to plans in the next thirty days. We received an enforcement notice to that tune the following week. The deadline took us to the end of December.

When the council realised we had done absolutely nothing to comply, they informed us of their intention to pay us a planned inspection visit on 20th January (3 months from A-Day). By then all of the supplies had been brought in, including illegal armaments. We had additional boats and sailing vessels in the quay and very large tanks at the shore storing enormous quantities of diesel, marine diesel and kerosene plus a smaller one containing bleach. The quay looked more industrial than it should. Following the brief inspection Peasebody formally hand delivered a court order; a notice of demolition scheduled for April 19th. Peasebody added he would be bringing legal action against Sir Patrick Hastings-Crawley, and he had already been issued a summons to attend court to begin proceedings on March 15th. Simes and I shared a look, the timing was near perfect. We would lodge an appeal, and it would take us past the deadline nicely. The court rejected our appeal, and the demolition order was reinforced for Monday April 19th, just T-4 days.

As the days passed, I received several calls from the team worrying about those we couldn't accommodate and how we could help. I really couldn't budge; we couldn't allow any more people in; I empathised with them. I also needed to say goodbye to some of my friends, my elderly mother, and my in-laws. How would Kate react when she realised they couldn't be saved? It would be a catastrophe. Imagine the issue ten-fold when all the guests realised at the party. The most difficult issue was Drake's son. He lived with Drake's ex-wife, and they barely spoke. He had not accepted the invite, and Drake wasn't sure he would make it. Drake was becoming distraught.

By the end of March, all the supplies were in place, all the vehicles were garaged on site or in our supply facility onshore. The pickups had been adapted with heavy-duty off-road tyres, winches and fixings to allow protective cages to be fitted to cover the glass. Our project was very nearly finished. The Haven was kitted out, and Phil sent me a photo of the sign above the main entrance which read:

> "The Summer Haven
>
> A peaceful dwelling from which to safely observe the end of the world"

The sign made me laugh, and then a minute later almost cry, my emotions were always awfully close to the surface. It was poignant but really quite funny too. Phil had a wicked sense of humour, but I sensed a little Spall in there too. We were all riding an emotional rollercoaster.

Spall had ensured all of the defensive positions were in place with weapon mounts ready, both on the island and at our facility on the mainland. The perimeter fences were installed with regular supply stores holding kerosene, fungicide, sulphur, bleach, and ammo. He was ready for everything the world threw at us.

The tourist boat trips would notice the changes we had implemented; to mitigate the risk we had remarketed the venture as a survival space, needing to defend itself from attack. It gave us the excuses we needed; folks would assume the weaponry was fake, merely for illustration.

Party preparations were well underway. Kimball and Simes did a double act and decorated the island with every imaginable kind of bunting, flags, and banners. They decorated the atrium with beautiful fabrics, plants, and herb gardens. It was simply stunning. Their daily photos showed clear improvement each time. The food was ordered, a catering company was managing the entire event, their personnel were on strict orders to depart the island by 9pm on the day of the party.

Deliveries were made to the other Summer Islands, including large quantities of soil, fertiliser, seed and construction materials for outbuildings, pens and equipment. We maintained it was an error by one of our suppliers, it would be rectified before the end of the month.

On the 19th of April, the scheduled demolition planning visit was due. As the boat approached the island, Spall and I sat in the crow's nest above the Haven contemplating the morality of our agreed approach. Spall hefted his Barratt M82 sniper rifle and sighted the boat through his long night vision scope. He chambered a single sub sonic round; the weapon was suppressed to ensure a near silent shot. "Are you sure you are ok with this?" he queried. "Yes, just don't hurt anyone".

When the boat was half a mile from the island; Spall stabilised his breathing and took the shot midway between inhalations. The rifle recoiled, and the report of the weapon was quite loud even though it had a suppressor fitted. The heavy round took the boat in the forward section at the waterline and blew an eight-inch hole through the hull. The sub sonic round was virtually silent, there was no sonic boom; the first the pilot knew of their predicament was a large explosion in the front of the boat followed by the vessel sinking rapidly. They swam or floated back to shore holding large pieces of flotsam. Hopefully they would think their boat had suffered a collision in the water. It was the last we ever saw of them. "I didn't know it would feel *that* good", Spall murmured.

A few days later, Peasebody woke in the night to the sound of his baby crying again. He and his wife sat up in bed and were surprised by the presence of a young lady dressed in camouflaged army fatigues gently holding their baby close to her chest. He then felt the muzzle of a Sig-Sauer pistol thrust into his forehead. Spall explained to him he shouldn't get too involved in pursuing the Summer Haven development, or things might not go well for him and his family. "Please don't hurt me", was all he said. His wife was terrified but didn't fail to notice he was more interested in saving himself, before the lives of his family. We wouldn't hear from him again. I know it sounds like an act of extreme callousness; I don't really approve of what Spall did; but I must admit, sometimes I wish I had been a fly on the wall for that encounter.

IV. The Moment of Truth

"If God does not exist, everything is permitted"

Fyodor Dostoevsky

1. The Last Day of Normality

A-Day was almost upon us, we were all getting more than a little tense. Even though now we believed the events would really happen, there was always a small nagging doubt. Our phone calls became frantic. What if it didn't happen? What if it did? We had threatened a member of the local council and discharged a weapon at their boat? We had also broken all the planning rules and might have to tear down the building, leaving no residual funds other than the escrow, and the equity of the island itself. Yet I still dearly hoped I would end up in court for these transgressions, as it was vastly better than the alternative. In such a scenario, I would shoulder the blame.

Drake remained in a bad place, worrying about his son Jake, though there was still some hope. Jake was considering attending the party, as the vehicles and weapons did interest him, but a couple of days in the middle of nowhere seemed too dull. He also wasn't sure about spending time with Drake, they had argued quite a lot recently, he was disgruntled about the outcome of the relationship breakdown with his mum.

Neither communicated their feelings very well, and silence filled the vacuum. They never really got to the bottom of their mutual unhappiness, nor did they really let each other know they still loved each other. A common problem across all walks of life, but more acute for Drake because of the situation we were facing. Drake hadn't given a second thought to inviting his ex-wife, even though I had tried to encourage him to include her. Something really bad had happened there. I was confident Drake hadn't been unfaithful, but I couldn't say the same about Trish, his ex.

Phil's wife, Robyn, had a slight stomach upset in the morning, but it was looking like she would be ok to travel. Kimball's spouse, Bryan, was urgently mandated to an important business meeting on the following day, but he made a robust rebuttal to his boss; the days had been booked for several months. He opted to call in sick and face the fallout on his return to work, which would obviously never happen.

On the other side of the spectrum, Spall's long-suffering partner, Jane, was really looking forward to such a fantastic high-profile party and nobody could keep her away. Simes' wife, also named Jane, was another lady getting overly excited. She was keen on the celebrity participation in the party; as a keen autograph collector, she was always looking to elbow her way into a high-profile bash. Personally, I found her a little obnoxious and lacking in tact. I couldn't understand what Simon saw in her, if I'm honest. He was such a thoughtful, tolerant guy, there must be far more to her than I had been able to see in our few short encounters. Perhaps I should spend a little more time with Jane and get to know her better. I guess we were all going to be spending a little more time together over the next few years.

Steve's wife, Kulbir, was someone I hadn't met, I assumed she must be a very tolerant lady or had her own interests. Steve would spend endless hours tinkering with his old rusty Triumph Spitfire car, which he kept on the road by sheer force of will. He also invested a lot of time working on his computer studying all kinds of subjects. It was only later I found out they were birds of a feather; they shared these interests. Kulbir's knowledge of fabrication and welding was born from an interest in metal sculpture. She had moved into engineering, though it didn't extend to IT. It was Kulbir who recently resprayed the Spitfire.

The seven families were preparing for the party, plus the vast majority of the local professionals I had invited. We included the families of two doctors, a surgeon, a couple of farmers, a biologist, a blacksmith, a couple who were professional sailors and a few more who helped fill the gaps in our skill set. Spall sent a joke text to us, "So we've got all the scientists, engineers and doctors in this ship, where do we send the estate agents, lawyers, salesmen and social workers?" The Douglas Adams reference started a long chain of childish banter, which raised our spirits. Drake didn't participate, which I must admit worried me a little.

I called Drake early in the afternoon to check he was ok. "It's my son, he won't come to the party. I've tried everything to persuade him, but he just couldn't be bothered. He is more into extreme sports; he thinks a fancy party on a remote island would be tedious". I suggested we could tell him some of the weaponry was live and there were unofficial shooting range sessions planned, to raise his interest. Drake was uncertain, but he agreed to make one last attempt. Drake was in a bad place; I hadn't seen him so down in a long time, since we started the project he had returned to his usual ebullient self. It worried me, I wanted him at his best for our last push. We all needed to show some real leadership over the next few days.

We arranged early transport, so we could be there to welcome the guests as they arrived. We aimed to be there by midday. The main dinner was at 7pm, the big announcement was at 10pm after the kids had gone to bed. Rusty would provide a ferry service to the island from our mainland facility for those who had elected to drive. A private helicopter service was transporting folks in from the airport in groups of ten. It was the last big splash; there was no money left, we were running on vapour. Kimball had taken a loan secured by the property for the food and festivities.

We agreed that following the announcement we would allow time for guests to make peace with their families. We installed a mobile phone signal booster, to improve the service from the island. By 11pm the phone lines would be overwhelmed, as people panicked.

We were finally ready. We had done our best; we were leaving it all up to fate now. Steve had rigged up a large radio mast from the crow's next and had installed a top-quality ham radio. He would now be able to chat to survivors all around the world. Spall's wire fencing encircling the Haven entrance diminished the event, however Rusty and Sheena had threaded coloured ribbons through it in an attempt to make it more attractive.

That evening I sat at home feeling tense; Kate presumed I was concerned about the big launch. If only she knew the full extent of my worries. Tidying up after dinner seemed pointless, as this life would soon be gone, but I had to keep up appearances. I attempted to read a book, but nothing would settle my nerves, what was the point when I would never be able to finish the story? We ended up curled up on the sofa watching drivel on the TV. I looked around the house, wondering if we would ever be back. Would it survive the meteor storm or the ensuing craziness? Would it ever be our home again? Would we ever be as happy as we were here?

Sleep didn't come easily. I had nightmares again, but this time they really were just bad dreams. None of the vividness or clarity, just my brain trying to make sense of all the information.

Eventually, I managed to get some sleep but woke early. Then everything changed and not for the better. As Churchill once paraphrased, 'no battle plan survives first contact with the enemy'.

2. A-Day: 23rd April 2021

As usual, we had the news on the TV in the kitchen whilst eating breakfast, the presenters were discussing the promised show of shooting stars at 11pm. They elaborated that no one needed to worry as the larger of the bodies would miss Earth. Like the previous tranche, the meteors would briefly touch our atmosphere before slingshotting across the solar system. It promised to be a clear night and would provide a spectacular display worldwide. The show would be most intense in Asia, as it would be daylight in the USA, and they would miss much of the drama. They claimed was a chance in a lifetime to see such an event.

My family paid little attention to the report, as they were going on a fantastic trip to paradise island. Although they were only allowed a small overnight bag each, they planned to cram in a months' worth of clothing. If they knew the truth, they would be attempting to pack their whole life and a few friends in the bag. Kate touched up her makeup and we were ready.

Leaving home was easy, getting to a place of relative safety was paramount this morning. My team and I were keen to ensure our families arrived at the airport in good time. However, it was hard not to show weakness in front of them, I tried to suppress a few tears for those we were leaving behind. Kate commented, "Why are you so worried, Paul. It's going to be fun, a big party, lots of drinks". I replied, "Yes, but there is lots to go wrong. The lighting, the travel, the event we have planned. I guess I'm on point for the festivities, and I really need it to go well. Our leader won't be too happy if the party proves to be a disaster". She understood and tried to settle my nerves. "Sir

Thingy-Bob is running a party for you all. It's a thank you. He won't mind if there a few setbacks, just so long as everyone has a good time". "You don't know him, he is meticulous", I responded. The conversation helped; it distracted me from a myriad of issues. Kate and the kids jumped into the limo; my phone rang, it was Drake.

Drake was distraught, at the end of his tether, "Paul, Jake isn't coming. When I pleaded with him to keep his old dad company, you know what he said?" "Go on", I gently enquired. "He said I hadn't done much for him over the last five years since the divorce, so why the all the fricking fuss now".

I tried to calm Drake down, but it was clearly having no effect. I really feared for him, he was at the island and unable to act. He had done so much, and I couldn't leave him like this. My brain went into overdrive. In the heat of the moment, contrary to my plans and the risk to my family, I promised I would sort it for him. He texted me his ex-wife's address in Stoke. I turned to Kate, "I've got a massive issue I must resolve. I need you to go to the airport and take the flight. I'll meet you there". "Meet me where? In some island in the middle of nowhere? With people we don't know. I really don't think so!"

I explained to Kate I had a couple of places to visit to collect some replacement parts for the event, I promised I would be on the next flight, guaranteed. She wanted to wait for me, but I couldn't allow it, I knew the next flight wouldn't arrive in time. I managed to calm her down, she realised she was unnerving the kids. She agreed to take the limo to the airport. It was 9am by the time I formulated my plan, my time was limited.

I drove to the address Drake had texted me in Stoke-on-Trent city centre. My big problem was it would take at least eight hours to drive to Ullapool, even if I could get Jake on board and we left at 12pm, any delays would be fatal. I needed to travel at speed to build up contingency, regardless of the national speed limits. But on the other hand, what were the consequences?

I knocked on the door at 10:00 sharp, Jake's mum answered with her phone pressed against her ear. "Hi Trish, remember me?" "My god, Paul. I haven't seen you for donkeys' years! What are you doing here? How the hell are you?" I explained all was well and I had a really urgent message for Jake from Drake, who was indisposed in Scotland. At the mention of his name, her face darkened a little. "How is the old bastard?" "He's fine, he is doing some philanthropic work; in fact, we're running a charity project together. We have a big launch tonight and Drake really wanted Jake to be there, it's really important to him". "If it's that important, why didn't come himself?" I explained he was in the Highlands making last minute preparations, I had chosen to miss my flight to try to help, but time was precious. "So, you have dropped yourself in a world of pain, just to help that old reprobate?" If she only knew.

Jake ambled downstairs looking groggy. I explained the situation with his dad, but Jake just shrugged, "So what?" "Don't be like that Jake, Paul has come a long way to talk to you. Show a bit of respect!" yelled Trish as Jake grabbed a coffee from the kitchen. I could smell it when the door opened. "Wanna cup? It smells like it's just brewed", shouted Jake. "Sure", I replied looking at my watch. Trish left for work. It was getting ever closer to 11am, the clock was ticking, we had so little time. "Look Jake, I know you don't want to come, but I want to make you an offer you can't refuse", I explained. "I know you like crazy sports and spend most of your waking time planning dangerous events and trips. So, if you are game to come to the party, I thought we could thrash a superbike up to the Highlands". "What about the cops and the cameras, man? We'll be in prison before we even get there!" "That's my problem, I've got countermeasures", I said flatly. His face lit up at the thought of this, especially as were going to break the law. A fast bike could make for quite an exciting day. "It's your license. What sort of bike is it?" he asked. "Let's go and buy one now, you can help me choose". "Really?", he queried, "Can we get a Ninja or a Fireblade?" I explained we had an eight-hour ride, and a sports bike may not be the comfiest option, but we could have a look to see what is available.

I explained I worked for a guy who thought the end of the world was coming and made us jumpy. It was the reason his dad was so emotional about Jake attending. I offered to pay Jake generously for his time. It quickly became a done deal, £500 cash, and a fast bike ride was irrefutable. Jake grabbed a few things, and we jumped in the car. "Don't forget to send your mum a text to explain", I added.

On the way, I called the biggest motorcycle dealer in Stoke, "What's the fastest long-distance bike you stock that's ready to go?" "We have a one-year-old Suzuki Hayabusa and a 3-year-old Honda Blackbird. Both are 200mph superbikes". I consulted Jake and we opted for the newer of the two. Jake enthused that Hayabusa was Japanese for Peregrine Falcon, the fastest animal in the world. It was so cool, because its hunting dives were spectacular and could reach 200 mph. I offered to pay the bike's full ticket price if the showroom would prepare, fill the tank, and tax the bike for me in 15 minutes. He agreed to provide the first week's insurance for free.

I called Spall and explained my position. "Christ, you are really pushing it mate. You need to red line it! Keep your speed down to ten percent over until you get to the Wigan junction, or the police will see you on the smart motorway cameras and get an interceptor out to stop you. I'll drive down and leave some 5-gallon drums of fuel every 50 or so miles from here down to Stirling, a friend will do the same down to Penrith. Expect the GPS coordinates, I'll send them to your phone. I'll ensure someone leaves you a firearm at you first pitstop, if anyone stops you, need to shoot them and get going! Don't even think about it and don't waste a goddamn second negotiating. Please keep safe, you idiot!" "Thanks Spall, I'm on it", I affirmed. My god, he was harsh, but he was always one who was good in a crisis. We would rely on that skill rather a lot over the next few years.

We arrived at Suzuki Stoke at 11:15, I paid for the bike immediately on a credit card, assuming I would never see the bill; it was actually quite satisfying in a surreal way. The salesman was clearly over the moon, making an unexpected sale of a £15k bike at the drop of a hat. We equipped ourselves with Bluetooth helmets and leathers and hit the road as soon as the bike was ready. I skipped the bulk of the safety demonstration and headed out, leaving the salesman flabbergasted. I sellotaped my iPhone to the handlebars as soon as the route came in from Spall.

I fired up the motor; it was quiet but roared when I pulled back the throttle. The bike had quite a reputation in a straight line. I had ridden lots of bikes over the years, but I was a fairly cautious rider. I was going to have to push myself on this ride, way beyond my normal limits. I didn't know if Jake was used to pillion riding, but he had a reputation for being a speed junkie. The engine was remarkably responsive, but I avoided revving the engine as we made the first leg of our long journey. I kept the speed down to 77MPH until Wigan, as Spall had suggested. We still had half a tank of fuel remaining, due to driving economically. As Spall intimated, when we really started to burn, the fuel wouldn't last as long. The bike was a little uncomfortable for my long legs, so I needed to stretch them from time to time. After Wigan, the M6 motorway cleared, the frequency of cameras receded a little; I opened her up. "Whoa" shouted Jake from the back through the headset. I think the first acceleration burst caught him by surprise with its intensity, and he grabbed me and held on tight. My god it was fast. According to the salesman it could do 0-60 MPH in 2.76 seconds, but it felt so much faster even two up. We passed cars in a blur, and we stayed in the fast lane. The speedo was hitting 180 MPH, the buffeting was extreme, it was going to be very tiring over the long haul.

We hit Penrith after 90 minutes, and we still had just under a quarter tank of gas. It was 13:48, and we had a long way to go. As we approached the waypoint on the motorway I slowed. There was a big red arrow sprayed on the hard shoulder; it pointed to the partly hidden drum in the shrubs at the side of the road. Very subtle, but at least I didn't miss it. Jake thought it was funny. I advised him to stretch his legs while I filled up. I grabbed the drum and found a Glock 9mm with a spare clip beneath it. The pistol was in a plastic bag, and it had a belt slip. I slid it inside my leather jeans, so it was less conspicuous, but it made my trousers really uncomfortable, especially against the hip armour. I dumped the fuel into the tank, closed the lid and threw the drum into the undergrowth. Car passengers stared at us; it must have looked suspicious.

We jumped back on the bike and streaked off towards Stirling at virtually 190MPH. We arrived at 15:01, we had made good time, but the single carriageways on the A roads were slower. I maintained a high speed, I was forced to concentrate to ensure we took the long sweeping bends at a sensible pace, though the foot pegs were nearing the ground on a couple of occasions. I felt like my heart was in my mouth a few times, but we were still alive. Jake thought it was hilarious. We arrived at Dalwhinnie at 16:27, but the miles were really starting to take a toll. We grabbed some power bars, had a quick jog and drank water, I avoided the excellent local whisky.

At the halfway point we stopped to eat something more substantial, time was not on our side. I'd lost count of the number of fuel stops we made; the bike was guzzling fuel at such speeds. We set off at pace again, as we approached the shores of Loch Ness, I nearly lost the bike on a sharp bend. Jake pointed out we would be dead if we came off at that speed, as if I didn't know. We hit Inverness at 17:59, that's when we ran into serious trouble.

In England we had been spotted by the authorities on the M6, it was inevitable. A vehicle travelling at over 150 MPH is conspicuous, I just hoped to outrun any trouble. The police tactic was to block the motorway ahead and wait. However, we were already in Scotland by the time they mobilised. They had prewarned Scottish police, we were still breaking speed limits by a significant margin. Police interceptors blocked the road south of Inverness as we approached on the thin stretch following the top of Loch Ness. Jake muttered, "Shit", as we approached the roadblock, I dropped the throttle and brought the bike to a halt. We dismounted the bike; I quickly removed my gloves to allow mobility. Three police officers approached, looking more than a little angry. "We've been chasing this wee bike for 300 miles, you have been going at nearly 200 miles an hour for the whole way, laddie. You have also been filling up illegally on the hard shoulder. You are in all sorts of trouble; you pair of bloody idiots".

The words of Spall echoed through my mind, just shoot them, don't waste any time. I understood his point, but I just couldn't kill people in cold blood. I calmly explained to Jake, "We need to keep going, if anyone asks, say I have kidnapped you. Don't worry I have a rational explanation for this". I pulled the Glock, I heard Jake say, "Shit, what the fuck are you doing?" Jake looked like he wanted to run but couldn't make up his mind.

The police turned white and froze, as they were only armed with tasers and batons. I ordered them to drop their radios and kick them over to me. I instructed two of the officers to get in the boot of their patrol cars, and the other to cuff them and close the boot lids. I smashed their radios so we would gain some time. No doubt they had already reported to the operations team that they had pulled us over. With my Glock pointed at his face, I instructed the younger lad, who was more nervous and less experienced, to move the car. I blasted both the in-car radios, which made the lad wet himself. Jake looked extremely distressed. I tossed the keys and handcuffed the police driver to his steering wheel. I also shot the front tyres for good measure and inserted the second clip into the pistol. I now realised the value of Spall's weapon training. Jake climbed on the bike, afraid to challenge me. I remounted the bike and thrashed it all the way to Ullapool, with a single fuel stop, arriving at 19:59, we were running extremely late.

We soon reached the facility near Achiltibuie. Spall was waiting at the gate, "Thank Christ you're here. Everybody's waiting. I feared we might lose you". He looked at Jake's face and intuitively understood what had happened. "Don't worry Jake", he said quietly, "You will understand very soon why you are here and why Paul had to kill the cops". "Kill? Jesus, he didn't kill them", retorted Jake, "But he locked them in the boot of their car. You should have seen their faces. It was bloody priceless! We're going to get in a lot of trouble over this. He pulled a fucking gun on them". "Trust me", said Spall, "You're not in any trouble, we are on an MI5 assignment", he added with a wink. I felt obliged to say, "Thanks mate, your quick thinking saved us yet again. The fuel and the 9mm were absolutely priceless".

Spall already had the RIB engine running ready to roll, I quickly locked up the facility and boarded. Spall took us out to sea and pushed the boat up to 70 knots. We were at the island in a shot. Drake was waiting on the pier with tears in his eyes, "Oh you wonderful man!" he sobbed. He grabbed Jake in a bear hug, much to Jake's embarrassment, "Steady on Dad". He then hugged me. We were late, it was 20:41. We had missed part of dinner, but not the main event. My legs were stiff after the long and cramped ride and my nerves were shot. But we were ready, as ready as we could ever be.

3. A Romantic Night of Shooting Stars
(Francisco)

From the writings of El Tigre

We spent Christmas at Valletta on the island of Malta, together in our new rented home. Lucy had managed to get a job in the local hospital, and I had taken a bar manager's job in the reputed Grand Excelsior Hotel by the waterside. I had easily acquired the job, as I was a fluent bilingual with significant bar and restaurant experience. The staff hadn't heard of me or my infamy, it was bliss for a while. However, the management started to become more inquisitive when a number of guests recognised me, it was inevitable. Luckily as it was a high-class hotel, the clients were more interested in telling their own tall stories. They very quickly switched from recognition to, let's talk about me!

Colletta started at her new school, which she didn't like too much initially. We gently explained it would take time to settle in, and she would soon be happy when she got to know everyone.

Valletta itself was magnificent; the whole city is a UNESCO heritage site with amazing fortifications around a lovely quaint old town centre. Late Autumn was pleasant, but I had heard the winters could get cold and breezy, but the weather remained good. We had moved all of our belongings, and we were starting to get the house tidy again. Most of our possessions were shipped in by the removal company in a container, but we still carried quite a lot of our stuff on the plane.

The hotel had a stunning view of the water from most rooms, and I could clearly see the ancient fort on Manoel Island from there. As the winter progressed, building work started on the little island and the fort, there were workmen coming in and out at all times of the night. The hotel manager started to get really grumpy about the disruption and on occasion the noise. Live and let live. One evening, I strolled over to the fort with Lucy out of curiosity. It appeared that they were improving the fortifications on the old building. There was something going on with the bridge too, but I couldn't quite make it out through the large construction fences, they were covered with white plastic drapes. No one was particularly friendly, they certainly avoided discussions regarding their plans. I hadn't witnessed such extensive modifications to a listed building.

We weren't settling in quite as well as we had hoped. There were strong Italian and English influences in Malta, and it was going to take some time to get used to. My lunch breaks were the highlight of my working day, I would pop into the old town and grab an arancini and a coffee at the café in the square. I tried to ensure I was assigned first break, as the arancini sold out quickly. The hotel was very formal, and I missed the relaxed easy days in Alicante. I reprimanded myself with the memory of the terrible statue in the square at the front of the hospital.

A show of shooting stars was predicted on the 23rd of April as a large group of meteors passed Earth and fragments dipped into the atmosphere to burn up on entry. Lucy organised a babysitter for Colletta, and we booked dinner in the hotel's finest restaurant, 'The Admirals Landing'. The babysitter was a young local girl, who like most people on the island, spoke really good English. I wanted it to be romantic, as I had bought

Lucy a diamond eternity ring as a surprise, she had been hinting she would like one, but it was the last thing she was expecting. It turned out be a night to remember, but sadly not for the romance.

We left Colletta playing Monopoly with Mina. She was a lovely inclusive girl; kind and understanding and she gracefully tolerated the brazen cheating that went on. We walked to the hotel via the great entrance of Valletta city, passing into the square featuring the impressive Triton fountain, which was grandly illuminated. We followed the Great Siege Road into the hotels main entrance and strolled up the grand stairway to the restaurant for dinner. We had great seats, by the huge glass windows enjoying a wide view of the waterside. The time passed quickly, we finished dinner at around ten thirty and ordered one last glass of wine, we readied ourselves for the meteorites. I hoped it wouldn't be a disappointment, as I had wagered my reputation and half my month's salary on the dinner.

At 23:00 the staff dimmed the lighting as the shooting stars streaked across the sky. There were many more shooting stars than I was expecting, the sky was full of them. It was a magnificent display, everyone in the room remained in a constant state of awe. "This is so wonderful, how romantic", Lucy snuggled into my arm. "It was so kind of you to arrange this", she added. I presented her with an eternity ring in a small velvet box. She smiled, "It is the perfect evening, how could possibly improve on this?"

The show continued for some time, until the meteoroids started to break through the atmosphere and physically strike Earth, this development wasn't quite what we expected. It caused great alarm in the room. Scientists had assured us there was no danger whatsoever. Many lights seemed to be heading for Sicily and over our heads towards Tunis on the north African coast, but some struck here too. Malta was getting off lightly, it seemed, on balance. A number of explosions came from the direction of the city. Valletta had taken two or three hits, but Gozo, the nearby island, took a huge pounding. Valletta's defensive walls were metres thick and had taken quite a shelling over the years, from the Ottomans to the Germans and then the Italians in WWII. They could easily take a few meteorites, presumably.

Suddenly Lucy exclaimed, "Colletta". I instantly understood, and we headed for the hotel entrance at speed. I left cash for the meal plus a generous tip on the Maître D'Hôtel's desk and we ran home. We sprinted up the steps onto the Great Siege Road and up the hill into town. We ran through the old city gates and past the theatre and into the old streets. The Bank of Malta building had taken a significant hit, and the front of the building was smashed, fragments of glass littered the street. 'Small' meteoroids! I thought to myself. We ran through the main square of St George; the Grand Masters Palace was surrounded in confusion. It may have taken a hit towards the rear; a moderately sized dust cloud was rising from the back. We passed through the square, down the steps and turned left into St Nicholas Street and up to the front of our building. There was no damage, Colletta was safe, thank goodness. We stopped for a moment and caught our breath.

Suddenly, we heard shouting and screaming from the main square. It sounded like there was a fight, many were shouting abuse at the top of their voices. The shouting intensified into a roar, as a horrific scene emerged at the top of our street. An old lady had been set upon by a married couple. It was a most surreal scene, a woman in a headscarf and Gucci coat was attacking the old lady's neck with her teeth like a feral animal. Simultaneously, the man was flailing his arms at her. The old lady toppled to the ground, I tensed, about to offer help.

Lucy yelled, "Francisco, we need to protect Colletta. There are dozens of people up there screaming and attacking each other. It's too late for her, there is nothing we can do". I knew Lucy was speaking sense. From the opposite end of the street, a man ran towards us emitting a hideous guttural scream. Lucy fumbled but managed to open the door. We were inside just in time, the raging man pounded on the door. The door was thick oak, he was not coming through that. We were safe, for the time being.

We headed up the steps into our apartment. The scene before us was harrowing; forever etched upon my soul. Never a quiet moment went by without the image appearing in my mind.

The French doors opened onto our small terrace to reveal blood covering the floor. I held Lucy back with my left arm and moved into the opening, where an insane scene unfolded before me. Mina had transformed from a lovely, shy girl into a rabid, wild animal. She held my precious Colletta in her arms and she was ripping open her stomach, pulling out her intestines and eating them. Colletta was dead, and her head was lolling backwards as the monster fed ravenously. Her hunger drove her to the point where she didn't even notice our presence. I froze. Lucy appeared at my side and started screaming.

I grabbed the cast iron door stop and stove in the head of the creature that was once Mina. She collapsed to the floor and remained still. Lucy continued to scream. I was overcome by rage and hit Mina repeatedly. Blood splattered the room and extraordinarily little remained of Mina's face when my red curtains of rage parted. I dropped the door stop and looked at Lucy. She was sat in a pool of blood, crying and holding Colletta's remains in her arms, she cradled her as if she was a baby.

The desperate scene broke my heart when I saw the anguish on Lucy's face, I am sure it was closely matched by the desperate look on mine. How could life be so cruel? I took Mina's body and tossed it over the balcony, to join the chaos on the street below. The world was literally going to hell. I alternated between crying, raging, and whimpering like a child.

A frantic crowd formed below; they ignored the violated body of Mina. The strangest thing then occurred, as I watched Mina's body, a mushroom grew from the nape of her neck. It sprouted at an alarming rate, and within a few minutes it had reached a metre tall. The mushroom made a soft popping sound, and a cloud of dust was emitted. My animal instinct warned me to get the hell away.

I dragged Lucy and Colletta back into the room and quickly slammed the doors and crudely sealed them with tape from the dresser drawer. I ran around the apartment and closed all the vents, windows, and apertures. I then sat and waited. What in God's name had happened? The meteors must have carried some kind of disease which murdered my daughter and destroyed our lives for ever. There was no recovery from this.

Lucy was still wailing, holding Colletta whilst sat on the floor. I wrapped my arms around them both. Lucy found no comfort in my gesture and roughly shrugged me off. Lucy shouted, "It's all your fault. Bad luck follows you around the world, you bring it with you wherever you go like a plague. I wish I'd never met you, you pig". The exclamation shocked me to my core, I felt like I had been hit with a sledgehammer. I cried, whispering, "I'm so sorry", over and over. There was no forgiveness from Lucy, her face turned to rage. "I'm going to kill you, you bastard. You did this to my beautiful baby".

I was confused and bewildered. Lucy leapt to her feet, her face dark and hideous. She launched herself at me, attacking with her nails and teeth, intending to tear me to pieces. I stood and tried to wrap her arms in mine, to restrain her and help calm her. It proved to be a grave error of judgement; I had brought her in too close and she bit my right cheek. It seared with pain; I physically threw her across the room. She tripped over the Colletta's body, falling headlong into the corner of the sideboard. Her head snapped back with a crunch; she fell to the floor heavily; blood pooled around her damaged skull. She died on the floor in our apartment, next to the corpse of Colletta. All the people I really cared about had left the world without me.

I fell to the floor and gathered them in my arms. Everything was covered in blood: it was all over me, the floor and our furniture, like a scene from a terrible nightmare. My life was undone. I could see no future; my life was over.

The screaming and fighting outside continued unabated. I lay on the bloody carpet for hours with both bodies in my arms, numb. My mind had deserted me, it had departed in search of better thoughts and found none.

4. The Party for the End of the World

"Where on this damned Earth have you been?" demanded Kate, she was stood next to Kimball and Simon, they all looked anxious. "Sorry love, I had to drive, the flight was too late", I said placatingly. Instead, I opted to try to make her laugh, a risky strategy, "I ran out of gas! I got a flat tire! I didn't have change for cab fare! I lost my tux at the cleaners! I locked my keys in the car! An old friend came in from out of town! Someone stole my car! There was an earthquake! A terrible flood! Locusts! IT WASN'T MY FAULT; I SWEAR TO GOD!" I shook my hands, in a parody from her favourite classic, The Blues Brothers.

I managed to pierce the gloom and won a glimmer of a smile from Kate, she replied, "Come on, you need to make it up to me!" Drake decided to assist, in his usual ham-fisted fashion. He explained to her I had just literally saved his son's life, and he would always be grateful. Kate was confused but opted to ask me about it later. Jake cut in, "He even got in trouble with the Police for speeding across the country, he locked them...". Spall roughly grabbed Jake by the arm, silencing him, he then asked for his help with lifting the sound rig. Jake followed in Spall's wake with an evil grin on his face. Kate was utterly baffled, "Is he taking the piss out of me?", she asked. "Take no notice of Jake, he's having a laugh. Let's see if there is any food left, I'm starved".

The team had chosen to delay the main course for me. Spall knew my whereabouts all the time, he and Steve had tracked my mobile phone. We walked into the Atrium; it was beautifully adorned in gold and purple. Kimball handed me a 'Summer Haven' stretch Kevlar oversuit, which I used to hide my soiled clothing. I noticed the rest of the team were already wearing them, we were on brand. I really needed a shower, but I put a brave face on and continued. We sat down to a really excellent meal.

After dinner, at 22:00 precisely, the lights lowered. It was time for the main event. A large screen had been erected at the back; the projector was ready to display the live coverage. The banner 'Party for the End of the World' was illuminated in green. The doors were closed, and the whole complex was locked down. All eyes turned to me as I walked up to the stage, strangely energetic after a hard day. Adrenaline surged through my veins; I would probably collapse into a catatonic state afterwards.

"Good evening and welcome", I began. "Sir Patrick Hastings-Crawley and I would like to formally welcome you to the launch of Summer Haven. As you know this is a working commune designed as a prototype to test the possibilities of survival in the face of global disaster".

"I would like to begin by informing you all that my narrative is a complete and utter sham, everything I have told you about this place over the last few years has been a necessary lie". A few confused looks were exchanged by the audience. I continued, "The first of the lies is Sir Patrick Hastings-Crawley does not exist", the audience gasped, "The seven of us have led the build of the project under our own funding". I gestured for the others to join me on stage. "It's a remarkable achievement, completed under great duress. I hear you ask, why would we create a charitable foundation and fund this amazing facility? In order to answer the question, I will have to wind back the clock a few years".

"It all started with really bad dreams. My wife will attest to the many nights with broken sleep and vivid nightmares, as she got little sleep too. My dream warned me of a great disaster where meteors from space would strike Earth and would spread an infection that would kill every person on the planet, except in a small number of locations. This island was one of them. The dreams showed me how to raise the money, using a few well-chosen bets and investments. I had a winning streak that led me to build up a fortune of almost a hundred million pounds". The crowd gasped collectively at this point; they shared looks of utter disbelief.

Kate was astounded and dumbstruck. "So, seven of us set out to build this fully operational, fully armed fortress. We began in a state of disbelief, which I'm sure you are feeling a good measure of right now. But we made sure we had our feet on the ground to measure the extent and damage caused by the first meteorites when they struck Earth". Someone in the crowd shouted out, "They didn't strike Earth, they flew past!" I continued, "Well yes, they did strike Earth, and the Russians covered it up. If you remember we didn't actually see the light show we were promised. Here are the messages sent to us secretly from our friend in Russia. As far as we can tell, he died collecting this information for us. I displayed the communications from Sergei on the screen. It caused an uproar, "What the hell is this?" "It can't be true!" I interjected in an attempt to quell the unrest, "I'm not saying it's true! What I am saying is we thought there was enough of a risk to warrant building this facility, sufficient to bring you all here. What we are doing is securing our friends and family whilst we find out".

BBC news was displayed live on the big screen. "We are interrupting this program to announce a worldwide emergency! Tonight at 11pm a shower of meteorites was predicted; however, we have breaking news. Many meteorites will physically strike Earth in about 40 minutes time. Don't panic! You must stay in your houses and lock the doors until the emergency passes. We will keep our reports running live so you remain up to date, and we will notify you when the risk has passed. They are small meteoroids, most will disintegrate before they hit Earth, but there is a high risk of collateral damage". The sound in the room dropped to a murmur. Worried looks were exchanged. It was no longer a question of me making up an outrageous story, our friends and families were seeing the threat unfold in front of their own eyes. The timing was impeccable.

I explained, "Don't be afraid, we are sat under hundreds of tons of rock and steel. You are all perfectly safe in Summer Haven, it was purpose built to withstand such an event". The crowd chattered nervously, there was a lot of noise. People pulled out their phones and rang their families and friends.

At 11pm we switched the sound system back on, and the crowd quieted. BBC reported that meteorites were striking around the globe, thousands of them. From time to time, we could feel the ground shake a little. They weren't large rocks, and they eroded as they travelled through the atmosphere, however, they still hit the ground hard with significant momentum. After 30 minutes or so, the bombardment stopped, the reporters were visibly relieved. The TV centre itself had taken an impact, we could see the cameras shake and the dust moving around. In true BBC fashion they kept the updates coming regardless. They reported many buildings all over the country had been damaged. It was the emerging pattern across the world. The USA and Asia had taken the worst of the battering.

The first UK TV footage showed a crater in the centre of London. The reporter spoke anxiously, "You can see the groove where a meteorite hit the ground and made its final crater here. A profusion of dust was driven into the air on impact, but it has now subsided. The worst of it looks to be over". An onlooker peered into the hole, wobbled and started to gag. The camera cut back to the TV centre and reported on the catastrophe globally, it showed footage of the damage to homes, supermarkets and office blocks in several large cities. The scenes were dramatic, many had lost their lives, but on the positive side, most of the country was still standing.

At 11:35, the first infection appeared. The BBC were filming live from the crater near television centre and one onlooker went berserk: clawing, tearing, and biting another observer. The attack was feverish. The victim was taken down quickly, but the fatal wound was inflicted by the grip of the attacker's jaws on the victim's throat. However, once a deeper laceration emerged the attacker began tearing and biting. Blood sprayed as the victim's carotid artery was punctured. The sight on the display was hideous to see, someone screamed in the room behind me. The camera remained on the scene far too long, but to us it provided important information. Finally, the camera cut back to the presenters in the studio who were horror struck and completely lost for words for probably the first time in their entire careers.

I again attempted to placate the terrified faces in the room, "Don't worry, we are quite safe here. None of the meteorites have collided with the island and we are far enough from the mainland to avoid the infection. However, because of the threat I am forced to impose martial law for the time being. You are not prisoners here; we are all friends and family. Any of you can choose to leave at any time, but I wouldn't recommend it for obvious reasons.

"As part of martial law, we can't allow anyone who has been on the mainland back to this island under any circumstances, so choose your next action wisely. Everyone on the mainland is potentially infected and we don't know how long to apply a quarantine for. We haven't had the opportunity to study the infection, though from the information from Russia we do understand it behaves like a parasitic fungal infection. The closest resemblance we have seen in nature is a fungus called Cordyceps. It is a killer fungus that invades the body of an insect to grow and spread, it can wipe out an insect population in a short period of time. It enters the body of the insect through the eyes, mouth, or any cuts and abrasions. It grows in the brain and spinal cord. The pressure on the brain leads to insanity and finally death. The fungus then propagates via a fruit in order to spread".

Steve displayed the video clip of the development of the infection and commented, "Fungal spores can last for many months, so we can't approach the mainland for a year or two and even then, we need to take great care. We need to be self-sufficient. Therefore, we have provided plentiful stores, agriculture, and livestock to help us through. We will need to be careful, as there are a lot of us, but no one will starve. Please be assured you are quite safe here".

I continued, "From tomorrow we will need to work together as a team. It's imperative we learn to defend ourselves against the threat from the infected, as they may attack. Self-defence and weapons training are compulsory for everyone. All adults will always be required to carry a firearm, so you will need to learn how to use them safely. We will also issue clothes", I indicated my oversuit, "which are made from stretch Kevlar and have a high neckline. They are bite resistant and they will also protect you from blows and sharp weapons. We aim to quickly build farms on the three adjacent islands, which I believe are also uninfected. We have deposited all the materials we need in advance. We all need to pull together to make this work.

"However, enough for tonight, you must rest. The only thing you need to know for now is the sound of the klaxon. An intermittent tone like this", Steve demonstrated the sound. "This indicates you must stop what you are doing and get to a safe place quickly. Those nominated will need to gather weapons and man the defence positions. If you hear a continuous tone like this, then you should prepare for battle as we are under imminent attack. Don't worry we will have plenty of warning, the crow's nest has radar and enhanced optics; we also have CCTV and motion sensors. Spall can hit a target a mile out, we don't plan on letting anything near to our island. You are safe, get some sleep, we start at 7am".

The first of many questions bubbled up from the group, they were close to panic. "Why is this happening to us?" "We're all going to die!" I managed to calm them down a little, and then the more intelligent questions started to emerge, we were quite unprepared for some of them. "Astrophysicists have been studying the movement of planets and meteors for hundreds of years. Why did they not know they would strike Earth? Why did we not receive advanced warning?" said Janus, one of our potential science team. There was a hush after this question. "Are you saying someone, or something changed their direction?" came from the crowd. No one knew how to answer that question, and it was left hanging. "Why didn't the dog get infected? Are animals and plants immune? Is the fungus targeting us specifically? Was it done on purpose?" demanded another voice. It left an even more disturbing thought with the group. None of us would sleep too well tonight. "We don't know. Our focus is to survive right now. But you must take comfort in the fact that someone somewhere is trying to help us".

As if it wasn't enough, Jake pitched in with a cutting blow, "So why didn't you save more people? Why didn't you warn everyone? You kept it all to the seven of you and let everyone die, including my mum". I choked at this point, but Spall chose to wade into the debate. "Listen up. There is no point in asking that kind of question, space is limited. Who the hell would have believed the story anyway? It sounded more than farfetched to me. I only went along with it because I got to work with my friends, and it was well paid. This man has bravely fought to save all our lives, he deserves our undying gratitude, not our criticism and dissent". "Here, here", came from the crowd, and there was a much more supportive mood falling over the group. "We now need to get our shit together. Life is gonna be tougher than most of you have ever experienced. We're going to have to work hard. Get some rest! Think positive, you are alive! The fungus *might* kill us, but negativity will most definitely kill us!"

Some of the crowd milled around, they were worrying and sharing their fears. Some went to find their sleeping quarters. Each family had been allocated a room and their belongings had been placed there. Children woke up, "What's going on Daddy?" "Go back to sleep, its ok love". We lie to children routinely to make them feel safe, to imply the world is a cosy magical place. It was odd that even in a world of chaos and danger, we still resorted to the same behaviours. It's programmed into us in the deepest places in our psyche when we become a parents.

Some of the crowd attempted to phone their loved ones. The calls were never going to connect, due to everyone in the world trying to call each other simultaneously. Frustration set in, one by one they followed the cycle: dialling, frustration turning to anger, desperation, denial, then deep sadness as they realised they weren't going to connect, they would never speak to their family again. Grief would come, but only when things started to calm down, when the urgency gave way to routine.

Kate and I followed the directions to our allocated room. She was gently pleased Spall had managed to acquire a few personal items, to attempt to make a rudimentary room look a little more like a home. The kids were fast asleep and seemed to be utterly unphased, they saw it as a big adventure. "Nice mattress", Kate observed. I wondered how comfortable it would be after 20 years, when it would be stuffed with hay. Kate looked sleepy, but I was expecting more of a fuss. After all I had lied to her for nearly three years. I think she was simply happy for the four of us to be alive. After a while she did cry quietly to herself. "It's ok love", I said comfortingly. "It's Mum and Dad. I will never see them again. Nor Terri". We wouldn't see any of our relatives again, except perhaps in the next life. I started to think about my family too and became upset. I knew Jake was particularly upset about his Mum. He had given Drake quite a hard time about it. It was why he had hit out at me so brutally in the atrium, a totally natural reaction. Drake would take any battering Jake dished out; he was so happy to have his son here alive. Even Jake was starting to accept what must be accepted, we were all on that long and windy road. We were grieving.

Normally, in a stressful situation you learn to cope; you get on with it. It tended to be the point when everything had settled down that the wall of emotions finally hit. It was often the case with individuals who had beaten horrific illness such as Cancer. The full shockwaves hit when you get the all clear, it's part of being human. I felt relieved we were safe; we had a home, and we had managed to assemble our families. The last three years had been leading up to this, and now it had happened I could relax a little. Until tomorrow…

5. The Destroyer (Francisco)

From the writings of El Tigre

I woke in the same room, a place where of the worst of all horrors had been enacted. I had been ill, with a raging temperature, I remembered feeling like my entire body was being eaten from the inside out. The wounds on my cheek, arms and chest hadn't healed fully and had an unpleasant green tinge, though I was fairly sure they weren't septic or gangrenous. I think I had spent three days and three nights in my blood covered state. I had eaten nothing, and I didn't care. The smell of the room was enough to choke a normal person, but I existed in it as the stench grew. A gradual change was not so discernible, plus I really didn't give a damn. All I ever wanted was here, dead in this room.

The room was full of spores that had erupted from the back of Lucy's head. I had been breathing them for days. Was I on the turn into something rabid, a monster? I considered ending my life right there. I had nothing to live for. I kept running the events through my mind over and over again. At the fringes of my vision, I could sense a presence bending over me, looking at me. I could almost make out an expression of deep concern, but it faded in and out. "There was nothing you could have done my son", the vision said. "Don't blame yourself; it was the infection. There are others who need your help, you need to find them". "Go and f...", it wasn't even worth the breath to say it.

A day or so later, I felt a little better, the sickness and burning sensation had abated. I stood, with a little help from the chair. I saw my reflection in the mirror. I looked like one of the infected myself, covered in blood, dishevelled and angry. I had to get out of this place, it was killing me, it was a morgue.

I gently lifted Lucy and wrapped her in a sheet and laid her on our bed. I then lifted Colletta and did the same, wrapping her tenderly in another sheet. I kissed their foreheads and closed the door; it was the end of a chapter. Probably the end of the book for me. I cleaned myself up a little and took some food from the fridge. It was five-day old pizza from the evening Colletta had spent with Mina, it was close to being rank, but it filled a hole. Mina had been a victim here too, but I couldn't get the image of her with Colletta in her arms from her mind. It was driving me insane.

I purposefully strode to the spare room and accessed the back of the wardrobe; I retrieved the locked wooden box that held my katana. The lock on the box was not a code, it was like a Chinese puzzle box, a few pieces needed to be moved before the mechanism could be slid to unlock it. The katana was pristine. It was held in a leather saya, a traditional Japanese scabbard, I secured it to my back with its soft leather straps. Never again did the blade look so clean and new. The letters on the blade were in Kanji:

ザ・デストロイヤー

My Sensei's wife had said the logographic translated to: 'The Destroyer', which always seemed a little theatrical to me. It was time to see if the blade lived up to its name.

I left the apartment and walked into the street. It was like shouting 'free meal' at the top of my voice. I was utterly silent, so it must have been their sense of smell that led them here. Fifty or so infected ran down the street towards me. I didn't run, I became angry. This moment was my suicide, to end to the pain of my rotten life. The rage was fuelled inside me by the horror the infection had inflicted, and these creatures personified that evil. The sword chopped them down but still they came. I was turning left and right and cutting them down, like the stalks of maize at the end of harvest. There was no subtlety, no feints, no clever sword work. I just cut them down and walked over their bodies to get to the next in the queue to be executed. I started to tire as the street was choked with cadavers. They kept coming, and I kept cutting them down. If I continued, I would die here. The thought didn't faze me, perhaps somewhere deep inside I wanted my life to end here. The presence of an old friend finally lured me into making my escape. "Manoel Island. They need your help, go there my son. It is a haven from this storm".

I was in such a state of fury, I found it hard to back away from my harvesting, but I managed in time. "So long guys, I'd love to stay but...", I shouted as I turned and fled. I left many of the monsters behind me, but a few were fast. They were gaining on me rapidly. Let them come, I thought to myself. I allowed the distance to build up between me and the main horde, then stopped, turned and fully vented my vengeance. The first, I decapitated as he came within range, but strangely its body continued to charge me. I sidestepped the corpse, and it ran for a short distance, like a headless chicken. I sliced the legs from under the two that followed, I stepped back and took the last one with a parry straight into its chest. I screamed into the face of the infected man; he was held upright by the blade of my sword. I retracted the blade and jogged away. I was moving northwest along Triq il-Fossa, by the waterside. Three more infected came gurgling at me from down a side street, I took their heads and continued. I run up to Marsamxett Harbour on my right. I was hoping the ferry would be in, but no such luck.

I was left with a simple choice. To swim to the island or take the long road around the inlet to the other side. My brain started to process data, which in turn led to the rage dissipating for the time being. What had I done? How many had I killed? Was it murder or simply a mercy killing? Was I becoming a monster?

The swim would be tricky, with a sword on my back. The longer road route around the large marina was about four kilometres, and fraught with dangers. I was tired and low on energy, so the long route was out. I hadn't seen a normal human being yet, I hoped they were safely hiding in their homes, away from those wicked spores.

The infected were everywhere. I decided to head for the Grand Hotel, I knew there was a small wharf adjoining it where there might be a boat I could take. I ran the kilometre without crossing the path of any more abominations. I was becoming tired. I decided to break into the hotel Tiki bar and look for food. I climbed the fence by the side entrance to the conference centre. The trouble was everyone in the hotel at the time of the meteors were trapped in the hotel building. The creatures didn't seem smart enough to find a way out. They just lined the windows and screamed and gurgled, it was creepy. The infected went crazy when they saw me and followed hungrily along the glass mashing their jaws. If we hadn't left the hotel so quickly, it could well have been our fate.

The Tiki bar was unlocked, but there were two creatures inside. I walked through the door brazenly and they attacked. They were easily dispatched; I chopped the infected man to the left almost in half at its waistline. I stepped back to create space from the other and took the blade up diagonally, which cut off the top half of his head from jaw to ear. I looked more closely; I had worked with this guy. It had been Ali, the night manager. I needed to move fast before one of those damned toadstools popped up. I ran to the fridge and emptied it. There were olives and a slice of cold lasagne, probably Ali's supper from 5 nights ago, it had become little ripe. I grabbed the food and some bags of crisps and headed out of there.

I walked along the small jetty and looked for an available boat. There was a very large yacht, which I didn't know how to pilot. I would also only be able to disembark by standing on the prow and jumping off when I rammed it into a quayside. It was no good at all. A rowing boat was accommodated on the yacht, but it looked like it needed the winch to lower it, which would require keys. There was another rowing boat in the water, but it had half sunk, as the hull had been damaged. The only vessel I could find was beached a hundred yards beyond the jetty, adjacent to a restaurant. I ran past, shoving crisps into my mouth, which made it hard to breathe and run. The sign had been damaged and was hanging from one side, 'The Haywharf'. My transport was a hot pink pedalo with a solar panel roof. When I got aboard, I found there actually weren't any pedals, it was solar propelled. Just great! But then it didn't matter if it was slow, it was safe once I was on the water.

I arrived at Manoel Island. Can you imagine the sight that befell the defence force? Here comes the cavalry! One lone warrior on a cerise pedalo, a blood-soaked lunatic eating cold lasagne with his fingers. My reception was a little less than warm. I arrived to find four Kalashnikov rifles pointing at my tomato and blood covered face.

6. The First Few Days of the Rest of Our Lives

We gathered after a basic breakfast, It was 7am and the sun was coming up. It was shining brightly through the green tinted windows, a glorious spring day. Was it good to be alive? *The jury was out.*

Spall and I addressed the group. "I hope you all got some sleep last night. I'm not sure I did", I added a rather strained laugh. "You will see the rota on the wall, with your names assigned to duties". There was a groan from a couple of the younger folk. "We will do self-defence and weapons training every day at 7am sharp at the practice ground. At 8am, we will start the duties on the rota. Sunday will continue to be a day off, except for the catering team, who will take Monday instead. To my left you will see a poster which contains our basic laws. Simon will preside over any disputes or non-conformance with our laws, he will form a jury comprising of your good selves as and when needed. I'm sorry it's such a rude awakening, but we need to start as we mean to go on.

"We don't have an opportunity to take it easy for the time being, it is war. When the threat of the infection has died down, we will move back to democracy and I will stand down at that point, you have my word. You can then elect who you want as leader, but until then we all have to be strong. I suspect we were talking about a couple of years before we can start to assess the safety of the mainland. We have a storage facility by the waterside, it's safe, but we mustn't go beyond the wire perimeter at any cost. The main body of the building is sealed, and we access via the waterside only. As I mentioned last night, anyone who leaves the island, or the facility perimeter cannot return. It's far too dangerous as the infection is airborne. The main duties which we will all partake in, including myself, are farming, cooking, defence, science & engineering and medical. Please head to the stores in the basement to collect your protective jackets and sidearm. You will be assigned ammunition after completing your first weapons training session. Look after our equipment and supplies, it's all we have. We have the facility to repair items, but we need equipment to last as long as humanly possible. When the gear stops functioning, then we will be forced to move back to manual old-fashioned means. Take time to familiarise yourself with the island and the locations of the larger weapons and stores".

Everyone headed out towards the training ground. It was near to the stables but not too close to upset the horses. The gathering was quite large, but Spall created four groups, led by himself, Rusty, Sheena and a guy I hadn't seen before called 'Wrench'. I never really understood where Spall's nicknames came from, but I just rolled with it.

Wrench was mid-height but really stocky, of African origin, a proper powerhouse. He had one of the biggest smiles I had ever seen; he was really friendly, and I took to him immediately. I joined Spall's group, we went through the safety basics, including the usual first law of firearms, 'never point your firearm at anyone unless you plan to kill them'. We all learnt how to strip and clean the weapon, load it, and remove the safety. We were issued with Sig Sauer P365 9mm automatics, though I had hung onto my Glock 19. The Glock had incredible reliability, was light, had 19 rounds in a standard magazine and it used the same 9mm parabellum bullets. The Sig was similar in every way, I just liked the idea of the Glock, I guess, it was made famous in some of the movies I had enjoyed. Both weapons were used by police and soldiers worldwide and were well tested in the field.

We practiced with targets pinned to hay bales at around 30 metres distant. Most of the trainees quickly learned a basic weaver stance and squeezed off a few shots, though they consistently tended to hit high. An accurate aim took a little practice, but over time they all attained a reasonable standard. The first time I fired a weapon was with Spall some years before, I adapted my stance and sighted the weapon. Squeezing the trigger gently and smoothly as I had been shown, my very first shot hit the target cleanly in the forehead. Spall seemed pleased; he said it was a great shot for a first timer. I didn't tell him I was aiming at the heart. The team would soon learn, as I had. They were all issued with a clip and were told where to find spares. They were also told not to throw away clips as they would need to be reloaded with ammunition from stores.

Following training, people moved on to their allocated tasks. The mood was surprisingly positive, the group responded well to the structure. I guess we were all pretty numb and tolerated being herded around like sheep. Activity took our minds away from the reality that life had become. The group started to pick up new skills, and they honed and developed them over the years to come. Some couldn't adapt to these skills, and we agreed to do swaps, but generally it worked out ok.

A large group used the ziplines to the other islands. There Phil showed them how to tend the livestock and build greenhouses.

They then spread the new humus rich soil ready for planting, the crops would be late this year.

I caught up with Rusty and Sheena after the training, I wanted to see how they were getting on. "This is damned doolally, bit a'd ower be 'ere than oan that pumpin' mushroom pit ower th' sea". "Yeah me too", I replied. Sheena laughed, "You can stop the Scots slang now, it doesn't work anymore. He's wise to it". "Oh well, it was really fun while it lasted", chuckled Rusty, giving her a noisy kiss on the lips. I was shocked, after all this time I found that Rusty had quite a gentle aristocratic Scottish accent. The absolute swine! It was funny though. I'm not quite sure, but I think his slang was where the word 'Shroom' originated, which we used to describe the infected folk. I guess adding a little humour into the mix helped us to deal with the horrors life was throwing at us.

The Islanders adapted to their tasks quickly. Spall was in his element, ensuring we were secure and vigilant. He kept track of the developments onshore using the cameras we had installed. Phil was unfazed, he seemed to be loving our new life. His wife, Robyn, and his sister, Iris, were always tinkering with the plants, irrigation, and planters. They were allocated an island each and ensured they were transformed into a useful expanse of farmland, working closely with their teams.

Drake diverted his attention back to fixing up older buildings on the island and took Jake under his wing. It was critical we shared skills, and it was good for Jake to pick up his dad's building abilities. Jake had been a bit of a waster, but the new life seemed provide the wake-up call he needed. He took the time to thank me for risking my life to save him and apologised for his harsh words. He seemed to accept the loss of his Mum, but then he was probably working hard to distract himself from bitter reality. He was going to be ok, and Drake never lost his perpetual smile. Having his lad by his side was a dream come true, it really completed him.

Steve locked himself away, researching fungi, downloading as much general information as he could before the internet went down. In those first few months, his team focused on grabbing and indexing as much information as they could. His printers were running at capacity and the tomes were stacking up. He continually tweaked the large aerial on the crow's nest for his ham radio rig, which Kulbir took a great interest in. She was often at the radio hoping to make contact with any survivors out there, but without success to date. Steve's new apprentice, Beryl, was Simon and Jane's daughter. She had an unending appetite for everything technical. She worked hard with Steve and Kulbir and their new friend Janus. They all took shifts manning the radio, hoping for contact.

Kimball ran the stores and the supply chain. He wasn't going to let anyone else squander his carefully built resource pool. He started to identify more places onshore where he could plunder, with Spalls help, once we were ready to go back on land.

Simes taught archery on Sundays, initially as a hobby, knowing it would come in handy in the future if we ran out of ammunition. Bow skills needed to be at a high level in order to hunt animals, as hitting a moving target was difficult. Some folk explored our collection of musical instruments, but I wouldn't go as far as call them a band. Simon helped out on lookout duties with Spall and his team, as did Kate and me. Several others joined look out duties to cover watches 24x7 and allow us to stay sharp at all times, we kept the shifts down to two hours.

Simes' wife, Jane, teamed up with Kimball's partner, Bryan, in the kitchen, with help from a couple of the younger ones. They were already putting orders into Phil for herbs and spices, though the latter was a little limited. They had a chilli pepper or tomato plant growing on every windowsill in the Haven.

Days started to pass quickly, and the numbness of A-Day faded, but not in our hearts. Life became a little more humdrum and routine started to settle. Karl, our blacksmith, took over Murdo's cottage. He and his wife Carla, our vet, enlisted Drake and Jake to convert the building into a forge and an animal surgery. Another cottage became a doctor's surgery.

We set up several meetings to review the state of the world outside. Everyone was either dead, or they were holed up in their houses trying to ride out the wave. The truth was probably somewhere in the middle. One thing that was painfully clear was how efficiently the fungus eradicated the human lifeform, whilst leaving virtually everything else intact, it almost looked deliberate.

Kimball was particularly keen to review the state of play in Russia. "What I really don't understand is how the Russians failed to capitalise on their advanced warning of the infection. They knew a lot more than we did about the nature of the asteroids and the threat posed by the fungus. They had a chance to analyse the fungus and spores before the second wave of meteorites hit. Why are they not faring better in this?"

We mulled it over, off and on, for several days but arrived at no concrete conclusion, as we didn't have any facts.

All we had was our supposition. Perhaps on the greater land masses the spores had superior efficacy, the winds around our island could have kept the spores away. Maybe the Russians couldn't lock down a specific area, as the whole country was systematically pounded by meteorites, the army simply couldn't cover enough space to be truly effective. Perhaps they were sitting there in bunkers, laughing at our feeble attempts to communicate our slowly evolving knowledge of the fungus to the outside world. Who really knew?

After a time, Kulbir managed to contact a couple of the other six havens. She had been in touch with a community on the island of Mont St Michel, just off the northern coast of France. She also communicated with a community in Malta, based on Manoel Island, the small isle between Sliema and the walled city of Valletta. She observed other activity but had no contact yet. It looked like Mont St Michel was very well prepared and had converted the old monastery into a fortress. The quicksand surrounding it had become a great defence once they had mined ingress points and fitted robot sentry guns to the entry road. Valletta was a little more problematic, as the island was awfully close to the mainland on all sides, and they were already fighting off raging masses of infected. It didn't sound good for them. I hoped they made it through, the Maltese were so resilient in the second world war, if they couldn't survive, then no one could. We had no real intel at this stage. Another signal seemed to come in and out of range, its source may have been moving around too much to lock onto.

The TV and short-wave radio signals from across the world were now completely dead. All we had were a few exchanges with our French and Maltese friends. There was no saying the others had installed a radio setup, but it might be they hadn't had time to get it online. The Maltese leader had experienced similar dreams to me, which had prompted him to appropriate Manoel Island. His team had barricaded the entry road but were finding it hard to protect the island from the water. It was also in a terrible place for spores riding the wind. How they could protect against that, I do not know. At least the fort had high walls.

The French were ready well in advance, and they had formed a small uprising to take over the island when A-Day came, their preparations were considerable; most of the commune were already resident on the little isle. It was like a small resistance movement all over again. For them, they were simply protecting their homes. They had stashed supplies over many months. It all started with dreams for their leader too, but no one believed him for quite some time.

A week later, we started to get weak signals from the last four havens. They were based in Formentera in the Balearic Islands, Zakinthos off the west coast of Greece, Isola Salina off the North cost of Sicily and an island in the Kattegat between Sweden and Denmark. They were the last outposts of mankind but were alive and kicking. The contact was patchy, but it was early days. I believed the four were working on it, and they would improve their communications, especially now they knew there were other survivors like them.

It was summer at the Summer Islands, but it didn't really feel like it. It was actually still fairly cool, even when the sun was high in the sky. We had seen lots of activity on the web cameras in Ullapool and the smaller villages near the coast. We experienced the same story, people tearing each other apart, some rabid and some becoming docile. It transpired that the creatures didn't need to eat flesh to survive, it seemed to be more a craving. The creatures survived as an animal / plant hybrid for longer than we expected. Although we were anticipated they would live for a few years, we hoped it would be over in a few weeks, and we could return to the mainland.

Still the violence continued. In a small village like Ullapool, you would expect all the community to be dead within a month or so. It was clearly not proving to be the case; it took time to hunt the uninfected people. The Shrooms' behaviour was odd, they seemed to go inert as the last of the people were killed, though they were particularly energetic and efficient in hunting. It appeared to be an olfactory sense that drove them, smell rather than sight. We knew we couldn't set foot on the mainland whilst the Shrooms were still alive. We needed to wait it out. There was no activity near our supply facility at all, as there were very few people in the immediate area. We had chosen the location well.

7. Redemption in Blood (Francisco)

From the writings of El Tigre

Manoel Island was entered via a small road on the south side of Sliema. There was a marina on the west side of the island and a fort on the east side. I landed on the rocks on the fort side. I don't think the guys knew whether to shoot me or fall over laughing. The first thing they asked me was, had I been infected. I explained that I had been exposed to the spores, but I was ok so far. They ushered me to a small hut, keeping a good distance between us. "Sorry sport, were gonna have to destroy your clothes, give you a spray and quarantine you for a week, if you want to join us". "Understood", I replied. I stripped, dropped the katana on the floor and let them spray me with disinfectant. None of us knew at the time that its efficacy was virtually zero, but it made them feel safer. The disinfectant burned my eyes, I had to rinse them with water. "The drinking water here is shite; I'll throw ya a bottle in a min".

"I'm Francisco", I offered. The Australian guy, Ted, introduced the rest of the team, "This here is Todd, the tall guy is Pete and the short fat hairy arsed one is also called Pete", "Steady on sport", argued tall Pete, mocking Ted's accent. "Not forgetting *Crocodile* Ted", chipped in Pete. "We'll bring ya some grub, but please stay in the hut or poor old Pete is gonna have ta plug ya full of some of Russia's finest lead" and winked. "He ain't a good shot, so it'll probably hurt a lot", he added. "Sounds good to me, thanks. I'm not in a hurry, I just managed to eat something". "You ain't finished ya meal yet sport, it's still on your facking beard!" he said and all three laughed. Forgive me, but I just wasn't feeling that cheerful. I also had a rumbling stomach from the rancid food I had been eating. "Thanks again", I said politely.

My week in quarantine wasn't much fun, it gave me far too much time to think. I almost considered calling it a day and testing Pete's marksmanship. The thought of escaping in a pink pedalo tended to put me off. Most days there were at least three or four attacks. I heard serious gunfire, it sounded like a big machine gun, one that threw out hundreds of rounds a minute, I'd seen them on TV. The sound of the shootings came from the other side, near the road bridge. I was really unsure the bridge was safe; it was too easily accessible. The place was a death trap. The team had hastily erected fencing which didn't look solid enough to me, it could easily be breached by hundreds of infected. I wondered what prompted the team to prepare; they must have been forewarned somehow. I started to think about all of the activity we had observed on the island over the last few months. A few questions started to come to mind.

There were lots of times I just sat there and cried. I always hid it when tall Pete came over with 'grub'. Pete was most interested in the Katana, "Is it a real one?" "Yes, from a Japanese sword master", I replied quietly. "Looks like it's seen a lot of action". "It was as good as brand-new yesterday morning". "Christ, you must have been busy then", Pete remarked.

My tears abated after a few days. I wouldn't say I had come to terms with my loss, or the blood frenzy that followed it, but strangely the killing was a therapeutic influence. I felt like I'd a measure of revenge and worked through some of the anger and loss. I was withdrawn but I kept going, what else was there to do? On the seventh day at evening meal, I was asked to join the community. Pete led me into the fort through the main gate.

I was surprised when I spotted the enormous stash of weaponry they had. "You must have been preparing for this for months. How did you know what was going to happen?" The Comandante, a big, bearded sailor called Rob, said it was difficult to explain. "It may sound nuts, but I lived through a series of visions in my dreams which told me what to do. I didn't believe a word of them until I received a series of juicy gambling tips. I amassed quite a fortune, which paid for this island. It seemed like the decent thing to do; after all, the visions had helped me win". "So, who warned you about the infection?" I asked. "All I could see was a man-like figure, he was too bright to make out his features. He appeared night after night with the warnings, I felt compelled to believe them. Sounds crazy, I know, but then he was right, wasn't he?" "Yes, I guess he was", I agreed. The figure in Rob's dreams seemed remarkably familiar to me, his words were not hard for me to accept at face value.

Rob explained his Valletta team had moved into their quarters on the island as they fortified it. When the first meteors were identified by astronomers, he knew his dreams were for real. His team had installed sentry guns on the entry road. They built wire fences around the island and weaponised the fort. They had plenty of firearms, the team believed they were good to ride out the storm. "We have forty guys armed to the teeth, and enough food for ten years", said Rob. They clearly hadn't looked at the best before dates. They hadn't thought their plans through rigorously, they were simply reacting.

"What happens with the spores?" I asked. "How do you stop them infecting you?" "What spores", he asked sincerely. Here was the heart of the issue, they didn't even understand how the fungus spread. I explained how a mushroom or toadstool projection grew from the infected cadavers to propagate the fungus. Even though the infected had fallen by the hundreds in the mainland close to the sentry guns, Rob's team hadn't noticed the mushrooms. I guess they hadn't got close and hadn't taken the time to inspect the corpses properly. One question remained, why had the spores not infected everyone on such a small island? Spores were light, they float around wherever the wind carried them. The only answer could be that the steady breeze simply guided them away from the island. It was pure luck these guys were still alive. What would happen when the wind changed?

I was interested in how the rest of the world was faring. "Do you have a radio? Is there anyone else out there?" "We haven't got it working yet", said Rob, "we can hear, but we can't transmit. Terry is on it; he'll have it operational soon". "How many countries are ok? Where are the survivors and how are they riding this out?" I asked. "As far as we can tell, the whole world is offline. A couple of people are transmitting, trying to find other communities, but they are small teams like us. Maybe we can't hear them all yet. There's a place called Summer Haven in Scotland and another in France called Mount St Michael; that's all". "Christ", I whispered anxiously. Things were much worse than I feared. Larger cities had larger populations, and the mobs of the infected would be numerous.

A group of fishermen returned with their catch and the barbeque was fired up. They had caught an array of fish:

bream, sole and fresh sea bass. Later, I ran into the fishermen who had landed the catch: Nidal, Gio and Rene. Rene looked how I felt, he had red rings under his eyes and appeared like he'd been drinking. We were having a good time until the sentry guns activated, their staccato was deafening. We ran from the fort, through the fence gate, grabbing weapons on the way. A mob of infected were crossing the road bridge to the island, they were getting mowed down by the sentry guns, but there were so many of them. The entry road was lined with bodies.

Finally, the first sentry gun ran out of ammunition. Rob's team started to cover with small arms, whilst tall Pete ran to reload with a large cannister of ammunition. He lifted the arm, removed the ammunition belt, threw the empty canister aside and started to load the new one. Meanwhile, the second sentry gun stopped, the ear battering ended, and I could now hear the cracks from the Kalashnikovs. Pete was in trouble, there were hundreds of infected and they weren't falling quickly enough. I drew my sword and ran to help him. "Hold on Francisco, you're gonna get yourself killed", shouted Rob. "We will all be killed if we don't get that gun back online fast", I shouted back.

I got to Pete just in time, as three infected approached him. I decapitated them quickly and stepped into the fray. I dispatched infected from the left and right, until Pete shouted, "Ready". I fell back and the gun opened fire, the sound was deafening at close quarters. How could the team communicate with each other when the noise was so intense? Pete and I fell back, I advised Pete to grab another canister, it was imperative the team got the other gun back online quickly or we would be swamped.

The number of infected swelled again. We sprinted to the other sentry gun; Pete started to clear the belt and reload. The first gun was effective in keeping the bridge clear, but the infected behaved like a swarm of wildebeest. They chaotically ran in all directions until a leader was successful in finding a way through, then they all followed. The leader survived by keeping close to the edge of the road, out of the sentry gun's field of view. The hoard followed in single file. I stepped forward, taking care to avoid the sentry gun's line of fire and took the survivors down, one by one. It was as if they were queueing for execution. Soon, I retreated as Pete brought the gun back online and the bridge was cleared in seconds.

"Holy cow Francisco, you know how to use that thing", Pete remarked, indicating the katana. "I've had a little practice", I replied. Pete thanked me, "It got a little nasty out there for a while", he added. Rob's team soaked the multitude of bodies on the bridge in kerosene and set them ablaze. After a few minutes, the large conflagration burned out. A man called Fallon fired up a backhoe; he cleared the bodies with the front scoop and piling them on the mainland. I realised the danger, a fifth of the bodies were starting to grow a mushroom and he hadn't noticed. I shouted, "Get the hell out of there Fallon, the cadavers are releasing spores!" He couldn't hear me over the rumble of the engine. His strategy probably worked well with smaller numbers of infected, but now large groups were attacking, the guns would be less likely to stay operational. The increased number of cadavers meant the dumper couldn't clear them quickly enough to avoid the spread of infection.

Fallon turned back with the dumper just as the spores burst into the air.

It was too late; Fallon was already back on the island when he was overwhelmed by his metamorphosis. He left the digger's engine running, climbed down and turned feral. He was taken down by the team before he reached them. "Struth", said Ted. The team were shell shocked, they hadn't witnessed the spores in action before. I dragged Fallon's body, threw it into the sea and ran clear. "Sometimes, the mushrooms start to emerge a few minutes after death", I explained. "If the spores touch an exposed cut or enter through the nose, mouth or eyes, then host is worse than dead", I continued. "We need to find a way to stop the infected crossing so easily, if they do, then we need to dispose of them quickly before they fruit. Have you got any explosives?"

With Rob's agreement, his team blew the entry road and used the digger to excavate the gap, to allow the sea to flood it. The problem was we could only clear fifty metres. When the hordes came, the dead bodies would fill the void and the infected would scramble across easily. We needed to take them down before they neared the water.

Rob and his team mounted the sentry guns onto makeshift rafts, enabling them to float the weapons over to the mainland, and pull them back when they were discharged, ready for reloading. I called out, "We need to make sure the guns are facing the right way when they are primed, or they will fire at us". The sentry guns would target anything that moved within the field of view of their motion sensors. Rob pointed out the recoil on the guns was significant, and the tripods needed to be well anchored. We agreed that as the guns discharged, the rafts would move in an opposite direction to the line of fire, which randomly swept from left to right. The team needed to brace the guns somehow. They managed to rig up steel arms fixed to the marina bottom that could be lifted up or down by rope. The guns would easily handle the recoil, but there was a risk the ramp would get jammed at a critical point, and one of the team would need to swim over to fix it. The further we were from the spores the better.

The team positioned a wall of sandbags to enable the team to function from the marina side, even if the sentries went offline. We needed an emplacement to engage the infected without withdrawing to the fort, which was our last resort. If we pulled back to the fort, then we would be trapped, and we could be under siege indefinitely. As a fall-back plan, we harboured a couple of large yachts at the rear of the fort for emergency evacuation. The island wasn't defensible for the long term, though it proved impossible to convince Rob.

Pete asked, "What would we do if the infected attacked the island from all sides, floating in on buoyant materials?" I had to admit all we could do was hope they didn't. They tended to swarm, but always went for the path of least resistance when they found it. That path was the entry road, the water was shallow and was easier to cross. But we couldn't afford to rely on that assumption.

I caught up with Rob privately later, "We have improved our defences today, but we have a massive problem". He looked at me quizzically. "When the wind changes, it will send the spores in Valletta towards this island, and we will all be infected. We can't make the fort airtight without suffocating everyone", I added. Rob asked for my advice. We mulled the issue over for a while. We agreed we should wear protective suits outside the fort. On the inside we would only occupy the airconditioned areas which used air filters, we must avoid the areas without such protection at all costs. But where would we get the suits from?

We examined the local business listings and found two possible candidates in the near vicinity. One was St James Hospital in Sliema and the other was a medical testing laboratory at the end of the inlet. Most of the distance could be covered by sea, which would avoid the attention of the infected, but it didn't mean we were safe from spores. Travel by land would be much more dangerous, especially when we entered a highly populated hospital full of infected people. It was a dangerous plan, but sometimes you had to choose your least dirty shirt.

We opted to deploy a four-man team. Gio drove the motorboat; Pete, Todd and I would execute the mission on the mainland. Gio aimed to drop us and dust off quickly, hovering in the water nearby. The next issue was protection from the spores. As I considered this, I realised just how lucky I had been not to be infected during my rampage. I remembered about the green tinge in the cuts I had endured, they had scabbed over and had healed normally; I had been more than lucky.

We managed to find several all-in-one decorating suits in the fort, liberated from an old painting project. We added latex gloves and high-top wellington boots. We taped the seams and added motorcycle helmets secured to scarves around our necks. "This won't work", interrupted Todd. "We have to breathe air, and it has to come from somewhere. It will have spores in it too", he added. It was the first sense I had heard from the guy while I had been there. We had to pilfer an oxygen tank and mask from the diving school to supplement our setup. We looked utterly ridiculous. The 'suits' were cumbersome, easily torn and hampered mobility. I had to temporarily abandon my katana and use a firearm, as I couldn't even move my neck without opening the taped seams.

I needed shooting practice before we dared depart, as I wasn't familiar with rifles or machine guns. On fully automatic, the machine gun felt like trying to hold a goat steady whilst a blind farmer castrated it with a blunt knife.

We adopted our makeshift suits, not knowing if they would be effective, and went in search of better protective gear for the entire team. We opted for the medical lab first, we figured there would have been no one working when the infection had struck, as it was at night. Gio piloted the boat through the marina to the end of the fork, leaving us on the waterside, it was all clear so far. Gio withdrew to stop the infected from boarding the vessel.

The lab was two streets back from the marina, we headed there as fast as we could. The lab was easy to find, it clearly advertised its services on the front of the building. I jemmied the front door with a wrecking bar, and we gained ingress. First, we systematically checked the building was clear.

We finally located the storeroom; we found fifteen brand new coverall suits. They were thick plastic and shouldn't rip too easily. The suits allowed mobility, and they were equipped with sealing straps at the neck, sleeves, and ankles. We also found surgical facemasks and hats. Another store in the main lab contained half a dozen air filtering masks. It was not sufficient for our needs. We headed back to the island and deposited the safety gear, then departed for Sliema and St James hospital.

The hospital was situated five streets back from the waterfront. The best ingress point was a rocky beach, we didn't need to land, the water was shallow. As we approached the shore, we could hear the sentry guns firing again. Perhaps we had stirred things up with our first excursion. Luckily, we were in and out very quickly and missed all the fun. Gio dinted the boat when he dropped us, "Why worry, I'll just steal a new one", he laughed. We scrambled up the rocks and climbed the railings onto the promenade. All clear so far. We headed inland and were accosted by a pair of creatures who had been tramps. One short burst from the rifles and they were down, we moved past them quickly and noted to return via a different route to avoid any spores.

We reached the hospital and entered through the front doors. The scene was chaotic. People had been locked in the building when the infection struck. Seemingly, they had killed each other, but we couldn't afford to depend on such an assumption. Many bodies on the floor had been part eaten. There were no mushrooms to speak of, which came as a great relief. I could hear activity coming from the next floor. The infected seemed to be waking as we entered the hospital. We followed directions to the labs. I dispatched a couple of infected along the way, but we found no serious threat so far.

Our suits were so damned clumsy, it was really hard not to rip them; a tear meant an early bath. We found more suits in the lab, some medical masks and glasses but no filtered breathing apparatus. I guess the hospital technicians didn't work with anything too toxic.

When we returned to reception, twenty infected were waiting for us. We opened up on them as they charged. I took down two, they fell down and the ones behind trampled over their fallen. I shouted to Pete to watch our backs, he turned and immediately opened fire. The infected must have heard the gunfire and came along for canapes. I shot the first who climbed the mound of bodies and launched himself at me. He fell on top of the others and so we continued with an ever-mounting heap of bodies before us. Todd ran out of ammo, and so started to change his magazine when he got side swiped. I shot his attacker, but Todd's mask had been dislodged and fresh mushrooms were starting to emerge from some of the bodies. We mopped up the stragglers, just as the first mushroom popped. We dragged Todd outside, Pete and I went back in. Finally, we picked up the supplies we had dropped when the fun started.

As we emerged from the building, Todd attacked. I hit him full in the face with the butt of my rifle, I felt the seam of my makeshift suit tear beneath my right arm. I quickly clamped my elbow down against my chest, as Pete shot Todd in the face, taking the back of his head off. Pete looked at Todd's body, he was shaking. "I just shot Todd", he screamed. "You had to; he wasn't Todd anymore. This stuff acts fast, you had no choice. He would have killed you without a second thought". Tears appeared in Pete's eyes, but his face hardened, and we continued our retreat to the waterside, avoiding the street where the tramps had attacked. We stepped onto the boat and Gio asked the inevitable, "Where's Todd?" We explained as he reversed the boat out. The sea had become choppy, and we were jostled by the waves. "Don't be sick in that stupid mask", shouted Gio. We were soon back at the island, where the team had mopped up the remains of the small party of infected that had attacked them. We disinfected, stripped off the makeshift suits and examined our acquisitions.

"Where the hell is Todd?", asked Rob. When I explained we had lost him, he looked stricken. Gio took me aside and explained Rob and Todd were intimate. I placed my arm around Rob's shoulders and apologised, but I explained there was little we could do. Pete's eyes welled up as he explained he had been forced to shoot Todd. Rob gently thanked Pete and he felt he had released Todd from a terrible torment, it had been a kindness. Pete sat down and became pensive as *hairy arsed* Pete sat next to him.

We hadn't managed to locate a sufficient supply of suits. We collaged about twenty suits; the surgical masks and glasses weren't deemed adequate protection. The air filtering masks were very good, but they hampered our field of vision. It was the best of a bad lot. If the wind changed, then we could only exit the air-conditioned facility when suitably dressed. If there was a significant attack, we would have to prioritise our defence and take the risk with the spores. The situation was awful, but it was better than we previously faced.

Over the next few weeks, we managed to fend off thirty or so skirmishes. We were resisting adequately; the sentry guns repelled many of the attacks on their own. We became more skilled when fighting in the cumbersome suits. I craved a decent hazmat suit, with flexible joints.

Rob finally managed to make contact with the Summer Haven team. It seemed as though they were ready for anything, they had a really good setup, I wished Rob had invested in the same planning and preparation. He mostly spoke to Steve or his wife Kulbir, but occasionally we talked to their leader, Paul. He sounded familiar, but I was certain we hadn't met. Often I find can instantly like a person if they remind me of someone else I know, perhaps it was merely that. The Summer Haven team called the infected people 'Shrooms', which we thought was hilarious and it stuck. Families were fully accommodated on their island, so they could continue to live as time moved on. We didn't have that luxury here; this place was doomed in the longer term. Let's hope we got through the short term.

The Summer Haven team informed us that we could use sulphur to irradicate the obscure type of fungus which emitted the spores. The problem was we couldn't find local sources. There were no natural deposits on our island; the chemists stocked it, but only in small quantities. The knowledge proved to be of little use to us in the end. The only opportunity was to investigate Sicily, Sulphur was likely to be plentiful near the volcano, Etna. However, it was a whole different story, Sicily would be really dangerous as it was a larger land mass, the numbers of Shrooms would be inconceivable.

Terry managed to make contact with two more havens on the radio. Isola Salina, off the north coast of Sicily, was our nearest neighbour. There was also another island near mainland Greece. Both communities appeared to be faring well enough for the time being.

Rob's team started to notice an increase in Shroom activity, they had become faster and more dangerous during the day.

Summer Haven confirmed our suspicions that attacks were unlikely at night. It helped our organisation, as more of us could rest at night, with a minimalistic watch. We continued as we were for a few more days, eating fresh fish and canned vegetables. Then the wind changed, and all hell broke loose.

8. The First Incursions

I heard the intermittent klaxon sound in the mid-afternoon. We were startled as the loud noise emitted from half a dozen horn speakers placed strategically around the island. The team ran to their allocated defensive positions, mine was in the crow's nest, the main command position. Children were herded back to the main atrium and safety. We didn't worry too much about the other islands, our Haven was closer to the mainland, plus they were largely uninhabited much of the time.

The creatures seemed to sense the location of their prey. Spall was already manning the crow's nest with Sheena. Rusty and Wrench joined us there. It took quite some time for everyone to get to safety, running from the extremities of the island. Those in defence positions would cover the stragglers in the event of an attack; everyone carried a sidearm, but it would only defend against one or two assailants.

Spall noted a vague radar blip at the coast near Badenscallie. The guys were using their optics to identify the nature of the contact. Spall used the large telescope, after a while he figured how it was playing out. Three figures in a small inflatable boat were heading our way. They were probably locals who were trying to escape to our island, knowing we were equipped to defend ourselves. It was a clear example of our clever marketing not helping us. Behind the tiny boat were a small cluster of Shrooms.

Shrooms lay on pieces of wood, paddling on their stomachs, like surfers striving for the long-awaited big wave. Their total lack of coordination was offset by their sheer energy and the rage driving them. The Shrooms were slowly catching up with the boat. Rusty explained the sniper rifles couldn't be used to take out the Shrooms, as the margin of error at that distance might mean they would hit the people in the boat. As they were almost on the horizon the smallest error could prove fatal. Spall reminded me that we couldn't let anyone land on the island, they were likely to be contaminated with spores, if they were not infected already.

We waited patiently. The dilemma was acute, we couldn't just kill them but saving them presented more significant problems. I couldn't stand by and watch them be ripped apart. I needed to be strong and decisive. I really didn't feel strong, my stomach was in knots. As the boat approached the half mile line, the Shrooms had caught up with them. I gave the signal for the team to take out the leading Shrooms as best they could at long range.

The three big Barratt rifles boomed. Two Shrooms' chests exploded, like a watermelon hit by an axe. "Shit!" shouted Rusty, "I was two inches out, it might as well have been a mile". "Just calm your breathing and take the shot again", explained Sheena. Rusty adjusted his scope by a click and resighted his weapon. His Barratt boomed and the third Shroom blasted apart. The snipers chambered a new round and fired again. We knew Spall could shoot. Wrench appeared to be a natural with lots of experience, but for Rusty it was a new skill; he had been quick to build his long-range ability.

Three more Shrooms exploded and fell into the unforgiving sea. The folks on the boat were looking around to see where the projectiles were coming from. Their eyes settled on the island, and they waved their thanks tentatively. Spall reloaded and took down the final Shroom. "Now we have a strategic problem", he said.

We waited as the small boat slowly approached. The folks onboard appeared relieved and continued to wave at us. How was I going to explain that we couldn't accept them onto the island? Suddenly, there was a commotion on the boat, one of the passengers turned ape shit and started attacking the others. The boat overturned and there was a lot of splashing. The guy at the prow of the boat had become a Shroom. It had attacked the other occupants of the boat, and they all went down together. It was clear the Shroom was unable to swim, but its victims couldn't escape its death grip. "Problem solved", declared Sheena, unfazed.

I stood down the klaxon to all clear, and the debate started. "It just proved our theory; we can't let anyone in. We don't know how to quarantine them and for how long", argued Spall. "But it's hard to just kill everyone heading over, isn't it?" I countered. "Nope, I'd ice them in a second rather than let them loose here", returned Sheena making a gun with her fingers and miming a shot to the back of her head. She was proving to be a regular hard case, even Rusty was a little taken aback. "One day you'll put a round in my head", he said. "Yes, I bloody well will", she fired back, "and you would be bloody grateful if you had that shit in your veins". Rusty ceded the point gracefully to avoid starting an argument, but the thought still hadn't dispersed fully. "At least you'd be a fun guy then Rusty", Spall interjected. The oldest joke in a bad book, but it made us all laugh and cleared the air. We did, in the end, agree to take out anything approaching the island in future with total prejudice; we couldn't afford to take chances. The events of today had proven the point, though we needed to explain to the wider group what occurred and why. We were an honest, open culture and we didn't want to appear like judge and executioner, however the others were surprisingly supportive. They were very worried by the situation and were relieved at the outcome. "If these people come here, we will all die", said Maisie Downall supportively. "We need to protect ourselves and thank god we have some of the armies best to help us". Sheena whispered to Rusty, "Aye 'n' some real rank amateurs playing fighter tae". Rusty smirked and winked to me when he noticed I had overheard. "It is just the start, buckle up!" asserted Spall, it was a wakeup call for us.

Days went by, filled with lots of work and training. Simes created a school for the little ones, and many of us took turns explaining our speciality areas, whilst my half-brother Kirk took the responsibility for the general education of the younger kids. He had been a teacher in the past and had given it up for a career in marketing. Kirk hated farming, so he found teaching a useful contribution.

Everyone was becoming a little more upbeat, and socials started to appear in our calendar. Phil finally got our still working, using some of the grain to distil whiskey. It was not a bad brew, but a little rough and peaty. It certainly raised the spirits as folks sat down together! We pulled together a 'band', I played the drum, a Peruvian Cajun, whilst a few strummers hammed their way through the chords and Simes cousin Eileen sang. She had a good ear but a poor memory, so the verses were often repeated. It was fun; we laughed a lot and many danced. It was a small step back towards normality, if only for a little while. On one social, the night went on, a few more drams, a few more dances, a few more drams. The room bounced along with a dodgy version of The House is a Rockin' Don't Bother Knocking, a classic Stevie Ray Vaughan song. Spall's brother-in-law, Barry was really enjoying himself, he encouraged everyone to get up dancing and really made it fun. It was a happy night, until Murphy's law was invoked, and the Klaxon blared out a single tone.

I ran to the crow's nest, taking the stairs at a sprint, arriving out of breath. I sobered quickly when Spall updated me; a military submarine had been sighted off the west coast of the island. It was 01:00 when the boat bubbled to the surface. It sat there quietly for a number of hours, and at first daylight they hailed us.

It was a British Navy Astute class atomic submarine, a nuclear deterrent loaded with 38 weapons, a choice of spearfish torpedoes and tomahawk cruise missiles. It was one of the newly deployed subs made in Barrow-In-Furness, it had tracked our radio transmissions. The submarine was capable of taking down a city at 1000 miles range, the reactor was able to sail submerged with full propulsion for 25 years without refuelling, the only issue was having sufficient food on board. When it first arrived, Rusty could see the optronic mast piercing the water about 2 clicks out from the west coast through his binoculars, it was largely invisible to radar until the flag, or conning tower, partly emerged from the water. It was a beast. We didn't know the intentions of the crew, but I wagered they would be in need of supplies.

Steve patched in the ham radio transmission to the crow's nest. "This is Captain James Capper from the warship HMS Ambush, do you read me, over?" Spall replied, "Affirmative. This is David

Sipall and Paul Collin from the Summer Haven speaking. How the devil are you guys bearing up? over". "It's good to hear another human voice Mr Sipall. We're not so good, but all the better for finding not everyone on this continent is dead or infected with the goddamn virus. Do you have any cases of the infection on your island? over". Spall explained we didn't, and we were well prepared for the events that transpired. "I'd like to hear your story over a dram sometime gentleman. Of all our naval vessels, we are the last remaining, though I can't speak for other countries. Of the three subs in service on the day, we were the only one fully at sea and submerged. We were updated by radio, just before the shitstorm. We pulled into Southampton took a recce via the scope and saw the chaos. Over". Spall explained, "Call me Spall; Confirmed, it's S.N.A.F.U. out there. Our CCTV locally shows the fungal infection is going crazy. Over".

It was weird hearing the 'over' phrase, it was something from old war films. However, Spall was talking on a ham radio, so he wanted to keep the communication simple and only speak one at a time. We explained how the infection worked and about the spores. "So how many are aboard, Captain? Over", enquired Spall. "Just the six of us Spall, we didn't have a full crew before we set sail. Over". The hairs went up on the back of my neck. I looked at Spall, he was thinking the same.

A submarine doesn't set sail with only six staff. Submarines are normally crewed by at least ninety people and usually have enough food for three months. There was a flaw in the fact they had to leave in a hurry, yet they were out at sea when A-Day struck. Something wasn't right. "Permission to dock in your main port, Spall? We have sounded out the depth with sonar, and we should be ok to make port there. Over". Spall replied calmly, "Negative Captain. We cannot accept new people on this island, for fear of infection. We can ferry out provisions for you, it's the best I can offer, sorry mate. Over". "That is not acceptable Spall. I repeat, it is not acceptable. As the last remaining officer of the Royal Navy in a wartime situation, I am in command. Begin preparations for us to make port immediately. Over". "This is not a military installation Captain. You have no authority here", barked Spall, dropping the convention. "It's not the point, we are at war. I am assuming command. Make way for us to port or face a disciplinary action. We are a fully armed assault submarine, and we won't tolerate insubordination. We are sending a boat out to your island with my First Officer, Kennedy. He will assume command of your facility until I arrive".

Spall's face hardened, "That's not going to happen Captain. If you approach the island, we will be forced to open fire". A lump appeared in my throat. "We have 4 Vulcan Gatling guns; they are in your direction. I hope the spray doesn't rip a hole in the side of your vessel. I have tracked your submarine as you arrived, using sonar. You confirmed you don't have a full crew; I assume it's because you have infection aboard. We can't take the risk, I'm sorry, we have over a hundred souls to protect here Captain. Please don't get unpleasant, as I said we will send over some food. You can dock in more northern waters, where the population is low, you would be safe to ride the infection out there".

We had no idea if further north was really safe, but it was a possibility. "Bullshit Spall. My warship is equipped with acoustic tiles, you haven't monitored our position at all. I also doubt you have Vulcans up there". Spall cut him off with the load bark of a gatling gun, the rounds made a splash in the water just in front of the prow of the vessel. "Stand down! Stand down! If you don't desist, then we will be forced to open fire. We can take out your island quite easily Spall". Spall nodded to me. I cut in, "Captain Capper, this is Paul Collin. I am the leader here at the haven. Stop making threats against us, we are a peaceful commune. I deeply regret our warning shots; they merely demonstrated our capability to defend ourselves. However, we would really prefer a peaceful solution. We won't relinquish control to you or allow you to come land side because of the risk of infection as Spall has said. Let's try to get along, we can send you supplies and keep in touch. There is no need for any unpleasantness". "Fucking air breathers", was the reply down the air waves.

The captain said no more, the guns on the submarine turned to train on the Haven. Spall nodded to Rusty, who ran at top speed down to the western defence pod. After a few minutes, I could see he was dragging a large cylinder from the storeroom and was launching it in the water. He held a laptop, with an attached wire spool, essentially a large makeshift fishing reel, connecting to the cylinder. God knows what he had rigged up, but it looked menacing.

"To the crew of the HMS Ambush. Stand down your weapons immediately, or we will be forced to act. A Black Shark torpedo is in the water with your fucking name on it". The submarine started to submerge. Spall became agitated, "If we let that sub bubble, he could pop up anywhere and catch us by surprise. We need to take it out right now!" It was the moment I had dreaded. I froze, I really didn't want to hurt anyone. "Those guys are Shrooms waiting to happen, we need to take them out!" shouted Spall. I nodded, "Do it". Spall waved a signal to Rusty, who launched the Black Shark. The sub was almost submerged when the torpedo took it amid ships. The explosion was staggering, and the flash blinding. The submarine's centre section turned white hot, even though it was under water. The sub went down in minutes, there were bubbles and a miscellany of flotsam on the water, but we could see no bodies. My heart sank along with the ship. It was our first act of murder; and it wasn't easy to live with.

The days that followed were busy, it distracted me enough to push the events to the back of my mind. We needed to explain the situation to the team, the situation, our actions and rationale. There were no dissenters; they were frightened by the event and felt grateful we had come out of it alive. Though it turned out Capper was misinformed concerning the status of the British Navy's fleet.

9. The Battle for Manoel Island (Francisco)

From the writings of El Tigre

Rob's team were occupied defending against a moderate band of Shrooms, when the breeze dropped and changed direction. I knew the outcome instantly. The twenty soldiers in makeshift hazmat suits continued the fight, the other six froze and started to gag, one was Rob our leader. Within minutes the Shrooms were attacking us again, and we were forced to open fire on them. Suddenly, both sentry guns ran out of ammo, and we found ourselves in a desperate situation. Pete and Rene resorted to grenades to take out the remaining Shrooms coming in from the mainland. Rene threw badly and took out a sentry gun as two guys were winching it back to the island to reload. Soldiers started to panic, in the commotion the guys picked up rifles to continue rebutting the attack.

We had taken down six Shrooms on our side of the water, when the other sentry gun fired up and cleared the rest of the land side mob. We quickly threw the bodies into the sea, desperately trying to avoid fruit erupting on the island. We were down to a group of forty-three; it wasn't sufficient to mount an effective defence, we needed cover shifts over a 24-hour period.

The guys were quiet at dinner. I carried the rations to the guys on night watch. "I guess you are in charge now, Francisco?" questioned Will, the younger of the two. "What makes you think that?" I enquired curiously. "Well, possibly because you saved us. We all know it, Francisco. Without these suits and the removal of the entry road we would all be dead". The older guy had a well-worn face with a mass of curly grey hair carried a measure of wisdom, he added, "Please consider it Francisco, we need you. The others will ask you after dinner".

The team had been discussing my role behind my back. They were unanimous and just needed me to agree, to which I felt obliged. My motivation was bolstered by keeping myself busy. The more work I had, the less time I had to reminisce on recent events. The role suited me, although I never wanted responsibility. Perhaps after this I could die in peace and re-join my family in whatever came next.

I wasn't at all comfortable with the next development, in the main hall during dinner a young guy called out, "Raise a glass to our leader, El Tigre!" They all cheered, which I found humiliating. It was like the floor opened up and swallowed me. They all chanted, it seemed to make them more confident and feel safer. It lifted morale and built comradery, but surely they could see it was making me desperately unhappy. I needed to man up, swallow my pride and show some leadership. I guess some of the group remembered the story, my face was instantly recognisable by my scars. Word had spread like wildfire.

There had been a change in the guys, they had a spring in their step, with more energy and more focus. Rob was a good leader, but not one they had chosen themselves. Selecting their own leader bound them together with common purpose; to survive. I couldn't tell them the island was doomed from the start; it just wasn't defensible. I wondered why the white being had selected this place as a haven. Perhaps it wasn't a conscious choice, maybe he or she had no control. Could it be that the being was simply showing us where the spores were less active because of environmental conditions, who knows?

There was a lot of activity land side. The infected were 'shrooming', as we now called it. Their numbers built up day by day, they were preparing for an attack. There was a kind of primitive intelligence emerging, which was a different behaviour pattern altogether. It was as if they were being directed. It was only a matter of time before we were attacked. We made sure the remaining sentry gun had reserves of ammunition ready to load, and we had grenades and spare magazines stashed ready for use. We were tense, we were all expecting a development very soon. The guys felt it, they weren't seasoned warriors, morale suffered as the numbers of our enemy built up. I used our down time to train the team in basic hand to hand combat. They, in turn, coached me in the use of firearms and grenades. The team were a rag tag bunch, but I would happily stand by their side at the end.

Will caught up with me one night after dinner. It was early autumn and there was a slight chill in the air. He was feeling morose, he asked, "Are we all going to die?" I responded, "We are always going to die; the question is a matter of when and how". I quoted from a self-help book I read when I was younger:

> "No one gets out of this life alive.
> So, leave a footprint of your choice.
> You are writing your epitaph.
> You are writing it now!
> Life is a process, not a goal.
> Live it now, or you will miss it!
> We have time to spend and no time to waste."

Several days later, when Shroom numbers had swollen significantly, they went on the offensive. They gathered at the waterside near the location of the old road bridge, carrying pieces of wood and items that would float, they waded into the water. The sentry gun wiped them out in their hundreds, but they kept on coming and soon the sentry was out of ammunition. The team pulled the gun back to the island and reloaded it, whilst the remaining twenty-five soldiers opened fire with their rifles. We had lots of ammo, but the Kalashnikovs were spewing out many, many bullets on fully automatic mode.

There were far too many Shrooms to mess about picking our shots. We would be buried in shell casings very soon. I stopped in my tracks as a thought occurred to me. Where were the casings going from the sentry gun, it was spewing out thousands every single minute? I called for reinforcements, and our remaining soldiers joined from the fort. It was a terrible tactical error in hindsight. We had forty guns targeting the Shrooms and the sentry gun was being reinstated. The team primed the sentry, and it opened up with a huge loud whine. It eliminated hundreds of Shrooms landside, where the bulk of the movement was, but ignored those crossing the water. It tore through the Shrooms, there was a significant mound of cadavers building up. We continued to take pot shots at those in the water and managed to curb the invasion after a while. The water was filled with Shroom bodies.

At this point, basic animal intelligence took over the Shrooms' attack formation. Their strategy completely changed, like a switch being thrown. Suddenly, without warning the Shrooms picked up the dead cadavers and started to throw them into the water. As the bodies built up, they created a rough platform, which they walked on, they systematically continued to drop bodies into the water. It was horrific to watch; they were building a pontoon from their dead. They dumped hundreds of corpses into the water, forming a makeshift bridge. The bridge was roughly ten metres long so far. I ordered everyone to open fire on the Shrooms carrying the bodies, which slowed their pace; but on they came. There must have been a couple of thousand Shrooms, all happy to take their part and die for the team. When the large pile of corpses was diminished, things took a turn for the worse. They started to grab living Shrooms; they threw them into the water to continue the bridge. It was like hell had emptied; its demons were all waiting on the mainland ready to torment us.

Morale dropped, I tried to encourage the guys, but it wasn't working. I was forced to take a more aggressive approach. "I know some of you are feeling like running right now. I know I am. But we must stand and fight. If we run, we are dead, I promise you that. We will only survive if we stand together. Gather your courage, here they come". I screamed my battle cry, "Death to them all", and my team joined me in the chant, but the sentry gun chose the wrong moment to run out of ammo. The guys tried to pull the gun back to reload, but the huge trench was full of expended cartridges and the raft jammed. They couldn't budge it at first, it came free and as the raft lurched, it tipped, and the gun fell into the water. "Keep pulling, you can right it later", I yelled, but they didn't hear me. They panicked and ran as the pontoon reached our shore. Their hazmat suits became dislodged, and the sheer onslaught of spores dissipated from the hundreds of fruits that had blossomed from the dumped corpses. It was catastrophic. All three guys who were operating the sentry gun stopped and gagged, before turning rabid, we were forced to take them down. Fruits started to grow from their bodies, elevating the problem.

How could we survive in the face of such an enemy? They weren't fast or skilled, but they were numerous and ruthless; they had basic cunning driving them. The spores would take down every soldier before we could engage in battle. I guess it was how the world was to be lost.

We continued to open fire as the Shrooms came over their makeshift bridge, they were unstoppable. They were swarming to the island in their hundreds. The horde was also growing on the land side. Terry remained remarkably calm. He seemed to be searching with his binoculars. I queried why he wasn't using his weapon. All able men and women fired on the Shrooms relentlessly, our grenades were making very little impact on their growing numbers. The explosions damaged the bridge somewhat, but more bodies were continually dropped into the breach and on they came. It was only a matter of time before the entire army crossed the bridge, and we would be overrun.

It was hard to hear Terry's words over the gunfire, but he seemed to have developed a theory that someone or something was controlling the horde. He swept the rear ranks of the Shroom groups and the higher ground. Eventually he found something of note. "Take a look", he suggested. We were managing to control ingress on the bridge at the moment, so I indulged him. At the back of the larger group, I saw a Shroom hanging back. I had to acknowledge its behaviour was different. The Shroom seemed to observe rather than attack, it was unprecedented. After a while we noticed there were six Shrooms behaving in the same way. Terry called them 'Shroom centurions', which seemed appropriate. I collared tall Pete, who was our best marksman and asked him to target the centurions. He used the scope to judge the distance, adjusted his sight and opened fire.

As each centurion was hit, a whole group of Shrooms reverted to their normal swarming behaviour, which was simply charging straight at us. As Pete took them down, the whole horde started to charge. "Destroy the bridge", I commanded. Crocodile Ted grabbed an RPG and targeted the makeshift pontoon. It blew a huge hole in the bridge, and the others followed suit. After three large explosions, the bridge was destroyed. Once again, the Shrooms resorted to using floats for transport to cross the gap. The problem they faced was they would soon run out of floating materials after the first incursion. We quickly reached a stalemate.

A couple of guys launched RPG's into the Shroom horde, which killed dozens of them, but it didn't really make a dent in the overall numbers. I shouted to the soldiers to desist and save their ammunition. I thought we might need the ordnance later, and of course we did. It wasn't long before the horde had nominated new centurions, and they again came under control. The bridge building began again in earnest.

It was then that I realised my error. There were screams from the fort side of the island, we had been flanked. Hundreds of Shrooms had gathered wood, lifejackets and rings, anything they could find, and had paddled in from Valletta. At least a third of them had been caught in the tide and had either floated out to sea, or into the marina harmlessly. However, there were sufficient numbers to present a significant threat. I signalled for a handful of guys to follow me; we took out a dozen landing Shrooms as they trudged through the ankle deep water. There were hundreds now coming aground.

The five of us pulled back to the fort; we were surrounded. I called the retreat, and everyone backed up from the marina. The Shroom bridge wasn't fully completed, but the Shrooms had started their ingress on the fort side of the island. We had no choice.

As we sprinted for the fort, the situation became even worse. Several dead on the fort waterside had grown fruits and they started to pop, the sound was ominous. The spores flooded the small island. Those who didn't have suits were instantly infected, they stopped running and started to choke and gag. We didn't have much time. As I ran, I took one last look. I saw young Jerry. He had hurt his leg, and hairy Pete was helping him. He wasn't going to make it. I turned and ran back to help. "Stop, you're going to kill yourself", screamed Terry. "Trust me", I replied. The others sprinted to the fort, opened the main doors, and entered the building.

I sprinted headlong towards Jerry, he was really struggling now, especially as he was constrained by his hazmat suit. Four Shrooms were running towards him. Pete fired and took one down. "Keep moving", I shouted, "Leave them to me". I hadn't got my sword, what was I going to do? I hit the leader head on with the butt of my rifle. He went slack and dropped. The second and third were upon me. I managed to turn the rifle enough to shoot one of them in the leg, which slowed it. I headbutted the third with full force. It smashed its skull, but also the blow broke my safety glasses and cut my forehead. Great, an exposed wound. I raised my rifle and shot the guy in the face. The third had recovered enough to attack, but Pete turned again and shot him in the chest. "Keep moving", I ordered briskly. More were coming. I dropped my rifle and took Jerry's other arm.

As we neared the fort door, I sensed activity behind me. Five more Shrooms were on the attack, the first was about five metres in front of the pack. I let go of Jerry's arm, spun on my heel and hit the shroom in the temple with an ushiro mawashi geri, a reverse roundhouse kick. I put significant power into the blow using the spin and nearly took its head off. I turned and ran flat out for the door. A fusillade from the doorway dropped the remaining four. "Thanks, hairy", I said.

The team expressed their mixed feelings in the fort. Partly because I had risked my life for two of the group, and partly because I had a cut on my forehead. Pete wiped my head with an antiseptic wipe and some kitchen roll soaked in fungicide. It made me shout, it hurt like hell. He then put a band aid on the cut. "Good as new, sport", said Ted. "Seriously, it could be infected. If I start to gag shoot me and throw me into the sea". "It shouldn't come to that hopefully", added hairy Pete, "the cut on your forehead was bleeding profusely. But when you are bleeding like that, it's harder for the infection take hold, everything is flowing out. Usually when the bleeding slows the problems start. Hopefully, we caught it in time". "We'll see", I countered.

Only twenty of us had survived the barrage. We barred the great banded oak doors and took stock. There was no way the Shrooms would get in through the doors, but perhaps the spores could. We decided to tape the door seams, just in case. We took a little time to relax. Pete spoke to me afterwards, "You crazy, brilliant son of a bitch". I thought for a moment and then responded to Pete, "In my book you were the hero, you helped poor Jerry without a thought for yourself. You couldn't have made it back to the fort on your own". We shared a grin and carried on.

10. Disappointing News from the Seven

Three weeks later, as if by magic, HMS Astute surfaced adjacent to the main quay; appearing just outside the salmon nets. I exclaimed, "It's like Deja Vu all over again, as baseball star Yogi Berra reputedly said". Spall chipped in, "Not to be confused with his ursine equivalent".

Any deployed nuclear subs were desperately searching for somewhere to call home, and the world had shifted tragically between one submerge and the next. Rusty was waiting by the waterside with another torpedo, prepared for action, when the dialogue initiated. Captain McCreedy was rather more pragmatic and clearly more human than his predecessor. He completely empathised, understanding that we couldn't accommodate his full crew of 98 sailors, but he was most grateful for a month's supply of rations and a few bags of sulphur. "Good to find some of us are still alive Mr Spall", he said. "Yes, you must stop by for a few drinks when the infection dies down". "That's a promise. Adios and keep safe", replied the captain. The submarine and its crew departed without realising the fate of HMS Ambush before it. Luckily, they arrived on the opposite side of the island, their sonar didn't pick up the signature shape of the Ambush's hull, perhaps the acoustic tiles worked in our favour. The surrounding ocean was much deeper than we realised, it was close to the North Sea after all. Maybe they did see the wreck and chose to ignore it.

HMS Astute departed for Iceland, as they their radio had picked up a static transmission from there. The captain took our advice seriously on how to avoid the spores. We had made an ally; we needed all the help we could get. Capper had said there were no other subs in operation, but clearly he wasn't fully aware. As we had only seen submarines, it became obvious that regular ships had succumbed to the infection. Ships tended to visit port frequently, whereas the point of the Astute class was always to be at sea, our hidden defence against nuclear threat. The subs could be in my backyard, and I wouldn't know it, so to speak. Yet, we had seen two in the space of a month. It was one hell of a coincidence they both arrived within a few days of each other. They were clearly monitoring the radio waves looking for survivors, trying to find a new home.

Communication slowed a little between the seven. We were all pulling through, with the exception of Malta. Their fort was too small and too accessible. They were trying to defend their haven in hazmat suits, but they were clumsy. When they were down to a handful, they had decided to abandon their base. Their leader had died and 'El Tigre' had taken over as Comandante. El Tigre was an unusual man, as he had experienced similar dreams as the seven haven leaders.

Spall and I submitted a motion to the commune to ask permission for the Maltese survivors to join us. We agreed it would take at least thirty days for them to sail here, and it was a reasonable quarantine on the proviso they stayed out to sea. If they docked in a port, then all bets would be off. They provided us with the ability to track their GPS signal. They had taken a large sailing boat, all their remaining supplies, plus a few fishing rods and set out into the Mediterranean.

I pondered why they were heading for Summer Haven, as Salina and Greece were more accessible. I knew the English and the Maltese were like brothers in arms and always had a close bond, but 'El Tigre' sounded distinctly Spanish to me. It turned out he was actually English, and the pieces dropped into place. It was the Spaniards who gave him his nickname after he saved the lives of twenty-six mothers and children when a tiger escaped its enclosure at a zoo, a year or two before. El Tigre was reported to have killed the tiger with his bare hands, it was in all of the newspapers and social media. Apparently, there was a video of the event, but I never had chance to watch it. At the time I found the story rather difficult to believe and I ignored it as fake news.

Isola Salina got back in touch; they'd had it really quiet so far. I guess the sea had provided them with a better defence, plus there were no visitors from the mainland on A-Day, it was only April, and the Med could be a little choppy. Most of the smaller islands probably got infected by visitors transmitting the spores, rather than experiencing a direct meteor hit. Sicily enjoyed limited tourism in April, but the more disperse islands tended to have a shorter vacation season. Salina's leader was Holy Father Giuseppe, 'Father Joe'. He provided gentle leadership to the folks inhabiting the island at the time. Joe regarded his leadership as guiding his extended flock. I wasn't sure he was sufficiently prepared for the impact of the infection, and he was too far away to obtain any meaningful help.

The island of Salina was just a volcanic rock in the middle of the sea that had become a green and fertile island over the centuries. But then, what was so different from our little island? Their island had over two thousand occupants though, so it might just be the largest human population left on the planet.

Salina was the singularly most important colony; we needed to find a way to protect it.

Salina was topographically characterised by its five inactive volcanoes, the two large ones that shaped the island were Monte Fossa delle Felci and Monte dei Porri. However, as with Sicily and the good lady Etna herself, the volcanoes brought a world of creation to the islands, and they were able to grow a great breadth of produce for somewhere so close to the equator. The volcano was really Mother Nature's chemistry set, where new species could appear without notice, due to a new combination of minerals in the soil, thrown up by the volcano when active. Father Joe claimed God would provide, and I dearly hoped he would. If nothing else, it looked like Father Joe might avoid any hand-to-hand combat. Salina had plentiful supplies of Sulphur though, provided by the volcanic activity in the long distant past. They had a small amount of recent activity, hopefully the island was safe. Isola Salina sounded like the perfect holiday destination for us, when it was all over. Giuseppe's English was excellent, which was lucky as my Italian was the usual lame tourist offerings comprised of hello, goodbye, please, thank you, beer, and cheers.

Captain McCreedy reported back, he found Reykjavik was a depleted but functional city with a couple of hundred residents, but there many of them couldn't communicate well as they were Inuit. They had seen meteors, but somehow the extreme cold seemed to have suppressed the worst of the spores. This didn't make much sense; we hadn't been contacted by Alaska or any northern European countries such as Russia. But it didn't mean they didn't survive, just because there was radio silence. Iceland wasn't one of the seven havens I had dreamt about, so clearly it was an unexpected upside. I guess the darker side of me started to wonder if the Icelanders just hadn't seen their share of the troubles yet.

Zakynthos had experienced a huge attack the following evening. The survivors had struggled to defend against the rabid population of the island. The meteors had brought the infection to those who had been living outside the confines of the main city. Perhaps their patron saint, St Denis, the great protector, was looking after his people. The team were managing to control the spores using large, atomised sprayers which filled the air with brine from the Ocean. The favourable wind conditions had created a prophylactic effect of saturating the spores, the additional weight driving them into the ground. The technique was ingenious, but it was a tactical solution not a long term one. The spores still survived and were lethal when they came into contact with anyone.

The Greeks had all but cleared their island of Shrooms. They were barricaded inside Zante town, which had been converted into a makeshift fort, when virtually the population of Shrooms from the isle of Kefalonia attacked simultaneously. The Shrooms used a familiar pattern of gathering pieces of floating debris and paddling over the sea. Many of them had been taken out into the wider Mediterranean by the currents, but still around a thousand had mobilised for the attack on Zante town. It was a huge battle, but luck or good forewarning ensured the Zante team had a large cache of functional weapons and ammunition. They had also dug fire trenches and used kerosene to kill the Shrooms in their hundreds. The creatures weren't too keen on fire it seemed; fungus proved as flammable as human flesh. After the attack, the Greeks joked that the Kefalonian's had always been jealous of their green pretty island and had always tried to set fire to it.

We heard extraordinarily little from the Kattegat and Formentera, I guess they were engaged with the infected. Of all of the locations, they would find it hardest to source Sulphur or Anti-Fungal compounds, I just hoped they had been well prepared.

Steve informed me that Kattegat is a stretch of sea between Denmark and Sweden. The haven was located on Samsø island, one of three islands in the straits. Samsø was the first island in the world to be completely powered by renewable energy and would be well catered for in the electricity department. Samsø was large, it has nearly four thousand occupants; but the messages we had received so far indicated there were only a handful of people in the haven. I had no idea of their circumstances, they weren't keen to talk about it yet, I suspected it was too painful for them.

It was December 2021 when the gates of hell opened. We had finished our harvest, gathered the crops, and prepared for winter. The grains were stored, the vegetables and fruit had been preserved by either bottling or storing in dark places. The stalks had been bailed in order to feed the livestock. It all went very well, but there didn't seem to be enough food to last out the winter by quite a margin. We would be relying considerably on our stores, which were extensive. We would need to improve our farming in the future. We enjoyed a small celebration akin to a harvest festival, where we all let our hair down and sampled Phil's famous whisky and his new batch of beer, which was hoppy and cloudy, but very drinkable. Life was simple and tiring, but very satisfying. It seemed a better world than the modern high-tech demand driven culture created for us. We gave an honest day's work and relaxed together in the evenings. The respite was good, it was much better after our hard labours. In my old job I was more stressed and found it quite hard to sit down at all, I always needed be doing something. After a hard day, a sit down and some conversation whilst the kids were running around was fine by me!

We had seen little activity for months on the mainland. Most locals were either dead or shrooming. As their prey had reduced, the Shrooms migrated. We weren't sure if they sensed the presence of our community, or if they were able to communicate our location in a rudimentary fashion. Whatever, the Shrooms were gathering in their hundreds at the closest point on the coastline, near to Polbain. They appeared to possess basic coordination, as if the island had been dusted with 'fresh meat here' hormone. On Christmas Eve, they collected pieces of wood or anything that would float and took to the sea in their thousands.

11. The Siege of Fort Manoel (Francisco)

From the writings of El Tigre

Fort Manoel was a limestone star fort, built by the knights of St. John in traditional French military style. In the shape of a square, with a pentagonal bastion on each corner, the bastions allowed the defenders to target the enemy in either direction along the walls. The Maltese had carefully restored it after WWII. Two bastions were located on the seaward side, facing Valletta. They had inoperable gun emplacements that were added in the war and served largely as a tourist attraction. The curtain wall linking the two bastions contained the main gate, which was protected by a two-faced defensive aperture. The other pair of bastions were located along the landward side of the fort. It was a well-constructed fortress, that could be easily defended against sizeable numbers, if there were sufficient soldiers. However, we didn't have enough troops, not by a long shot.

Rob had managed to bribe a senior member of Valletta's council to allow him to buy the fort before it became a world heritage site. He made some subtle alterations to provide a fully air conditioned and liveable space in some of the inner buildings and barracks. Rob also added a substantial machine gun onto the top of each bastion. The piazza on the inside of the fort contained a chapel, an armoury, and the barrack blocks. The latter had become our home. We were under siege in an antiquated fortress. We had time to think, because the Shrooms couldn't climb the walls nor penetrate the doors, we just needed to keep watch for developments.

An English Apocalypse - Paul JC Edge

We were hemmed into our fort until either we ran out of food, the spores penetrated the suits, or we went insane and ran away screaming. The latter was the most likely outcome, to be fair. The cut on my head had healed easily enough, but I felt a light fever and a familiar stinging sensation one evening. I kept my fever quiet; I knew I had survived it before. Perhaps I was developing an immunity to the small scrapes, perhaps I was just lucky. I didn't want to put it to the test.

The days rolled by, and boredom set in. Occasionally the guys would take pot shots at the Shrooms from the curtain. I discouraged it because of the spores produced, but what the hell, they were everywhere anyway. The Shrooms made a major effort at one point when they swarmed the fort from all sides and tried to climb, to no avail. They also tried to hammer down the doors with large pieces of concrete, also to no avail. The variety of attempts to overcome our defences was the swarm in action, there were only a hundred or so of them remaining on the island, the remainder were slowly building up at the marina. I knew there was going to be trouble, as the shroomings meant only one thing, with volumes came centurions.

We stayed in constant contact with France, Greece, and Scotland. We learned there was still a submarine floating around and there were actually seven havens, plus a small outpost in Iceland. It was an extremely poor showing for what had been an entire planetary community.

Rene had hit the bottle again; he was reliving pain from his past. I knew Gio was trying to hold him together, they were close friends. I didn't get involved; Rene didn't really know me. I was too psychologically shaky after losing my family, I would probably end up being brought down by him. Rene needed better support than I could offer. But we must make sure he knew we were there for him. I had to keep up the pretence of strength, being 'El Tigre'. I hated my nickname, but the trouble was, it had surely stuck, I needed to learn to deal with it.

As Jerry regained his feet, he took delight in winding up hairy arsed Pete, it almost came to a head at one point and fists were raised. The banter went a little too far, but they eventually calmed down and they became friends again.

The Shrooms were on the move, this time the centurions were too far out for us to take them, we didn't have a good sniper rifle nor the wherewithal to use it. Pete took pot shots at them but had little success. His aim just wasn't good enough, he had to allow for the parabolic drop of the bullet due to gravity, plus the prevailing wind, it was all too much for him at the distances involved.

The next morning at sunrise, the Shrooms came in force. There were thousands. They stopped at the walls, then started to build ramps, which was becoming a familiar approach. The Shrooms on the front line were smashed to the ground by those behind. The bodies dropped and the Shrooms moved forward and the same was done to them. The bodies were piling up. Normally there would be no army left after the enormous level of casualties, but there were so many it made little difference. They were cut down in their hundreds, but the pile was growing. Within an hour they would reach the top of the wall, and we would be overrun.

Pete questioned if we should open fire. I explained there was little point, because they were killing themselves, it would just add to the pile and waste a lot of ammo; it would ultimately help them. Our tactics evolved, we dropped kerosene onto the Shrooms and ignited it, but the smoke choked us. The burned bodies continued to add to the problem. When the cadaver ramps were getting high, I gave the order to open fire. The two guns on the land side bastions opened up, and they spewed death across the infected. They dropped many hundreds of Shrooms.

Our teams had reloading down to a slick machine-like process, and we continued to wipe them out. The problems started when a gun jammed. Thousands of dead were lining the walls, but the shrooms pushed on regardless. Pete struggled with his machine gun as the rest of us opened fire with our rifles. The second machine gun kept firing but was going to run out of ammo sooner or later. This tactic couldn't continue indefinitely.

When nightfall came, we were ready to fall over, we were in agony through sheer exhaustion. As the Shrooms were inert at nightfall, we passed around food and additional ammo. Hairy commented on the vast quantity of fruits growing, the air was laden with spores.

Jerry made a huge error of judgment by taking off his safety glasses to wipe his eyes, the lad was shattered but had fought well. "NO!" I shouted, but it was too late. He started to gag and was at the point of turning feral, I had no choice but to place a bullet between his eyes. It was a horrible moment. Pete failed to let us know about a small abrasion, he had caught his hand with his screwdriver whilst fixing the machine gun under extreme pressure. He thought no more of it, it was trivial accident. Intricate work whilst wearing big heavy gloves was impossible and he'd allowed himself to get frustrated. He was with Doug when he went off the rails. He slashed Doug's face and bit Ted's neck before we shot him. That night we were down four, there were sixteen soldiers remaining, and tomorrow we faced another day. I moved all the ammo to the other machine gun, and we finally got some rest. Terry couldn't sleep, so he kept watch. It was all quiet, so he waited until just before sunrise to wake us.

It was like Groundhog Day. Thousands of Shrooms fell upon us again. The big machine gun took down hundreds of the enemy. Hairy dropped grenades over the walls to dislodge their cadaver ramps, which slowed them a little. The machine gun barked all day long, we were like the walking dead by nightfall. Our suits were wearing thin, and a couple had developed holes. We swapped out or taped them. Luckily, we had four spare suits which we recovered from our casualties before we committed their bodies to the ocean. We were alive and still surviving, I feared we wouldn't last much longer.

I gave the order for everyone to acquire brand-new weapons, to minimise the chances of our rifles jamming, we were too tired to clean them. It only took one faulty firing pin to render a soldier ineffective. The crap dry rations we ate tasted like paradise. Nidal stuffed three packs in his face, I hadn't the heart to stop him, we could be dead in a few hours. Nidal was a rotund guy. Have the food, you've earned it my friend, I thought.

The next morning, we began our last day at Fort Manoel. We manned the walls just before sunrise. The sight that greeted us was the most prolific army Earth had ever seen, there were hundreds of thousands of them. They had been slowly dribbling in during the night. Some Shrooms seemed to be capable of movement, even limited attack at night. However, as they got older and became more fungus than human, they needed more light to be active, they tended towards the inert. My heart sank as we looked upon the masses. Now I knew how Hector felt when he looked upon the endless hoards of the Greek army from the walls of Troy.

As the sun rose, so did the army and they charged the walls. The big machine gun sang its song of death long into the morning, but still they came. We started to run out of ammunition. It was just after midday when they breached the walls. The Shrooms killed as they came; we had no chance. In the end four of us remained, we were barricaded into the top of the bastion on the Valletta side of the fort. Only Nidal, Rene, Gio and I had survived the onslaught. That morning, I had strapped on my katana, I just had a feeling I might need it when the munitions supply chain failed. The Shrooms pounded on the door with something heavy, the hinges were weakening.

We were locked in the radio room, where Terry's precious ham radio was set up. We switched it on, it was tuned to the frequency band Summer Haven was using, as luck would have it. Gio managed to contact a guy called Steve. He explained Valletta had fallen, we were down to four and had decided to abandon base. Gio let them know our leader had died and I had taken over as Comandante. Steve had heard a little about my cursed life journey before joining Valletta. After a discussion with his commune, Steve informed us we were welcome at Summer Haven.

Gio had selected a large sailing boat called 'The Eagle'. He advised Summer Haven we would see them in about a month. We smashed out the windows and dropped a rope to the ground below. Gio explained he'd loaded the boat with supplies, a little over a week ago; he also packed plenty of drinking water and some good fishing rods. "Well, what the hell else was there to do", he exclaimed. "I always figured I would be forced to run at some point", he added with a cheeky smirk. We clambered down the rope, after lowering our ammo and the rifles first. Luckily the Shrooms hadn't surrounded the water side of the fort, they tried to avoid water whenever possible. We made our way to the boat, which was moored at anchor just out to sea. Unfortunately, a group of Shrooms would see us before we got close to the boat. We also realised we couldn't swim with the guns and wearing our cumbersome suits. We needed a plan and fast, before they caught wind of us. Thankfully, the suits had an additional benefit, as well presenting a barrier to the spores, they also kept our odours in, we hadn't washed for days.

In the end we opted for the simplest approach, even though it was risky in the extreme. We decided to wade into the water, when we were up to our necks, we would strip off the suits. Taking off our air filtering masks underwater would allow us to swim below the surface until we were close to the boat. Unfortunately, we wouldn't be able to take our rifles. Gio explained he had stashed a couple of Sigs and some spare mags in the boat's locker. We started wading, as predicted three Shrooms came lurching towards us with horrible guttural screams. I encouraged the others to keep going and ran back to get my rifle, but it was too late. The water slowed my steps a little too much. I had only one choice, I threw the mask and ripped off the suit and took out my katana. Before I could blink, they were on me. I decapitated the first, but its body rammed into me. I reacted clumsily due to the water constraining the movement of my ankles and the other Shrooms were upon me by the time I had untangled my legs. I dispatched the second with a vicious slash across its torso, which opened him up beyond its ribs. I spun and took off the head of the third. I quickly returned the katana to its scabbard, ran into the sea and swam for it. Gio and Rene helped me onto the boat via the small ladder at the keel.

V. The Truth Will Set Us Free

"One is never afraid of the unknown; one is afraid of the known coming to an end."

Jiddu Krishnamurti

1. The Gathering of the Shrooms

As if the mass of Shrooms heading our way wasn't enough, Steve announced he was out of cigarettes. He was horrified we had none in our stores and wasn't afraid to vocalise how selfish we were. It didn't occur to him we had more pressing business, or that food was higher priority. He'd had ample opportunity to resolve the issue or secure supplies for himself. Slowly poisoning one's body wasn't one of the things we had planned for, except for coffee of course. Spall ordered Steve out of the crow's nest, he was offended and perplexed until Spall hit the red button and the klaxon sounded for battle stations. Steve departed rather quickly after that, running for the relative safety of the main haven building. Kimball lost it when he saw what was coming our way. "Keep your shit together soldier", balled Spall. Kimball moved down to the forward defence post; he looked like he thought he was going to his death.

Spall and the team had rehearsed this scenario for quite some time, and the tactics were well ingrained into the teams. "Remember, in order to ensure a perfect aim, shoot first and nominate what you hit as the target", he joked. "For Pete's sake, call an air strike", hollered Rusty. How they could joke at times like this was beyond me. They opened fire with the sniper rifles to thin out the Shroom from just under a mile out. "It's like shooting a fish in a barrel", remarked Sheena with a smirk. Wrench arrived, "The trench is ready to flood with kerosene when we are ready". Let's hope they don't get that close, I thought to myself, it would be impossible to counter the spores that the fire would elevate into the atmosphere. I hoped the cold island breeze would carry the spores away. It was quite difficult to see the Shrooms on the water, the waves hid and jostled them around. By the time the Shrooms neared the shore, the snipers had probably killed fifty or so of them. However, there were hundreds still coming. "Wait until you see the greens of their eyes", Spall shouted down to the coastal defensive positions via the tannoy.

The Shrooms coasted in on their planks of wood and floated over the salmon nets; luckily, none got tangled so damage was minimal. They beached in their droves, the Vulcan gatling gun at the front-line coastal defence position fired up. It spread thousands of rounds per second in a scattergun pattern, it was built to bring down low flying aircraft. We had to be really careful to avoid 'friendly fire'.

Nothing was going to get through the colossal barrage thrown out by the incredible weapon. There were a few idle times when the ammunition ran out, and a new belt was loaded into the breech, but it made no difference. The infected went down in their hundreds, but extraordinarily little blood filtered into the sea. Many were bisected as they ambled along the beach. "Watch your ammo, fire in short bursts", shouted Rusty, as he joined the group. Other automatic weapons were opening up on the infected. It was a complete massacre. Hundreds of bodies lined the shore, they didn't have a chance. But then it became evident they were a decoy; we hadn't anticipated such a level of intelligence given our experience to date.

We had failed to realise that amongst the fray was a second group of Shrooms, they had beached on the northernmost coast, there was only a team of four manning the sandbags there. The team had no gatling gun, and the Vulcan had stopped firing, enabling us to hear the cracks of the M16's opening up. The Shrooms started to lift themselves up onto the shore. I sent a second squad to join them, led by Sheena, but it would be five minutes before they reached the defence team at full sprint. We needed to be better at anticipating their tactics. Sheena arrived to find the defensive position overrun by more than twenty infected. The monsters were crouched on the floor, feeding on our comrades. A hundred dead Shrooms littered from the shore up to the sandbags, the team had been overrun by sheer numbers. Sheena pulled the pin on a grenade and lobbed it into the defence post, Fire in the hole". The squad simultaneously dropped to the ground for cover.

The grenade took out at least ten infected and littered the ground with bodies, ripped apart by the blast and the shrapnel. One corpse started to grow the first showing of a fruit, there wasn't much time. The M16s fired, and the remaining Shrooms dropped. Two creatures were in a complete frenzy and sprinted towards Sheena. They were hit with at least four rounds each, but they kept on coming. They had really gone crazy, more so than the others. These Shrooms were fast and ugly. Their jaws were reddened by the blood of our comrades. Their eyes were monstrous, filled with hate and rage. Their clothes were ragged and flapped in the wind as they ran. They had only one purpose on this earth, and it was to kill.

Sheena's squad switched to fully automatic and took down the leader, Sheena stepped in with her wicked looking claymore and took off the other Shroom's head. She dropped the blade so it could be sterilised later, during the clean-up. The fruit grew scarily quick during the fray, and it popped. Spores were sent into the atmosphere around the base. Sheena ran to the defence point and fired the aerial suppressor. What looked like a flare was launched into the sky and exploded, the whole area was doused with yellow sulphur powder.

The team quickly covered the lower half of their faces with scarves, handkerchiefs or whatever they could lay their hands on. Although sulphur wasn't toxic in small quantities, the cloud made breathing problematic. The quick application of a damp cloth to their faces addressed the problem. The sulphur cloud suppressed the smaller mist of spores and would hopefully destroy them over the next few hours. Sheena's team needed to avoid the area for a while, they needed to dust off, much to their dissatisfaction. "We've already inhaled a shitload of this stuff, why are you spraying us with it?" It was just bluster really, they knew it was needed and wouldn't have it any other way. Better to be safe than sorry.

When Spall sounded the all clear, we donned hazmat suits and applied bleach and sulphur to the cadavers. Steve retained six bodies to which he only applied either bleach, sulphur, or a fungicide as an experiment. He waited with the bodies to assess the results; the test would help determine our best cause of action for the future.

The real hero of the day was Rosie, who found the ability to sniff out the Shrooms at distance. The miraculous olfactory senses of a dog! We washed her down in fungicide and later let her swim in the sea. We also isolated her, as we weren't completely sure if animals were affected. She wasn't happy; she whimpered all the way to the cage and started to howl. Our assumptions proved correct; after a week, the dog was fine. We treated her to a large meaty bone. I hoped more of the dogs would develop her most useful ability.

Steve's test demonstrated sulphur was indeed the best method for destroying the fungus and spores. Two other fungicides were also reasonably effective but took more time to act. The bleach had little effect. Steve covered the bodies in sulphur and treated them. We all dusted ourselves in sulphur before showering. Forewarned is forearmed. We set up a fifty-metre perimeter around the bodies, to reduce the risk of becoming infected. We also had around the clock observation to look out for any fruits emerging. Luckily, the sulphur did the trick. We were safe for now, but there was lots of clearing up needed afterwards.

After a week, we had burned the cadavers using kerosene. We then used spades to bag up the remains and the adjacent soil and dumped them at sea. We hoped they wouldn't come back to bite us, no pun intended. What a bloody mess.

We shared our experiences with the five other remaining havens, confirming the efficacy of sulphur as a means of disposal and control of the spores. Some had access to Sulphur, and some had the appropriate fungicides or a similar product. Isola Salina had found some natural deposits of sulphur from their inactive volcanoes. Only Mont St Michel was left relatively defenceless. Luckily, they had the natural barrier of quicksand and only three Shrooms had come within 100 metres of the island.

The havens universally adopted the term 'Shrooms', but it sounded really comical in a French accent. Their approach to disposal was novel, they bagged the corpses, inflated the bags with air and floated them out to sea. The biodegradable bags slowly leaked, and sank after twenty minutes or so, by then they were well out in the deepest part of the ocean. They also proved that the mycelia remained local to the host and didn't infect the surrounding soil, they were lucky enough to have biochemists available with the facilities to analyse it.

The scientists at MSM also concluded that the fungus wasn't known by biologists and had many unusual properties. It somehow attached itself specifically to human DNA and shunned other animals and plants, although how it achieved this wasn't clear. As suspected, the fungus was targeting only humans. The fungus trickled nutrients into the host for sustenance, the host didn't actually need to consume flesh, providing the fungus got regular daylight. It explained why the infected were most active on sunnier days and preferred to be out in the open. It also showed why the Shrooms tended to be less active at night-time, when the fungus was less able to provide food. The Shrooms exhibited low energy when the fungus wasn't performing photosynthesis. It was the most unusual fact; fungi are typically incapable of photosynthesis as they possess no chlorophyll. The fungi used another mechanism which was alien to us. The answer was simple, if we were forced to venture out onto the mainland, then we should go at night.

Spall observed very few infected on the immediate shoreline over the next few weeks. But the number started to build up gradually. Luckily, our island was remote, or we would have been overrun very quickly. When the numbers reached tipping point, we knew we would face another attack, but it wasn't imminent.

Late in December, Steve picked up a radio channel. It turned out to be a blast from the past, showing someone out there had a keen sense of humour. The channel faded in and out and it claimed to be Radio Caroline, the old pirate radio station. It was originally run from a ship in the North Sea to avoid the broadcasting laws imposed by the UK, until the dawn of digital radio. It transmitted from an oil rig, way up in the North near to the remote sandbank, Dogger Bank. It didn't offer any commentary on our predicament; it was a simple message of defiance. It was a ray of hope for the few who were left. I'm not sure the facility was manned; it could have been just a playlist automatically set to transmit on a loop. There was never evidence of human voices on the transmission. The pickup trucks had radios and were always tuned in, hoping for a recognisable song. To hear the voice of Britney Spears was actually something we valued a lot these days!

The radio transmission turned my mind to considering the plight of men and women aboard oil rigs. Safe from the bombardment and the spores, they would be manning the rigs until they died of starvation. There was nothing we could do to help the poor souls, other than hope there was still a helicopter aboard the rig, and someone able to fly it. The issue then became, if they reached mainland would they contract the infection. Sometimes the painful transition period would soon pass, but on other occasions those infected would make the change more slowly and be hunted by packs of ravaging Shrooms. It was not a fate I would wish on anyone. My deliberations motivated me to call McCreedy, who immediately understood what I was trying to achieve. He agreed to visit the rigs he was passing, but didn't hold out much hope. Over the following four or five months McCreedy saved some sixty souls in this way. Beyond that period, anyone he found was dead from starvation or dehydration.

Samsø Haven finally decided to share their plight. They had experienced no meteor strikes whatsoever, but a pair of travellers, who were island hopping from the smaller adjacent island called Sejer, brought in the infection. They became ill at the harbour side, and both sent up a fruit within fifteen minutes of collapse. No one knew what was going on and simply stared at the couple as the situation developed. The growth and the fruit were a most alien and curious sight to the onlookers. Nobody would instinctively think the fruit were harmful, it was merely a toadstool, but still they avoided touching them. They naturally assumed a toadstool was potentially poisonous.

The spores from both fruits emitted a cloud which infected the whole of Ballen within hours. The haven itself was based in Nordby and used webcams to keep look out. They were well warned, but the whole island was overrun in 24 hours. In Nordby they had built a modest underground complex near to the highest point at Ballebjerg, in close proximity to a small decorative tower.

The team had excellent views from the tower. However, they were too slow in locking down and a member of the team was infected and became a carrier. The team managed to control the spores with fungicides, but not before the infected guy had taken down fifteen people. There was only seventeen people in the facility, everyone else on the island was dead or infected. It was a terrible story, but they had been lucky. I suspected, however, that they didn't impart the full tale. It was a simple microcosm of occurrences everywhere. The team had controlled the fungus well, once it entered their haven, it showed control was possible but only with foreknowledge. I asked how they received advance warning of the infection; it led to a curious story.

Their leader Lars-Åke experienced recurring nightmares of an apocalypse as I did. However, Lars-Åke had also seen a wider view and remembered an implication of someone or something being behind the attack, and it was merely the first phase of something much bigger. The message was deeply concerning for us. Our numbers were so small; how could we fend off anything else? As a race we were depleted to the point of near extinction. My other worry was I had received no warning of the additional threat. Perhaps we had time before our helper would be in touch again.

2. Escape from Valetta (Francisco)

From the writings of El Tigre

"It was some rumble out there, dude. It was wild", said Nidal with a kind of surfers admiration in his voice. "It certainly was", agreed Rene, "but what about the damned suit, you probably infected yourself now, you stupid camel's asshole!" He wasn't being nasty; he was deeply worried about me; it was the way he expressed himself. "We all need to watch each other for a few days, we've taken a few too many risks. As soon as I get aggressive, you need to kill me and throw me overboard". "We best do Rene now then, he's always nasty", smiled Gio. "Fuck yourself, you Italian peacock bastard", retorted Rene. Gio didn't take his remarks as an insult, it was merely banter between two good friends.

Gio took out the boat and showed me how to set the sails. I soon got the hang of it; it took two to sail the boat. The yacht could accommodate ten, so there was plenty of room for us. Nidal bragged that he had the comfiest room he'd had for two years. "I should think so", said Gio, "this boat would set you back a million dollars and then some!" At least we had a modicum of comfort for our long journey.

"So why are we heading to Scotland?" asked Gio. I explained something was drawing me there, and it wasn't the haggis or the beautiful countryside. I just felt we needed to be there for something important. "What about Isola Salina?" he asked. "It's not far away. It's in Sicily, it is beautiful. There isn't any infection there at all, and it is too far away from Sicily or Italy's mainland for the Shrooms to travel there. We can swim in the warm seas and eat the olives and figs straight from the trees. Imagine a plateful of lovely focaccia with a little balsamico and pancetta, it would be heaven". I agreed it sounded like a dream, but nowhere was heavenly at the moment. Everywhere was under attack, it would only be a matter of time. In the end I cheated a little in order to cut the discussion short, I said my dreams told me to go there, and Gio desisted. In a way it was the truth, I couldn't explain my compulsion rationally.

It was hard seeing our friends die at the fort. It was harder for the others than me, I had faced the worst loss I could ever have to deal with already. My crewmates had sad moments and happier thoughts, recounting precious memories together. I was simply numb; I had been since the day that my family perished. I'm not sure I'd learned to grieve properly; I was just walling it off. It hurt too damn much.

I suffered a temperature again that night, and I hardly slept. I was devious in keeping my symptoms from my friends, irresponsible even. I had a strange, almost misplaced, faith I would come through ok. I had before. By morning, the temperature had gone, but I was poorly rested. I just shrugged it off, I was worried and couldn't sleep, which was understandable to them. As with all good lies, it told a partial truth whilst obfuscating the real facts. In my heart I was sure there was no threat to them, I had been through it before on two occasions.

As we traversed the Straits of Gibraltar, Nidal was keen to make port. He seemed to forget the peninsula would be shoulder-to-shoulder with Shrooms, eager to take a bite from our lightly tanned flesh. Summer Haven certainly wouldn't take us in if we made port. It would be too risky for them. Nidal complained we had given them our GPS tracking signal, if we hadn't, then we could have stopped for tapas. It did make us laugh.

Sailing for thirty-nine days and nights was tough. To be fair there were times when it was pleasant, when the sea was calm, and we could drop the sails and swim or fish. However, there were also hard times, especially when we passed Gibraltar and we entered the Atlantic Ocean, when the sea was rough and at times terrifying. I was sick at least three or four times on those days. I was forced to stand in the centre of the ship and keep my eyes focussed on the horizon. I was no sailor, not like my friends. Even they were seasick at times, but they had long been able to control it and keep functioning, whereas I lost my balance and my ability to eat. They just carried on as normal. I gained a lot of respect for them during the trip.

Despite the GPS, as we neared the north of France and Brittainy, we considered the possibility of making port at Mont St Michel and visiting the small community there. There were risks, of course, as they may see visitors as a threat. I felt I could overcome this by explaining we were from the Valletta commune, but there were no guarantees. We knew the island was tidal, and we could only access it from the sea during high tide. However, in 2006, a hydraulic dam was installed and was followed by a new light bridge, which provided improved control of the flow of waters around the island from the Coesnon river. Therefore, when we arrived, we found the island was less tidal than expected. We couldn't identify a port or a means to land the boat, proving it was not easily navigable. We were forced to abort and continue our journey. After several weeks at sea, I was craving to put my feet on solid land and to sleep on a still bed. Little did I know, when I finally slept on land, it would feel like the bed was rolling at sea for days. Gio hadn't sailed the Atlantic before, he frequently commented, "Christ, why is it so cold?" Then Rene resumed his banter, "We're not in the Mediterranean or the Aegean hot bathtubs now, this is the real ocean!" "Do they call the infected champignons here?" asked Gio, with a grin.

A few days later, we progressed up the coast of England, then Scotland via the Irish and Hebrides Sea. The further North we travelled, the colder it became. We were freezing even in our multiple fleeces and insulated jackets. Our gloves had poor traction on the ropes, and from time to time we were forced to take them off, our hands felt like ice cubes and soon ceased to function properly. By the time we entered the region that Rene called 'The Minch', between the Isle of Lewis and the Highlands, we were frozen solid. Eventually Rene called "Land Ho!", an old English sailing term that seemed appropriate to him, even though we were in Scottish waters. Gio fell in a fit of the giggles, we couldn't shut him up afterwards. Laughing helped keep out the cold. It was a cold spring, not a great time to set sail.

3. A First Expedition Onshore

We experienced a number of smaller attacks over the following month, but then our situation settled down for a while. We became efficient in dealing with the Shrooms. Around mid-January, roughly as expected, a six-man sailing boat appeared on the horizon. Spall called for me on the tannoy. He didn't sound the alert; the boat was expected.

I headed up to the crow's nest. We had anticipated El Tigre and his small team's arrival, but we needed to be sure it was him, and they hadn't set foot on land during their journey. It was impossible to tell until they reached hailing distance. The sailors held up a white flag and shouted greetings. "Hello Summer Haven. We are your friends from Valletta, seeking to make port". "Head for the other side of the island and dock there, we are expecting your arrival. Please confirm you haven't been on land and haven't been exposed to the spores". "Hell no, suicide isn't a part of my vocabulary", El Tigre added with a big smile. The crew were clearly aware we might not be so friendly to potentially infected strangers, from first-hand experience, they didn't want to start a fight in error. It was easy to see it was El Tigre; through the binoculars I could see the red claw scars on his cheek, just below his left eye. The tiger had left him quite a souvenir!

The boat sailed around the island and soon arrived at the main port. The crew threw their ropes to the guys at the quayside, who wrapped them around the cleats and hitched them securely. The four men crossed the plank onto the main quay. Spall exclaimed, "What the", as El Tigre crossed the plank. The guy looked almost exactly like me, like a lost identical twin. It was surreal. I could see El Tigre experienced the same confused thoughts. I stepped forward, "Well met Mr Tigre", I spoke mock formally in time honoured fashion and offered him my hand. "It is so good to meet you at last; it's really wonderful to be here. Especially after our long voyage. I know it's cheeky, but I could kill a beer" he said. "We can sure help there Mr Tigre". "Call me Francisco", he pleaded. He looked at me knowingly on arrival but seemed to be holding back on something. I opted to investigate later.

Francisco and his comrades, Rene, Nidal and Gio, settled in very quickly. They were like minded souls. After they were dusted in sulphur, showered and enjoyed a good meal, they were as right as rain. The team were great fishermen, and the harvest from the seas became plentiful. Nidal and Gio were rock solid, Rene had suffered a few issues, though he was improving in the face of the horrible events. The difficult times taught him a sense of perspective by a baptism of fire. Rene had no time to worry about the past, when the future consisted of so much risk and danger. We all suffered with a little anxiety, but it was normal in the face of potential danger at any minute of the day.

Francisco fitted right in with Spall and his team. He wasn't quite what I expected. I guess I had preconceived ideas of someone with his nickname, especially with the stories I had heard from the guys. The reality was he was humble, almost a shy man who had been through a lot. It was strange to find someone else who looked and behaved so like me. If the clarity of childhood memories were less vivid, I would have thought we might be brothers.

A minor rumble coming from of few of the commune was we had gone against our principles and had let in outsiders. However, there was sense in the fact we knew the crew and were expecting them. Additionally, they had spent thirty-seven excruciating days at sea during a bitter winter and no infection had materialised, so the minor risk was worth taking. They were comrades in arms, the survivors of one of the seven havens.

The following year progressed as quietly as we could hope for, in the circumstances. We experienced half a dozen raids from the shore, but they were dying down. The attacks were also becoming more predictable, typically a sunny day was followed by *shrooming* near to the coast. None of the raids were quite as large as the one on Christmas Eve, but we still lost a couple more of our team. Attrition, as Kimball would put it. Heart-breaking, I would call it.

In the fall, Sheena and Rusty were married. We managed to make the wedding a special day. When anyone celebrated in our community, we all contributed. Days were ordinary and humdrum, so we tried hard to make sure we celebrated when we had cause. The atrium was decorated with autumnal colours: brown leaves and dried flowers, it was really quite lovely. The difficult part was being asked to preside over the ceremony. Not having a priest in our commune, it fell to me to do the honours. I did my best, with a collage of the sentiments Kate and I remembered of our marriage vows and service. We winged it, it became the de-facto wedding ceremony, which evolved as time passed. It was a lovely, heart-warming day. The first commune baby arrived the following summer. We didn't christen the child, so to speak, but we held a naming ceremony. Baby Chloe was a delight for us all. She was the first of many young souls brought into the new life we were building together.

A couple of years after A-Day, the shrooming slowed dramatically. It was hard to tell from the CCTVs, but the Shroom looked like they might be weakening. Kimball, Spall, Francisco, and I discussed if we should take a look. Perhaps run our first scavenging trip. I was keen to check first, before we committed ourselves to a course of action. We had no idea of the dangers we faced out there.

Kimball outlined the areas of our stores that were starting to look depleted. After all the attacks, levels of sulphur were low. Munitions for the big Vulcan guns were critically low, they ran through belts of ammo like an elephant charging through the undergrowth. There were plenty of rounds for the pistols and the M16's, but there was nothing as effective for tearing through large volumes of Shrooms as the big gatling guns. Food stores were significantly down, but not quite critical. Farming on the island was going well, but we didn't generate as much food as we needed. If it weren't for the bounty of the seas, we would be thinking about rationing. An experimental excursion was necessary, although the risks remained high.

Francisco had seen plenty of hand-to-hand action with the infected over the last few years, he felt a sword was more effective in close combat than a gun, as it didn't need constant reloading. His thoughts were inconsistent, how could he have survived if he had been in such close proximity to the creatures. He favoured his sword as it was razor sharp, it could cut straight through a Shroom and not get snagged. Caching a sword in clothing or flesh meant death in a combat situation. I didn't feel comfortable getting too close to the creatures.

Francisco, Spall, Kimball, and I took the first look at the mainland together. We faced a number of objections, as we represented a large part of the leadership of the haven. The commune saw it as an unnecessary risk, they thought we should wait a few months; but then they hadn't seen our stores lately. Wrench piloted the RIB across to the mainland facility and we climbed the steps to the defensive position at the highest point of the building, overlooking the front gates. It was all clear, there were no Shrooms in the vicinity. Wrench primed the Vulcan on the top of the building in case we came back with a crowd of admirers.

We loaded a big pickup with a few basic provisions and fitted the M3 .50 Calibre Machine Guns onto the pre-fitted bracket on the back of the cab. We then moved to the other pickup. The guns could be operated from the modified sunroof or the bed of the pickup; the bracket was versatile. We wore our standard stretch Kevlar oversuits, carried our Sig-Sauer 9mm pistols, night vision goggles with air filtering masks and M16s. Francisco sported his katana strapped to his back. Spall's large hunting knife protruded from his boot. Kimball sported a map and some insect repellent spray. Spall advised us to set the goggles to light intensification mode rather than infra-red, as the Shrooms were likely to be cold blooded, and wouldn't show up on the display.

Our inaugural trip was exploratory. We headed into the nearest villages at dusk, Badenscallie and Polglass, passing the Summer Isles Hotel on our way down the coast road. There was little Shroom activity, most had probably been mown down on our coastline. After only two years the plants and animals had started to take over. Gardens were overrun by long grass and weeds, the houses and buildings looked slightly run down and unkempt. The roads were largely empty, as the meteors had struck at night. I guess we would run into blockages when we moved into a more built-up area, as some locals could have been returning home from a night out. We travelled slowly at 30mph, the truck windows were down, our fingers on the triggers. In Polglass we found our first Shroom. It seemed to be inactive as we approached, but we were extremely cautious. Kimball held antifungal spray at the ready.

Polbain was a small collection of white thatched and slate tiled cottages, a lovely view of the Summer Isles could be experienced in daylight. We headed south into Polglass. A Shroom was in the middle of the road near the village centre, it was tempting to ram it with the huge bull bars on the front of the vehicle, but we didn't dare due to the risk of spores.

Francisco advised us, from his experience, the only way the Shrooms produced spores was through their fruit, but we chose to be careful. We approached the Shroom, weapons at the ready. Kim was about to spray it, but Spall stopped him. Don't waste your weapons, it doesn't pose a threat at the moment. We moved within a couple of metres of it, illuminated the Shroom and fitted our goggles. There appeared to be no activity whatsoever. When we looked more closely at the Shroom, the human host appeared dead, fungus was evident mainly in the mouth, ears, and eyes. We weren't certain, but it almost looked rotten. Was it a dead one? We backed off and returned to the truck. There was no evidence of a fruit, which confirmed that the fruit only occurred when the host was killed by more direct means such as a bullet.

We headed south again to Badenscallie which was almost a continuation of the roadside cottages of Polglass. We found nothing of interest, so we headed to Ullapool. We knew we weren't likely to obtain sulphur without a longer trip to Glasgow or Grangemouth. The nearest military base containing munitions was at the RAF base in Lossiemouth, on the other side of Inverness. Otherwise, it was a long trek to Edinburgh which we were loath to attempt. So, we decided to hit Tesco in Ullapool.

We entered Ullapool on the North Road; all was quiet. We turned right along Market Street and headed towards the supermarket. There were signs of a struggle here, the population was much larger than the tiny crofting villages. Numerous, torn open, rotten cadavers littered the streets. One body's empty eye sockets seemed to be looking at us, and the blackened teeth showing through the cheek seemed to form an evil smile. It gave me the creeps.

The troubles seemed to have stopped here some time ago, it was most unlikely there were any fresh spores. We avoided the bodies where possible, but we were forced to rumble over a few with the oversized off-road tyres. It seemed disrespectful but needs must. We couldn't start moving bodies and burying the dead, they were too numerous. It was possible they were diseased, the idea was far too risky, and we had so little time. We needed to be back before sunrise, to be safe. We rolled into the supermarket car park, which was empty other than a few rotting bodies. Obviously, the building was locked up. There was a small break in the glass doors where the security blinds had been levered.

An English Apocalypse - Paul JC Edge

Safeties off, night vision on. Francisco manned the big machine gun, to cover the team as the three of us headed into the building through the main entrance. Spall used a large wrecking bar to prise open the roller shutters and create enough space to climb through. He also used it to clear the sharp edges of broken glass on the windows. Kimball whispered, "God what a stink, everything is rotten in here". Spall gave a dry laugh, "If you were expecting fresh produce at bargain prices, you've come to the wrong shithole".

Clearly there had been some looting, and rotten foodstuffs were scattered on the floor. "Head for the loading area, we might find larger packs of dried and canned foods there", suggested Kim. As we headed in, we heard a crash and some scurrying, we froze and searched for the source of the sound. We moved behind the racking, and we saw a cat desperately trying to get into a foil container. The cat ran as soon as it heard us, startled. Kim used a knife to open a few packets. "Softy", smirked Spall. We grabbed as many trays of salvageable foodstuffs as we could and took them back to the 4x4 in four separate trips. We managed to find canned soup, stews, beans, vegetables, and super noodles. Many dried goods had perished, but some were ok despite being way past their best by date. We grabbed bottles of fizzy drinks and beer. "We can also reuse the bottles", remarked Kimball. I headed in for one last recce as the team ferried the goods back to the pickup.

As I entered the loading bay, I heard the bark of the big M3 machine gun. I dropped my stash and ran back to the entrance, then slipped through the roller doors. My night vision was highly effective until there was a bright light, the muzzle flashes from the M3 were interfering with my ability to see, so I flipped up the goggles. Around thirty or so Shrooms were splattered against the splintered fencing across the rear of the car park. Francisco shut down the gun and reloaded a new belt. He shouted, "Get in, there a whole bunch of them coming our way. They aren't the screamers, but they're quick. Don't hang around guys!" We scrambled as another troop of Shrooms ran across the car park. We opened up with our M16s on automatic. "Save your ammo", shouted Spall. One shot will usually do it, if you place it right. Aim for the centre of the chest, it's a bigger target".

I jumped into the vehicle with the others; Kimball took the wheel. More were coming, probably twenty or thirty. We raced back down Market Street and took the North Road back towards the facility. The Shrooms gave up the chase at that point, I guess their energy levels were low as it was nearly dark. They could still function up to a point, so were still dangerous. As we left, we could see a couple of fruits starting to sprout on the bodies we had taken down. So, the mainland wasn't spore free yet, not whilst the Shrooms were still active. I guess it would be better to avoid shooting and leaving them to rot.

As we approached our onshore facility, Wrench called on the radio. "Get the hell back here pronto, they are shrooming, they must be aware of our presence". "Roger that", responded Spall. Kimball drove fast through the front gate, and I jumped down to shut the gates. A couple of Shrooms charged me as I attempted to close up, I hadn't seen them lingering in the undergrowth, I should have put my night vision back on. Spall and Francisco opened up on them, and they hit the ground. As we headed into the building, Wrench opened up with the big gatling gun, "Sloch this ye bastards". Oh god not another one, Wrench had been around Rusty too much. The remaining twenty or so Shrooms disintegrated under the sheer destructive force of the Vulcan. The bodies splattered onto the tarmac. Spall shouted, "Are there any more?" "Can't see any", responded Wrench, "be careful". Spall opened the gate and doused the corpses with sulphur, and then quickly closed up again.

We sprayed ourselves, the vehicle, and the supplies with fungicide. Luckily, the food was packed in polythene, which kept the actual contents clean. We loaded up the boat and headed back as dawn started to break behind us.

4. Venturing into the Big Unknown

Steve was keen to hear of our experiences on the mainland. We were grilled for two hours by the science team. They wanted to be represented on the next scavenging trip. It was obvious it was still extremely dangerous out there, but survivable. We could start to scavenge if we were careful. It would be more hazardous when we headed into a larger city such as Inverness. Janus was interested to find out about the rotten Shroom we had observed, "Did you bring a sample for analysis?" We hadn't thought to, it was another oversight we needed to learn for the future. We would need the means to take a sample, but keep it safely contained to avoid infection. If one Shroom had rotted and died, there would be more. Did it mean as time progressed, the more active ones in the city would start to die? A glimpse of hope entered the room but chose not to linger.

Steve had previously identified a manufacturer of sulphuric acid in Grangemouth as a potential place to liberate serious quantities of sulphur. If our following trip proved a success, the sulphur supply was the next item on our hit list. Sulphur could be found on the ground in Indonesia, near volcanoes, but it was harder to find in bulk in Scotland.

I was curious about something that Francisco had said earlier, I decided to gently broach the subject with him. Simes' sister, Ellen, had taken quite a shine to Francisco, Kate felt Ellen had always had a thing for me, and he was the next best thing. How on Earth could she know these things? I don't know what it was between Kate and Ellen, but they always seemed to keep in touch, and they always knew all of the gossip. We sat down for dinner with Rusty, Sheena and Francisco when Ellen joined the table. Rusty looked at his plate, "Mushroom risotto, really? I've had enough of these rotten things for a lifetime. Can't we carve up a couple of cows?" I explained with a smile, "It's springtime, the cows are giving birth, so you would be losing the 2-4-1 deal". Sheena asked, "I wonder what the Shrooms taste like. Do you think they are more oyster or chestnut?", which made us laugh. "Toadstool", said Francisco, "they're toxic. A member of the Maltese team tried to roast one. Personally, I think he may have used too much butter, and it gave him acid". Sheena laughed so hard; she almost lost a mouthful of risotto. Kate quickly passed her a tissue. "Nice catch", said Spall, moseying past with his wife arm in arm like it was their first date. *I completely forgot why I wanted to talk to Francisco, after all the nonsense.*

Francisco clearly wanted to tell me something but was holding back. I broached the subject with him a couple of times, but he was pensive. After three weeks, it was nearing summertime, we attempted another foraging trip. Kate worried I was joining a brigade of soldiers, and the trip would be extremely dangerous. She made me promise to be careful. I didn't really need to promise, I was always careful. I wasn't brave enough to be anything else.

On the next trip to the mainland, we headed for the RAF base in Lossiemouth, with a planned shopping trip in Inverness on the way home. We used the same team, but with Janus and Wrench in a second vehicle with a large trailer. "How are you going to use the M3 when you are towing a huge container full of stuff", challenged Spall. "I guess he needs to go in front, then Wrench can operate the gun forwards; we can point our gun towards the back. If anything comes from the side, it will get double rations", offered Wrench. "Ok, but if it hits the fan you need a way to ditch the trailer in a hurry. If you do, let me know first, or I'll be having an early bath!"

We armed up. We remembered to take nitrile gloves and a sterile sample kit this time. We drove straight through Ullapool and onto the main route. Roughly a couple of miles into the hills we found a car smashed into a wall, fully blocking the road. The area seemed quite safe other than the Shroom in the driving seat. When we got out of the trucks it seemed to come to life and tried to scramble its way out of the car. It had no idea how to open the door, so it simply flailed its arms against the glass and the dashboard. It howled in anger and frustration, especially when Wrench started to laugh. He thought it was hilarious, and a deep rumbling chuckle started in his stomach. It was the most infectious laugh. Spall instantly roared at us, "Focus guys, this is deep shit we're wading in!"

Wrench attached the winch hook under the car bumper and dragged it onto the grass at the side of the road. We put safety's back on and got rolling again. There was another abandoned car on the road, but it only partly obscured our route. Janus managed to gently nudge it out of the way using the bull bars. There was no one in the car, but the doors were open this time. We bypassed Inverness and headed straight to the RAF base.

The sign read RAF Lossiemouth. It was the only remaining supersonic RAF base in Scotland. The red and white striped barrier blocked the entrance. There was a rotted Shroom in the gatehouse. Janus suggested a theory whereby the Shrooms were starting to decompose in the quieter places, where the battles had been much shorter, and no one was left to attack. But why would fungus just die, it could survive indefinitely as a microorganism, as long as it had source of nourishment. I was unsure about these 'deaths' and needed to better understand what was happening.

We broke the barrier and continued into the main base. Wrench and Janus parked the trucks, and we continued on foot, ready for anything. We didn't split up to make the search faster, as we felt it was too dangerous. We searched each of the buildings by the airstrip. There were several Typhoon fighters, a couple of light aircraft such as Cessnas, lots of plane and jet parts, a canteen, and several dorms. The canteen kitchen had nothing of use. Wrench noted it "Stank lik' a pigs bahookie", as Rusty would put it. "I'm sure a pig's arse would actually smell a whole lot sweeter than this", remarked Spall. Even Spall was getting with the brogue now.

We finally found a shed presumably containing weaponry. It had a strong steel door with massive locks and hinges. "How the hell are we going to get in here?" asked Kimball. Wrench suggested we popped a grenade on each hinge with some gorilla snot to hold it in place. "Save me from idiots, this place is full of bloody explosives! You can't just blow the doors. It would be like the Italian Job all over again", remarked Spall. "You were only supposed to blow the bloody doors off!' Kimball and I recanted simultaneously. "How about through the door", said Janus after he'd popped around the corner and appropriated an oxy-acetylene cutter.

Janus carefully cut a section from the strong steel plate wall, big enough for us to walk through at a stoop. We still hadn't seen any Shrooms. Perhaps the base was deserted at the time of the meteor strike, or they could have joined another troop elsewhere. We climbed into the shed and found all manner of ammunition. But none would work with the gatling guns. Instead, we appropriated another pair of large machine guns with numerous cartons of ammo. No one recognised the model, but they looked rather dangerous. Probably antiaircraft guns for the airstrip that had remained unused. We also liberated several boxes of grenades and 9mm parabellums. "Load 'em up and move out", called Spall with a wide grin. We drove the trucks round and loaded up the trailer with the weaponry. Wrench thought it was Christmas as he hefted one of the large machine guns. "Bring those tripods for the guns too, we will need them", reminded Francisco.

Francisco took off his katana and climbed into the rear truck. We all followed suit, then headed into Inverness, where things didn't go quite to plan. Spall decided to give the hospital area a very wide berth as there might be a concentration of Shrooms there. We headed straight to the big Bookers cash and carry, as we figured it would hold numerous trays of food, grain, and other less perishable items. It proved to be the case, and we easily filled the trucks and any remaining space in the trailer with all of the above plus bottled drinks and long-life products. Huge bags of rice, flour (though some had been invaded by mice, it looked ok if you didn't mind silverfish), noodles, dried meats, plus underwear which was rather depleted in the Haven. We also picked up some prerequisite electrical components for Steve, then we were good to go. We started back towards the A9 which took us across the bridge over the Beauly Firth to Tore and Cononbridge. As we turned off the carpark and moved up the road, a large troop of

Shrooms blocked the way in front of us. There were hundreds of them.

We doubled back and took the other side of the loop down Longman Drive as an alternative way around, trying to avoid the confrontation. When we looped back to the road, there was another large troop of Shrooms. They had cornered us. They started to move towards us, some ambling some running at full speed. They looked like a ragtag band, but there was a basic organisation going on. "They are coordinated", whispered Francisco, "they do this when the group gets to a certain size, they move from the basic chaotic swarm mentality, where they randomly gather and do different things, to a more organised hive behaviour". One of them, that Francisco called a centurion, started to influence, and control the group from the rear. "If we take the centurion out, they will all turn chaotic again like throwing a switch", he added. "How do you know?", I asked. "Been there and done that", he replied with a pained smile, "tell ya later".

Spall arranged both trucks side by side on the road. "We'll charge at them at 40mph, big guns cutting a path through the middle. 20 metres before impact, we reform into single file. We'll take the front, and we'll keep hitting them with the big gun to clear a path. The rest of you face backwards and take out the ones who get on the vehicles. We need to keep our speed above 20mph, or we'll get mobbed. It's going to get bumpy people!"

We stood in the vehicles ready; we tried to loop an arm or our belts to something solid. Kimball drove the first truck, Spall took the M3, which was fitted to the top of the front part of the cab and faced it forward, he was standing on the footwell to the rear set of seats. It was a squeeze, as Wrench and I were facing backwards in the same footwell. Francisco did the same on the other truck with the trailer, we needed someone in the second truck. Wrench switched trucks, giving Spall and I a little more room. In the second truck Francisco handed over the position behind the M3 to Wrench, "You're more used to this big stuff than I am, I'd sooner take them with a blade", he said, strapping on his sword.

"Go!" shouted Spall, and the big guns opened up as we hurtled towards the Shroom troop. The Shrooms fell in their dozens. We hit them at speed, and the big trucks careered over their bodies. The big bouncy tyres took a lot of the jarring impact but then the suspension started to oscillate up and down as we rode over the Shroom's cadavers. In the back, we were jostled all over the place, I acquired several heavy bruises. Janus tucked in behind us. I really needed to be careful, as I could easily hit him with friendly fire as the truck lurched up and down.

At first, we went rapidly, the sound of the M3's was deafening. Wrench stopped firing when we took position in front of his vehicle, and he turned the gun all the way round to cover the rear, narrowly missing Francisco's forehead with the hot muzzle. The big 4x4 pickup bounced over the bodies. As we slowed the Shrooms gained confidence and started to cling to the sides of the vehicles. We opened up with the M16s, but it was really hard to target them whilst avoiding everyone else. Wrench opened up again with the big gun and he mowed down many of the infected. Spall shouted down the radio, "Don't waste ammo on those behind us, focus on the ones in front!" Finally, the first truck emerged out of the group, and made a little ground. The second truck driven by Janus struggled. The M3 was firing but the Shrooms were starting to slow the momentum of the truck to a standstill.

As we started to lose hope, Francisco jumped down from the cab into the back of the pickup, weaved his way through the supplies and onto the trailer. He fought off a couple of Shrooms trying to climb on and picked up one of the large heavy machine guns and loaded a ribbon of bullets into the breach and opened fire. What a weapon! It cut through the Shrooms like a hot knife through butter, and within seconds the truck accelerated again. We were clear. How El Tigre held the huge gun steady in his hands I will never know, it was amazing to see.

We high tailed it back onto the A9 and headed across the bridge crossing the Firth. We had made it in one piece. The trucks didn't stop until we were back at the facility, where Rusty opened the gates for us. We offloaded the cargo, sprayed it and each other and headed back across the sea with a huge sense of relief. Rusty said he would go back with the barge to pick up the gear after daybreak. What a haul it was! Francisco had scorch marks on his jacket and mild burns on his forearms from the machine gun, I dressed his wounds as first priority. Our hearing was impaired due to the noise of the firearms, it took quite some time to return to normal.

We discussed the events of the day over a few medicinal whiskies. "It was really hairy for a while back there", Kimball started. "I didn't think we were going to make it, until El Tigre started blasting them with the enormous gun". "I'm not sure it went quite like that", said Francisco laughing. "No, but you really pulled our asses out of the fire with your crazy stunt!" added Spall, "Good job!". I added, "There were thousands of

Shrooms, and they were organised. I couldn't believe it; we were lucky to get out of there alive". The problem was it was the first of many longer trips we needed to make. It was going to be tougher than I thought.

The next trip was to Grangemouth and the sulphuric acid factory. The area was industrial and didn't a have big night-time population, so the trip was more or less eventless. We relieved the factory of an exceptionally large quantity of sulphur, but there was lots more for future trips. We were lucky. I must admit as we passed through Inverness, there was more than a little trepidation, we had seen very many infected there last time.

5. Inspiration

Barry would have been Spall's brother-in-law, if he was married. I didn't know him, but people seemed to like him well enough. He and his partner were always grateful for being saved, as he didn't feel he was closely related to the seven nor had significant skills he could bring to bear. He was almost gagging for a chance to prove himself; to make a difference to our lives, one way or another. Even if it was the simple act of making a cup of tea. I was always curious why a Chinese family would choose a name like Barry, but I found out it sounded similar to his Chinese name Bo-wing. It was a name that we could more easily relate to, though I liked Bo-wing well enough.

Spall, Wrench, Rusty, and Sheena were sat discussing safe ways to return to the cash and carry without being coated with spores or eaten alive. Francisco joined us. Sheena greeted him, "Hi there, Tiger Boy". She loved to tease Francisco; it clearly made him uncomfortable. We were at a complete impasse; our best outcome was a simple re-run of our first trip. The only improvement was to send in a third truck as decoy, making lots of noise and shining bright lights to draw the Shrooms away. The only other possibility was to ditch the trailer and have more runs, it was the extra weight that slowed the second vehicle and made it easier for the Shrooms to board it. At this point Barry pulled a 'Flemish Giant' rabbit out of a party hat.

Barry scurried past and half overheard the conversation and the problem we faced. He stopped, put his hand onto the top of his thick, straight black hair and suggested, "Why don't you crop dust them, they are just like fungi and pests". "Sorry", Francisco queried, "What do you mean?" "Well, fill a crop-dusting helicopter with sulphur and dust the whole area. You could cover five square miles in thirty minutes". "Who do we know who can fly a helicopter?" I asked rather too pointedly. He jovially added, "I can. I'm a little rusty but I can fly any civil aircraft". Spall looked over, Rusty smiled, "Don't start with the little Rusty thing, I'm just as tall as you are!" he added, "We could dust the larger towns and cities; then we only need to clear the countryside by hand if it presents a problem". There we had it, revolution! The power of diversity epitomized.

In the USA it was more usual to use light aircraft for crop dusting; my mind darted automatically to the plane stereotype. However, the UK tended to use helicopters as we have much smaller expanses of open space and the copters were more controllable. The issue was most of the crop spraying companies were based in southern England, which was too far away. A couple of helicopter tour companies were based on the east side of Inverness. Steve decided his team could build a sprayer which we could attach to the helicopter's undercarriage. "We could use a pressurised cylinder to spray concentrated sulphur solution though a simple pipe with jets. It would become gummed up and would need flushing every time we used it, but it is perfectly feasible", Steve said. He was on it.

The next question was finding a chopper which would fly safely after a few years of inactivity. Barry explained that helicopters should be maintained and stored in tip top condition at all times. However, the helicopters in Inverness hadn't been maintained since A-Day. We would need to be incredibly careful after a couple of years of not being used. We could oil all of the necessary parts and ensure they were freed up and try it out. After a few weeks Steve and his team had produced a working prototype duster. We appropriated compressed air cylinders from the diving school near to Dundonnell and took an exploratory trip, driving to the helipad near Inverness. The aviation company had two modern choppers, the very ones we rented for transport for the party on A-Day. We dragged the first of the choppers out on to the helipad using the winch on the truck. We fuelled it, Steve looked over the mechanics, oiled a few parts and gave it a very rough check, Barry jumped into the cockpit and attempted to start her up. No go. Steve checked the battery and swapped it out. The engine sputtered a little but fired into life after the starter motor had been running for a few minutes.

Barry grabbed the cyclic and collective handles and positioned his feet on the pedals. He twisted the grip on the collective to power the rotor, pulled the collective to change the blade pitch, giving the chopper a small amount of lift. Barry then pressed the left foot pedal to use the tail rotor to counteract the torque and stop the whole bird from spinning. He pulled harder on the collective and the rotor took the weight of the copter. Just as he left the ground, he touched the cyclic to move the chopper forward and there was a loud bang, smoke poured out of the exhaust vent. The chopper dropped and hit the helipad violently. Barry held up his thumbs, he was ok, just a nasty jolt.

We winched the copter off the helipad, prepped the second chopper and winched that into place. The second helicopter was ok, he managed to take off and fly it around in a tight circle before landing safely. We left it there for the day. Barry seemed quite calm, like it wasn't a big deal, but we nearly suffered heart attacks. It was really quite a dangerous venture. None of our team could maintain these birds, and in normal times there were many deaths each year in well maintained ones.

We returned the next evening with trailers attached to our trucks. It was only safe to venture into Inverness if we were confident. I decided we couldn't dust the whole city; we didn't want to damage the countryside with sulphur. We opted to use the chopper as air cover, the trucks would draw the Shrooms out and Barry would spray them. Steve cable tied the pipes of the spray rig to the undercarriage and mounted the cylinders. The assembly only needed to hold for an hour or so. Steve pointed out, "You will need a passenger to pull the trigger to release the sprayers, using this rope. You need to keep some tension on the rope and the spray will continue until you release it". He drilled a hole into the side of the fuselage for the rope to pass it through. Barry suggested we tied off the rope inside the cockpit, it could take out the rotor if it became loose. We were ready. Steve went along for the trip; they flipped down their night vision goggles.

The chopper could cover the ground much faster, so we took a head start in the trucks, M3s at the ready. Steve and Barry took off as we neared the cash and carry. We figured the Shrooms would surround us after an hour or so loading the trucks, like last time. Barry gave us a much better idea of our situation as he hovered 100m above the building. "All clear so far", he announced. We started to load up. Tinned meat, vegetables, fruit, dried pasta, noodles, flour, and clothing. We accumulated a huge load. Kimball was most impressed with the haul. As we suspected, a call came in from Barry just as we were tying the loads to the trailers and the pickups. "My god, there are thousands of them guys. They are shrooming from all sides of the town". "Time to go to business then", said Spall calmly.

We agreed if we got into trouble, we would ditch the trailers and run. We had previously installed a quick release mechanism on the towing hitches as a contingency measure. The chopper moved out.

Barry swept over the larger troops of Shrooms, and Steve dropped the payload gradually. The dust dispersed everywhere. Steve accounted for the downdraft of the rotor, but not quite enough. The sprayers dispersed a wide spread, but the rotor pushed the sulphur down in a tight vortex. By serendipity it was actually amazingly effective, due to the huge area of coverage for such a short burst. A five second shot dusted the whole troop of around seven hundred Shrooms.

We awaited the report from Barry on tenterhooks. Steve updated over the radio, the Shrooms had slowed and were behaving differently. A few minutes later they started to collapse. We heard Barry shout to Steve that he had seen another troop of several thousand coming from the riverside. Barry took a direct flightpath to the new threat and Steve doused them too. They then flew off and dropped a large cloud over the city centre and castle where we had observed Shroom activity. "We're out", Steve called on the radio. "That's it, buckle up gentlemen", announced Spall.

Francisco asked if we should take a look, to verify the effectiveness of the spray. Spall was adamant, "The hell with that, let's get out of Dodge in case it hasn't worked. We can come back for a recce in a truck without the trailer tomorrow, it's safer that way. Let's get rolling". We agreed Spall was right, it was better to play safe. We headed out to the highway towards the helipad to collect Barry and Steve. I was conscious they weren't soldiers, and they had no protection once they landed. They had the same thought and were hovering when we arrived. As soon as we cleared the building, they landed, and we got moving.

Wrench drove through the nearest troop of Shrooms, but we saw no trouble from them, they were preoccupied. Only a handful attacked from a group of a few hundred. They were soon mopped up by Spall's big machine gun. The drive to the Haven was uneventful. Rusty manned the crow's nest on the facility, and we received a huge whoop from him when we returned. We didn't need to disinfect as we were all covered in sulphur, so we just wiped down our clothes, the cabs and had a shower. "We could wash the trucks tomorrow, after our fishing trip", suggested Francisco. Rusty again agreed to bring the supplies on the barge later, so we helped him load up. We then took the RIB back to the island. Our families were waiting to check we'd got back in one piece and were overjoyed to see us, even if we did smell sulphurous. "You smell farty", laughed Matt.

The next day Spall, Francisco and I drove back to Inverness to see how things were progressing. We had used several bags of sulphur on our trip, but we had lots in reserve. We could easily take a visit back to Grangemouth if needed. The dusting had killed the Shrooms and left them in a rotting state, its efficacy had been incredibly good. The powder must have penetrated lots of other areas in the city as the wind had picked up. It had catastrophically damaged the Shroom population in the city, though there may probably still a few groups around, we didn't cover the whole area. At one point we passed the waterside, but we were forced to back track, there was a moderate sized troop in residence, they immediately proceeded to scream and charge at us. They couldn't keep up with the vehicle, they were easily outrun.

That evening, at the Haven a fairly conservative party awaited us, and Phil broke out the new batch of his beer. We celebrated everything these days.

"Today we've had a huge breakthrough in the war against the Shrooms. We've all but eradicated the Shrooms in Inverness and we can now start to move further afield and take them on in the other cities. I just wanted to say thank you to the scavenging team for their bravery. To Steve and the science team for rigging up the crop duster. For everyone who supported this activity back here and at the facility", Rusty and I shared an acknowledging glance. "But most of all for Barry Wong, for having the wonderful idea that might just have saved us all, and for risking his life in an unmaintained helicopter".

6. Annihilation

That year we waged war on the Shrooms. We hunted them in the fields and forests. We dusted the cities in Central Scotland, and we started to douse South of the Highlands down to Fort William. It wasn't all easy, there were a couple of chopper close encounters, in one Barry nearly lost his life. We also fended off a few larger firefights with Shrooms, though there hadn't been any attacks on the island for some time.

The last of the Shroom troops in the Highlands caught us by surprise when we took a more frivolous trip to Durness in the North. Our aim was to check for confectionary in the chocolate factory there. We thoughtlessly entered the small craft village in daylight and found chocolate that hadn't perished or gone white. I wouldn't eat the white stuff, but Phil liked it. He claimed it was white due to high temperatures separating the emulsion of sugar and fats, he said it was quite edible. We liberated quite a quantity of good stuff; the kids would be delighted. We also acquired a large quantity of hot chocolate powder!

It was a very remote location, so we didn't expect trouble. We found a few small groups of rotten Shrooms along the way, which always made us hopeful, it implied they had limited longevity, and we would soon be rid of them. After raiding the factory, Francisco and I were surprised by thirty or so Shrooms hiding at the rear of the little craft village that surrounded the chocolate shop. We rounded a corner on foot, with less care than we normally would, we were clearly becoming overconfident and possibly a little negligent. The Shrooms chanted their chilling guttural cry and charged at us. I emptied my M16 rather too quickly in the blind panic. I just sprayed all my magazine on full auto at the troop and felled nearly half of them, but then I was out of ammo. I regard Francisco as El Tigre in the following account, it was more than deserved, in homage to the ferocity of his actions. A tiger indeed.

El Tigre always maintained the sword was a better weapon in close contact with the Shrooms, though he never explained how he knew this or how he could survive such proximity. Whilst I was shooting wildly, he calmly drew his katana and dropped his M16. When my gun was empty, he charged the remaining twelve Shrooms. He leapt into the fray and beheaded the leading pair of Shrooms in a single stroke. He spun and took the legs from under the next and almost cut another in half along the waistline. He spun again and it all happened too fast, but I saw two more Shrooms hit the ground. There were six remaining, and by then I had managed to retrieve Francisco's rifle and prime it. I took out the two Shrooms who attempted to outflank El Tigre. The remaining four were dispatched quickly by his sword.

As the last one fell, El Tigre was attacked by the Shroom whose legs had been truncated. I guess in hindsight it was sloppy of me not to take the opportunity to dispatch it properly, but it was all in the heat of the moment. The Shroom managed drag himself closer using only his arms, it grabbed El Tigre by the leg and delivered a vicious bite to his ankle before I took him down with a triplet of bullets to the centre of his spine.

El Tigre suffered only a minor wound, but it was grievously infected. We needed to help him quickly; it was desperate. I stripped his leg and applied sulphur paste, but it was too late, the infection had entered his bloodstream. Francisco started to talk deliriously, "Paul, you need to save them, the Dark Ones are coming!"

As he started to fade, he added in a trance-like state, "There's something I haven't told you about...my birth mother, I was told she was an angel, though I can't remember her, I was too young. Her name was Beatrice. I looked for her, but never found her. I think you might be my brother". As his consciousness faded, I realised I needed to escape before my friend fruited. I ran back to the vehicles, I was forced to leave him there, after all he had done. He had saved me. More than that he had given me some kind of warning, one that I didn't fully understand. Was he reminiscing our dreams, or was it something new? I dearly hoped not.

Was it a coincidence that our mother's name was the same? The only brother I was aware of was Kirk who was a half-brother on my father's side, he was nearly a decade younger than me. It was remarkable that Francesco, and I looked so similar, like twins some said. It just left me confused, but more than that desperately sad. He was a good friend and a formidable warrior. We wouldn't be able to bury him in the manner he deserved. I returned to him and dusted his body with sulphur to kill the fungus. Spall shouted, "Get in! You have to leave him. They could throw up fruit at any second. Move your hairy ass soldier!" In the heat of battle, Spall was our commander and no mistake, so I jumped into the truck as the Shrooms started to bear fruit. Wrench headed back to the isle. Was tour trip really worth it, just for some damned chocolate? Ciara and Matt raved over it, so did the other kids and some of the adults... but not at the cost of someone that might indeed be my brother.

Life became a little easier, as we now had access to all the farms in the Highlands. The crops were a little overgrown, but they were still growing amongst weeds and were plentiful. We had sweetcorn for the first time in years, we had lots of meat and herbs. Things were looking up. The cattle in the fields had mostly survived, some had escaped into the countryside. Those left in sheds had died, as no one had come back to let them out or feed them. Many of the chickens had been killed by foxes and wild dogs. They couldn't fly as their wings had been clipped by the farmers, but a few had survived. There were plenty of geese and ducks as they could migrate and stay safe.

All in all, there was more food than we could possibly eat in a hundred lifetimes. We had a modest funeral for El Tigre, Simes' wife Jean worked with Kulbir to erect a statue in honour of him in the gardens of the Haven. It was a beautiful tribute to a great man. Little did I know it was the second of his tributes, one had been erected long before in another place another time.

We communicated our successes to the other havens continuously. Isola Salina had an easy time in general, compared to the rest of us. Zakinthos had a less easy time, they had no access to fungicides but had successfully suppressed the Shroom population on their island by burning the bodies before they could fruit using makeshift flamethrowers. The team hadn't ventured beyond their island but had been lucky. The small team on Samsø also struggled to stay alive, as they inherited an enormous population of Shrooms. But a handful survived and managed to make the north of the island safe. They acquired large quantities of industrial fungicide in sprayers but didn't have the ability to invoke the damage like we had. However, the Shrooms were starting to rot due to the lack of prey. Mont St Michel managed to set up a functional crop-dusting solution using drones, which proved to be an extremely effective and flexible weapon. They started to reclaim a few nearby areas in northern France but found it hard to keep hold of them for long. Formentera coped due to its small population and ventured into the island of Ibiza with limited success.

Iceland was business as usual, we hadn't heard from Captain McCreedy recently, but he had checked in roughly every month or so in the past. After helping the crew stranded on oil rigs, they had all made port in Iceland, where they helped to rebuild the habitable parts of town. There was little Shroom activity there due to the cold, they thought, but then the many geysers emitted lots of sulphurous gas, it could have been this that suppressed the spores. Some of the havens were getting a little stir crazy, and we talked about the possibilities of a face-to-face meeting. It seemed like a big ask, and it hadn't progressed. The time wasn't right, the communities remained nervous.

My half-brother, Kirk, finally met someone; he planned to be married in the fall. Rusty and Sheena had their second child on the way and Simes and Jane were expecting a fourth child! It was lovely to see life working out. Spall and Jane's kids were growing up and were getting quite close to some of the other older teenagers in the community. Since A-Day the bond between Spall and Jane became much closer. We would have to watch the space there. Barry still had a big smile on his face, and Spall's sister Fern said that it was like having a new and better model of her partner.

Phil and his family were still heavily involved in the farming with his sister Iris, there had been no change there, they were really happy. Drake gave me the biggest hug whenever he bumped into me, and Jake had started to follow suit. They were like the proverbial peas in a pod and were rarely apart. That was until Bessie, Kate's niece, had caught Jake's eye one party night after a few whiskies.

I sat with Kate on the quay with our legs dangling over the side. Once again, we wondered if Francisco could possibly be my brother. Why wouldn't I know something important like that? Why wouldn't my Mum or Dad tell me about it? I started to think about the scratches on his face, it was the only feature that differentiated his visage from mine. Kate asked, "Do you remember that day at the zoo, Paul? When you were frightened and thought there was something in the bushes". "Yes, it was an odd feeling, I felt like I was going to be attacked". She added, "You really had a bug up your ass about visiting the zoo that week, I have no idea why. It was the exact same day that Francisco was attacked by the tiger, I worked it out from his journal a few days ago. I forgot to mention it to you". I remembered the odd feeling I had at the time. "I had a sense there was someone with me, someone who made me feel stronger when we were together. I also remember the tiger attacked me and I squatted and hit out at it with my forearm". "Yes, just like his account", said Kate. I came to accept Francisco was actually connected to me supernaturally in some way, he was my identical twin. It sounded crazy, but I knew it was true.

An English Apocalypse - Paul JC Edge

One early evening, Rusty and Spall called me to the crow's nest. "You've gotta see this", said Spall. We were hailed from a small sailing dinghy approaching from Polbain. The man stood in the stern of the boat resembled Francisco from a distance, but it couldn't possibly be, could it? As he neared the island, we could see it was clearly him. He tied off his boat to a cleat and mounted the quay. "Permission to come aboard", said my brother. I ran over and embraced him. "How are you still alive?" I asked. "I guess I have some kind of genetic immunity to the spores", he said after pondering for a moment. "I have been bitten, scratched and infected by spores many times now, and I am still here. Don't ask me how. It's how I survived fighting the Shrooms at such close quarters, I guess". I was so pleased to see him, the whole concept of infection hadn't entered my mind.

A small throng gathered at the end of the quay, with Simes at the front, they wore a hazmat suits. "I'm so sorry Paul, but you can't come onto the island, you might be infected". I looked down and Francisco was coated in spores, and now so was I. Francisco apologised gravely; it was stupid not to realise. We had been reckless and now I was going to pay the ultimate price for it. Francisco optimistically suggested I might share the immunity genome if we were truly identical twins, which gave me little comfort at the time. But it was possible I would be immune too. Kate shouted, "You need to sulphur him quickly. Why aren't you doing anything?" "It's too late", I told her, "They are everywhere, I'm so sorry". A surge of panic hit me, but I looked at Francisco, and he was fine. Perhaps I would be too. We sprayed each other with fungicide and coated ourselves in sulphur. Our clothes were taken and burned, and we were issued with new ones. What a bloody fool I was!

So that was how Francisco and I really got to know each other, in a quarantine hut at the edge of the island. Francisco, the dog Rosie, and I stayed in the hut for two weeks. We couldn't understand how we came to be brothers, but we knew we absolutely were without question. Our views were aligned on most topics we chatted about, other than the finesse of using a sword in close contact with Shrooms.

We both suffered a mildly feverish couple of days, but soon shrugged it off. I had the fever much worse than Francisco did, but he explained it got a little easier each time. "When you were delirious, and I thought you were near to death, you mentioned the 'Dark Ones' were coming, do you remember?" I probed gently. He didn't, perhaps it was just a red herring. It was so boring in the hut, we played cards, we whittled wood, we even sung a few songs together. It was the time when folks became most grateful we were isolated.

As the week progressed, we started to experience dreams again. We shared the same dream, but Francisco found it unusual. His experiences with the white one were more notable when he was awake. The dream was more relaxed than before and was a suggestion. I suspect we were now open to his influence, after all the events had proven true, we were now listening. The being was reaching out to us both, together in the same dream. He wanted us to join with our brother on Isola Salina. He said the Dark Ones were coming, and we needed to protect the remainder of our world from them.

Francisco and I talked at length about the dream, which repeated in the early hours on the last three nights of our isolation. There were several disturbing factors. The first was the concept of another brother. The second was the vague being we had seen was physically present on Earth, and no mistake. The third was another threat we needed to face. The war was not over, not by a long shot.

Spall was greatly concerned about the story when we shared it with him; he felt we needed a plan, and we shouldn't just disappear into a dangerous unknown. We had no idea how to find our 'brother', but with Gio's help we could certainly locate Sicily, which was adjacent to Salina. We were discussing our idea when Wrench called us up to the crow's nest. "Take a look through the scope", he urged. We looked through the main telescope, each taking turns.

A figure dressed in black, was standing on the shoreline of the mainland promontory at Polglass. The figure inclined his head to the side as we peered at him. It was hard to make out any detail at dusk, but it appeared as though he was staring at us. Surely it couldn't be possible, he was a mile and a half away?

Wrench had already been weighing the situation up, "He is either a new form of Shroom that we haven't seen before, or he is a scout for someone else". "He is a threat", Francisco and I exclaimed in unison with absolute certainty. We knew he was a 'Dark One' from our dreams. "He's looking for Francisco and me, he aims to assassinate us", I added. We knew it for a fact, it was intuition. Wrench spoke into his radio, and we saw a muzzle flash out to sea, part way towards Polbain. Rusty had quietly taken a boat close to the shoreline, he had the figure in his sights all the time. As the bullet hit the figure, it spontaneously combusted and bright burning ash blew up into the grey sky, dancing like fireflies and followed the wind out to sea.

An English Apocalypse - Paul JC Edge

This story continues in Summer Haven II: A Doctrine of Fear.

Our World had largely been exterminated by a group of infected meteoroids from space, which carried an infection that turned ordinary people into rabid killers. This is a record of how a man, relentlessly pursued by demons, had been taken in and protected by the Catholic church so that he could play his part in the saving of mankind. Following the apocalypse, he joined his twin brothers and together they pursued a terrible truth until they were forced to face the abyss together, shoulder to shoulder.

Printed in Great Britain
by Amazon